PROMISE OF DEATH

Stryker's eyes shifted from the terrified expression on the driver's face to the look of intense pain on the man's partner's features—from chin to eyebrows he seemed one complex contortion of agony.

When the jeep came to a stop, Stryker yelled for the gate sentries to phone up to the rooftop MP. "Tell him the chopper's to be ready ASAP!" He was pulling out his own first-aid packet now. "I wanna be airborne in zero-five, got that?"

The wounded soldier grimaced as a bolt of pain lanced down through his bowels. "Hell, I musta taken a bazooka round, sarge," he gasped. "I can't feel nothing anymore but the pain. Nothin', sarge . . . I'm not gonna make it, am I?"

"You'll make it okay," Stryker lied. "But the people who did this to you—they aren't gonna make it at all," he promised. And that was the truth.

SAIGON COMMANDOS

BOONIE-RAT BODY BURNING

#5

JONATHAN CAIN

ZEBRA BOOKS
KENSINGTON PUBLISHING CORP.

ZEBRA BOOKS

are published by

Kensington Publishing Corp.
475 Park Avenue South
New York, N.Y. 10016

First printing: September 1984

Printed in the United States of America

During the pre-dawn hours of January 31, 1968, twenty-seven American Military Policemen lost their lives fighting to save Saigon from a surprise Viet Cong attack, launched in the midst of the Tet holiday celebrations. Another forty-four MPs were wounded in scattered street battles throughout the steaming metropolis of over three million Vietnamese. To those gallant heroes, all proudly wearing the green and gold combat patch of the 18th MP Brigade, this book is respectfully dedicated.

Though the author served as a Military Police sergeant with the U.S. Army in Vietnam, Thailand, and Korea, portions of this "novel" have been altered and fictionalized to protect the lives of those men and women left behind, abandoned during the surrender of Saigon in the spring of 1975.

Boonie-Rat Body Burning is a novel. But it is based on several true stories the author swapped with other MPs at Mimi's Bar in Saigon, where he was assigned to the 716th Military Police Battalion.

The phrase "Saigon Commandos" was a derogatory term invented by infantrymen in the field to refer to almost any soldier stationed in the "rear." But some of the Military Policemen fighting snipers, sappers, and other hostile hooligans across the sleazy Saigon underworld affectionately adopted the title, proud to be lawmen, and not jungle grunts, battling crime in the toughest beat in the world.

JONATHAN CAIN
October 1983
Malacca, Malaysia

SAIGON: . . . Excessive love for the exotic can destroy the American in the Orient. Many men think they go away from here with their souls intact—but they find in their own countries they've been profoundly changed by their experiences without knowing it. They become outcasts among their own people because everything at home seems insipid in comparison with the East. Then usually they're lured back again by the siren call of what has already ruined them. . . . These lands are deeply inhospitable to men with white skins . . . and too often that compels them to commit acts of which they can't be proud.

—Anthony Grey

curfew, bombed out of his skull on cheap Vietnamese "33" beer. Rocked and rolled by a brazen cabbie an hour earlier. Penniless. Helpless, with a back alley wild dog trying to rip his leg out by the roots.

Private Railroad Smythe managed to kick out at the mutt again, but this sudden, unexpected move only angered the animal more—excited it, more than anything, and Railroad's next unpleasant sensation was of a razor-sharp set of incisors slicing into the soft, fleshy cup under his knee.

Railroad heard his own scream as if it came from a distant man, miles away—the obscenities bouncing back at him as if from a dark and murky tunnel. He fought to raise his fist, to strike out at the canine, but even this effort defied what was left of his reflexes, and he found himself wondering if the army would mail a posthumous Purple Heart home to his parents, or if they'd even find what would be left of his body—he'd heard stories of the wild dogs of Saigon roaming the streets in deranged, rabid packs, attacking anything foolish enough to venture out after curfew. There had even been accounts of the animals sneaking into poorly secured shacks in the slums and dragging screaming infants out into the night—never to be seen again. And hadn't he overheard those crazy MPs from the 716th in Mimi's Bar just that evening talking about the missing persons case they had solved when two privates on routine patrol discovered the shredded carcass of an AWOL soldier that had been dragged down into the sewers beneath the Saigon Zoo? That's all he needed now: to be carried on the AWOL rosters and eventually the Deserter sheet, while all along some lousy VC mutt lay cuddled against his corpse in an underground pit, its paws draped lazily across his bleached-white thighbone, a satisfied gleam in its eyes as it slowly licked its chops.

Mimi's Bar. Just a tiny, dimly lit joint down from Le Loi on Flower Boulevarde, Nguyen Hue. The Vietnamese secretaries in the office had repeatedly told him to stay away from it. "Only MPs and CIA hang out there," the cutest girl had warned. "And MPs are bookoo *dinky dau*—number ten, for sure!"

"No lie, GI," another girl had agreed, though her smile belied her sarcasm, mixed as it was with perhaps a cherished memory or two. "MPs break your heart every time. . . ."

Even as the mongrel tore at the tendons and ligaments in his leg, Railroad Smythe was thinking back to the serious expression on the woman's face when she shifted her full bosom across the top of the typewriter—the electric keys had danced under the slight pressure of the smooth flesh strapped tight behind the silky flowered *ao dai*—and faced him, sitting at his clattering telex machine. "MPs from Seven-sixteenth bad news," she had said. "Experts at sweet talk, then *di di mau* out of the bedroom before even the sun rise! Numba ten, *ching ching!*"

It had been lost on him all along why they'd take the time to warn *him*—a "man," about hanging around some overrated, oversexed Saigon Commandos, and he had arrived at Mimi's early, telling the female bartender he was an MPI agent down from Danang for a short-7 and a little R&R.

He had never been given so many free drinks in his life.

Oh yes, they had just been rocketed that very morning in Danang. Several MPs wounded. The barracks blown to hell, the company headquarters still burning when he left. Routine pre-dawn VC harassment that the men "up north" had grown accustomed to.

The senior MP present had given him an open tab at the bar, and from out of nowhere two beauties clad in hot pants and tight halter tops had appeared across either arm, eager to please. "Anything, mista, anything you want. . . ."

He had settled back to listen to their stories. . . . The latest chase, which had totaled three jeeps and ended only after the suspect himself crashed and burned, a side-street robbery where one MP took a splinter of lead in the elbow and the suspect stopped eleven hollow-points before being slammed

11

face down in the dirt, the burglary where the tiny female tenant surprised the suspect and pinned his hand to the teakwood floor with a bayonet . . . routine incidents the innocent layman would remember with crystal clarity the rest of his life, but which the seasoned policeman would forget in a week's time.

The bar had been unusually crowded for a Tuesday night, but they eventually explained to him that another cop was biting the dust—marrying a local. In the past, they had held contests to see how many hearts they could break before boarding their freedom bird home. Now, many of the second-tour vets were coming to realize they couldn't do better than an Asian wife when it came to loyalty and blind obedience, and tonight one of them matchmakers from the embassy with his portfolio of high school cherry girls eager to meet an American husband was scheduled to drop by and show his collection of seductive poses to the lonely hearts club of jungle MPs fresh in from a month of clearing tunnels beneath Fort Hustler.

Railroad Smythe didn't drink that often. And after an incident in Thailand the year before where he had stumbled drunk right into a hostile anti-American housing project after attending his best friend's wedding reception, he had vowed never to drink to excess again unless accompanied by enough close friends who wouldn't mind carrying his overweight mass of flab back to Camp Samae San. But that was Siam. And this was 'Nam.

Who could resist all those free vodka-sevens? And Railroad would be the first to admit he was not known for possessing a strong willpower. The next thing he knew, it had happened again. All the wise old MPs had caught a patrol jeep home mere minutes before the midnight curfew went into effect, and the gorgeous bartender had slapped him silly and refused in no uncertain terms to take him home with her after he was unable to produce his MPA membership card or 18th Brigade patch. Two slender waitresses with seductive almond eyes and long jet-black hair had unceremoniously toppled him from his bar stool and drop-kicked him out into the gutter, where a gypsy cab driver had expertly scooped him up and driven off into the night, not even bothering to solicit a destination.

He could clearly remember the way both girls' firm, upturned breasts jutted out against their fancy satin *cheongsams* at him as they hustled him from the bar. He could remember the hint of smooth, muscular thighs revealed inside the wide slit that ran half the length of the tight Chinese dresses. But he could not, for the life of him, remember anything about the cabbie who had dumped him out in a back alley behind the towering American Embassy after rifling through his pockets.

A boot in the face, and the toylike blue and yellow Renault sedan was puttering off down Thong Nhut. Slowly, as if nothing out of the ordinary had happened.

Railroad smiled, forced a chuckle despite the mongrel now trying to rip off his big toe. Saigon. Saigontown after dark. Nothing out of the ordinary *had* happened.

There came a sudden beating of monstrous wings against the muggy night heat, and as the flapping of dull, powerful rotors sliced the thick air overhead, Railroad Smythe's dazed eyes focused on the Huey chopper preparing to land on the roof of the embassy. It hovered briefly just above the seventh floor helipad of the huge white building, and Railroad managed the motivation to raise his hand skyward—a muted plea for help from the beautiful angel in the sky. But the wild dog at his feet, excited even more by the sudden movement than by all the spurting blood, lunged at the outstretched fingers and clamped its jaws down across his wrist, snapping his arm at the same time the tail of the helicopter dropped slightly as the craft began its landing descent.

Despite the drunk stupor clouding his mind, Railroad's gears were grinding beyond the pain now sweeping aside the alcohol. He knew the routine, having worked at MACV nearly six months now: Three MPs would dismount from the nightly courier ship after it set down with its semi-precious cargo of classified documents and computer discs. One would accompany the warrant officer inside the embassy, while the other two would step onto the retainer wall encircling the pad and survey the quiet grounds below. It was a routine precaution, and the men had come to enjoy it more for its sightseeing benefits than as any security maneuver—no one expected the VC out in the night would risk breaching the perimeter of army MPs roaming the block and then the marine guards inside the main doors just to capture a briefcase full of documents. Even the wily Viet Cong knew the trips were sometimes made with an empty load—just to keep Charlie guessing.

Railroad Smythe took in a chestful of the humid, misty air—it felt like one lung had collapsed now . . . sharp pains were racking his body where there were no outside wounds—and just as he began his scream up at the glowing white letters on the black helmet, the huge mongrel ripped its teeth out of his twisted arm and finally did what all wild animals are eventually expected to do: clamped onto his exposed throat and slashed down into the jugular with frantic, almost desperate tears that grew more vicious as the hot, steaming blood was pumped toward the surface and out through the deep, gaping wound.

Railroad's eyes saw the MP seven flights overhead motion his partner over. They saw the second cop bring a set of folding binoculars out of his pocket. But even Private Railroad Smythe knew they could never race to his rescue in time. Even if they took the awesome responsibility upon themselves to fire down at the mongrel with their M16s, old R.R. knew what little was left of his lifeblood would gush out into the gutter before help could arrive to close the crater where his throat had been torn out.

But his mind's eye was seeing the floorshow dancers at the

Queen Bee. The young one wearing the black and orange bikini, in particular. He was seeing the silent invitation in her exotic eyes, a dare that told him to meet her after closing—if he was man enough. And he had never been man enough. Now he would never know.

Her bikini top, filled tight to overflowing with sweet, amber flesh, had always reminded him of his days as a boy back on the Kentucky hilltops, when he used to launch model rockets with his cousins, and delight in watching them float back to earth peacefully beneath their full, billowing orange and black parachutes.

Private Railroad Smythe's ears were hearing the growling, snarling dog swinging its head back and forth as it ripped free the cords around his larynx, but his mind's memory was hearing the din of voices in the crowded Saigon nightclub, the heavy beat of drums as the woman above him swung her slender hips and shook glistening breasts to the rhythm of a Vietnamese group, "Hammer," imitating the Status Quo hit "Pictures Of Matchstick Men." On a dozen occasions, usually after the third or fourth mug of *ba muoi ba*, he had envisioned himself following her home—hadn't she always left the bar unescorted in the past?—paying her to walk back and forth on his back, kneading tense muscles with her magical toes, before gently spreading those highly toned thighs and taking the legendary Asian plunge. . . .

So many chances she had given him, and he had always backed out at the last moment, saving himself for a woman back in "The World" who didn't even exist.

Now he was dying on a damp dirty back street in the Pearl of the Orient and, if his chances of seducing his princess from the Queen Bee nightclub were gone forever, he'd at least die happy—fantasizing about a feeling, an emotion he had never experienced, had only heard talk of. In Mimi's Bar.

The dog at his throat was suddenly dodging off to the left, out of sight, whimpering in pain as a board slammed down against its foaming snout.

15

Railroad Smythe could feel a presence hovering over him—a shifting in the oppressive layers of night heat that left him strangely relieved. He tried to make words with his lips, tried to voice his thanks to the MPs he was sure were gathering around him, but the pain pounding at his throat intensified with any movement of his jaw and the sensation melted into one of falling slowly, end over end, down into a black bottomless pit.

The shock from his injuries, mixed with the indifference of intoxication already flooding his veins, was quickly setting in, and it's doubtful Private Railroad Smythe ever felt the wine bottle filled with gasoline and shavings of soap being smashed down across his forehead by the phantomlike figure in black he had mistaken for a policeman.

1. MAKE MINE WELL-DONE

As he leaped down the last flight of stairs within the cavernous embassy lobby and raced out through the heavily fortified gates and around the block, the nauseating stench suddenly lacing the air sent Corp. Will Malboys's mind flashing back to that day months before when his combined-police patrol had come across a devastated village north of Gia Dinh that had had a hundred tons of napalm casually dumped on it.

At the end of the dimly lit block lay the man he had spotted from the roof with his binoculars—but now the body was a crackling ball of flames, its charred limbs still jerking about spasmodically, grotesquely, like some mindless demon vomited up from the depths of hell.

Tracers—glowing bright red as they sliced through the thick stillness—sizzled past, mere inches from the right side of his face, and bounced back and forth off tenement walls down the street. He turned back to see his partner firing past him, at some distant target an intersection away. The younger MP, a private with only three months in the 'Nam, lowered his M16 briefly to insert a fresh clip of thirty rounds before firing half the magazine again on full-auto, this time from the hip.

"What is it?" Malboys, a short, stocky twenty-year-old with a thick mustache the color of bamboo and wire-rim glasses, went instinctively down on one knee and drew his .45 automatic. Neither MP, in their rush to get down the seven flights of stairs from the helipad, had seen the mysterious figure spike the drunk soldier with a Molotov cocktail, but the private evidently felt—as did most policemen in Saigon—that the same rules governing a shooting scene applied to the malicious arson of a human being: Anything that moved was fair game for a bullet.

And the private had spotted a figure fleeing the spot beside the twitching cadaver.

Malboys, his own rifle still casually slung upside down over his shoulder, knew it would be a waste of time and energy to pop off a few pistol rounds after the brilliant tracers—he still couldn't see anything moving in the distant shadows. Instead, he cautiously moved up closer to the burning corpse, slipped the rain poncho from his web belt, and draped it over the victim, hurrying now to pat out the fire, to smother the flames before they could melt the plastic fabric. Immediately irritated that his partner was still standing still as he calmly chose his shots, Malboys waved his fist down the street in the direction the tracers were bouncing about and yelled, "If you see someone, chase his ass down! This crispy critter's toasted—I'll be right behind you!"

And as sirens from MP patrols across Saigon converged on the scene of sudden death, Malboys and his partner ran themselves out of breath down the maze of alleys off Mac Dinh Chi, unaware that their suspect was at that time safely in hiding, several blocks in the opposite direction.

Several blocks away, where Thong Nhut intersects Nguyen Binh Khiem, Sgt. Mark Stryker was getting bored as he sat back in his MP jeep, watching Pvt. Carl Nilmes throw kitchen matchsticks at the big apes in the orangutan cage. Last week, while cruising through the Saigon Zoo during an unusually quiet midnight shift, one of the overgrown monkeys had taken to lobbing a liberal glob of spit at the American with the black helmet and glowing

18

white letters. The discourtesy had come no closer than to splash across the jeep's windshield with a nauseating sound—something like the noise day shift made when they staggered in from an evening drunk along the nightclub row of Tu Do, only to take turns vomiting up their "Saigon tea" in the latrines at the end of the barracks—but Nilmes now went out of his way to patrol the district surrounding the zoo in an effort to teach the apes some manners by subjecting them to a nightly half hour of harassment in the form of flaring matches arcing in through their bars.

Stryker shifted his stocky six-foot frame about behind the cramped area under the steering wheel and glanced at his wristwatch. Nearly two o'clock, he thought to himself. Time to be heading over to Tan Son Nhut for a little of that good ole air force midnight chow. Roast beef subs and an iced-down coke'd do a number one job on my gut right about now—would really hit the spot. He ignored the sudden staccato of small arms fire in the distance. It was a common enough sound across Saigon after martial law curfew was clamped across the city of sorrows. Usually just the sidewalk militiamen cranking off some rounds, intent on killing only boredom and not Victor Charlie.

Stryker tugged absent-mindedly at the bullet scar in the center of his left earlobe and forced himself to look over at Nilmes, now face to face with the largest of the apes—separated only by the thick bars of the long cage. "Aw, knock it off, Carl, that big baboon gonna—"

"Nothin' doin', sarge!" The short, slender MP scratched his brown natural briefly before replacing the helmet liner in one fluid movement, "You aren't talking me outta boppin' this punk again—somebody's got to teach him a lesson, or this whole side of town's gonna go ta hell. . . ."

Stryker took the small brown mirrored comb his sister had sent him from back in The World and commenced brushing out his thick mustache in preference to arguing with his partner anymore. He resisted the impulse to inform Nilmes that the big monkey was a female, and instead began

19

humming a mellow Vietnamese tune that had been lingering in the back of his mind all day.

"Yep, gonna bop this motha with my billy-club. . . ." Nilmes boasted confidently, but using a tone that told the sergeant seated twenty feet away he had no intention of being cruel to the creature.

"Sure would be nice to eyeball them donut-dollies over at the Tan Son Nhut USO," Stryker mused out loud, leaning back in the jeep now as he tested the new zippers his housegirl at the Miramar had installed into his jungle boots. One thing he hated more than anything in this man's army was lacing up his boots every morning.

Nilmes knew the PX at the MACV annex had shut down at ten P.M., an hour before they had come on duty. That meant there wasn't anyplace to eat at the army installations, and the trek north to Tan Son Nhut was a short-7 every patrol looked forward to on graveyard shift. Not only was the chow a grade above army food, but the waitresses—yes, the air force actually gave waitresses to their men in blue— had to be some of the most beautiful Asians west of Bangkok. But Nilmes was obsessed with bopping anyone— man or beast—who had the gall to show any outright disrespect to a uniformed member of the 716th MPs.

Hadn't he sticked that full bird colonel from Hamburg for practically inciting a riot just because the MPs had been called in to break up his out-of-control birthday party down at the Eden Roc hotel? He still couldn't understand why an officer stationed in Europe would take his vacation in Vietnam, despite the propaganda he heard from Stryker and Richards every day about how Saigon was where it's at—the only place a *real* cop would want to work his beat.

"Yes sir, I can taste that platter of boiled shrimp and fried rice right now," Stryker yawned noisily and spoke the sentence so there would be no doubt in the private's mind that food was much more sweet at Tan Son Nhut than vengeance could ever be at the Saigon Zoo.

"But sarge . . ."

Just then the three-tone emergency scrambler broke the soft static hum coming from the back-seat radio welded to the inside of the MP jeep. ". . . *Any units* the vicinity U.S. Embassy on Thong Nhut, this is Waco. . . ." the dispatcher at PMO drawled out the final two syllables identifying the net call-sign so that it sounded like Wake-Ohhhhh. "Have report of MPs from gunship courier duty in foot pursuit of another torch suspect . . . now southeast-bound on Mac Dinh Chi . . . units to handle, exercise Code Zero: shots fired. . . ."

"Let's move it!" Stryker was already turning the jeep's engine over, and as the powerful patrol vehicle rumbled to life, the ex-Green Beret glanced irritably over at Nilmes—the man should have been "airborne" back in his seat by now.

"Jesus H. Christ! Help me, sarge! Gimme a hand!"

The huge orangutan—its long red hair dangling down a half foot in some areas, appearing hard as nails—had slipped its powerful hands through the bars and had clamped them tightly around Nilmes's neck when the MP had paused to look back at the crackling radio in the jeep. "This cocksucker's trying to *kill* me!" The big monkey was now swinging the short, slender soldier several feet off the ground and slamming him back and forth against the sturdy cage— the whole time seemingly ignoring the private as she grinned over at Stryker, shaking her whiskered jaws excitedly so that the spittle showered through the night air, sparkling slow-motion-like against the spray of security lights ringing the grounds' perimeter fenceline.

The police radio was busy cutting through static again: ". . . *All units* responding to the embassy identify to Waco at this time . . . you'll be looking for a subject clad entirely in black . . . nothing further at this time. . . ."

"Car Thirty-five responding from the Brinks BOQ . . ."

"Thirty-six from JUSPAO-Two . . ." The young MP gave the common pronunciation of the foreign correspondents' hangout without saying each letter individually, making it sound like "jus-POW."

"Car Niner-Alpha rolling from the ER at Seventeenth Field Hospital—code three!" and he slurred the code designation that announced he'd be activating his emergency lights and siren so there'd be no doubt the bored buck sergeant who hadn't even seen his nineteenth birthday yet was going to enjoy *this* hot run.

Stryker grabbed his radio mike instead of bolting from the jeep to assist his partner. If another Sierra unit—a sergeant's jeep—came across on the air announcing it was en route to cover the call, the quota for responding units would be met, and he'd miss out on the action. While he spoke into the microphone, his eyes remained on the wildly flying form of Carl Nilmes, still being battered unmercifully against the monkey house of the Saigon Zoo. "Car Tango-six en route from MACV annex number one," he calmly gave a phony location that was approximately the same distance from the embassy—but in the opposite direction—as they were now. Stryker didn't want them placed, on tape, at the zoo, in case he had to smoke the ape assaulting his partner. Then he slowly got out of the jeep and started over toward the cage, more irritated at the delay than concerned about Nilmes's safety—the MP was wearing his flak jacket and probably wouldn't receive any injuries except to his pride.

"Gimme a hand, sarge!" Nilmes was repeating now, "before this jerk-off breaks my neck. . . ."

"Yah, well . . . ya snooze, ya lose, Carl my man," Stryker answered, referring to the few seconds of carelessness that had allowed the monkey to grab him.

"Hey, eight-and-skate, boss-man," the private said, confidently now, his feet doing a little dance belying his nervousness as the ape ceased bashing him against the wall, electing instead to merely hang on to him tightly as she observed the second human moving toward her cage. The twinkle in the orangutan's eyes suggested that the beast was sizing the stocky sergeant up eagerly as opposed to experiencing fear. Nilmes was suddenly offended. He could "feel" that the big monkey was ignoring him now. Was in fact impressed by the sight of the tall buck sergeant stalking quickly toward the cage. "Try not to nick me when you dust this bastard!" he was saying, but Stryker was up against the bars so sudden and catlike that the bristling orangutan didn't have time to dodge the stream of mace that shot in through the cage instead of hollow-points.

The monkey dropped the American to the ground, and fell over heavily onto its rump, rubbing its eyes vigorously before pounding out at the bars angrily over being tricked so easily.

Moments later, the two MPs were racing down Thong Nhut, red hood lights blinking back and forth, but the siren off. "Thanks, Mark, I—" the private began, but his supervisor-partner cut him off.

"No excuses, dildo-breath. If it wasn't for that flak jacket, that overgrown baboon back there'd of made spaghetti out of ya! Just goes to show you what can happen when you slip out of phase yellow . . . Remember how I was tellin' ya . . ."

But the radio interrupted him. "Did you catch that, Stryker?" a hollow, metallic voice, clear and obviously close by came over the net.

Stryker recognized the voice as Gary Richards's, the cocky sergeant from the Decoy Squad who was lately overstepping his bounds again and jumping calls in territory usually guarded jealously by the front-line NCOs. Richards, in his thirties—like Stryker—and from Miami, was in charge of a four man "undercover" squad that was authorized to wear civilian clothes, carry exotic "sterile" weapons, and roam the city in a painted-over, souped-up jeep they affectionately called the Black Beast. They were already notorious in the Saigon papers for ignoring sacred district boundaries as they cruised the back alleys, hoping to entice an overconfident Cholon cowboy or two into pulling a stick-up on them. The game was to play drunk or flamboyantly stupid, wander the side streets in a "drunken" daze, and confront some of the worst characters the city slums had to offer. And Richards's men were good at their job. The squad

23

had already greased twelve undesirables.

Stryker picked up the mike clipped to the dashboard and pressed the side button in. "Delta Sierra Two, this is Tango-six . . . that's negative . . . you had background noise . . . ten-nine. . . ."

Stryker hated the new "Tango-six" designation. He was used to the Sierra call-signs, but headquarters' new foot in the spokes was labeling any two-man unit with a rookie aboard a "training" (Tango was the military phonetic for the letter "T") unit, so the men would know who they could really count on and who was still receiving on-the-job experience beside a seasoned sergeant. Stryker had protested the new radio guidelines—they didn't really apply to Nilmes, who had zapped a rooftop sniper out of his Ho Chi Minh sandals his first night on patrol—but since when could a mere NCO influence the chairborne warriors at Puzzle Palace?

The radio speaker emitted a scratchy and inaudible response.

"You're still broken, Gary. . . ." Stryker repeated. "Ten-nine your last. . . ."

"The suspect is now headed southwest down Tran Cao Van . . . toward the traffic circle . . . should be running right into you . . . can you intercept, over?" Lightning sent shafts of static across the radio net.

Stryker caught the street sign out of the corner of his eye: Hai Ba Trung. If he turned right and floored the pedal, he'd crisscross Tran Cao Van in two or three blocks.

The swiftness with which he swerved down the side street would have thrown his partner out into the air had they been turning the other way. As it was, Nilmes flew half into the M60 mounted in the bracket over the gearshift and half across his sergeant's poncho-covered back. Stryker calmly grabbed on to his flak jacket until the private could retain his balance, then cut off the engine, doused the headlights, and coasted down the hill, silent as a panther on the prowl, toward the target intersection. As if on cue, waves of warm drizzle began to blanket the city, masking the flares' sizzle loudly.

"Bingo . . ." muttered Nilmes softly as both MPs spotted the sprinting figure at the same time. The fleeing suspect wore a dark rain poncho that was so long it was difficult to tell if they were observing a man or a woman.

"This is gonna be a cinch," Stryker replied, surprised at himself for making such a statement when he knew from years of street experience that the most routine encounter could leave a twenty-year veteran dead on his back in the gutter.

"Run his ass down, sarge!" Nilmes urged eagerly, drawing his .45 now as the distance between the jeep and the suspect rapidly shrank. "I'll ram the barrel of the hog back there up his kazoo!"

"Settle down, bud." Stryker failed to fight off the grin. It wasn't often you saw a man with less than five years on the street looking forward to confrontation with the unknown. Give him another five years and he'll probably start reacting just the opposite, Stryker thought to himself. Once he's got *baby-sans* and a mortgage to worry about. . . . "We'll take him by the numbers. . . ."

"You can bank on it, sarge. . . ."

Stryker believed he was actually sensing the suspect's surprise and fear just then—could view the scene through the eyes of the caped figure . . . feel the *exact* moment *he* noticed the blacked-out jeep rolling down upon him—so in tune with the movement of time was he. It always happened that way. The action abruptly shifted into a kind of slow motion, playing across the screen of the mind's eye, whenever events or movements pointed toward gunplay and death. The ex-Green Beret knew he was coming to control that phenomenon . . . sincerely felt that, with time, he could enter a fire fight on *his* terms, critique the mistakes before they happened, alter fate, and cheat the devil. Unfortunately, he hadn't progressed that far yet. Events still transpired in a split second, no matter how slowly the mind deceptively perceived them as happening. And before he could master this dimension of combat-kill, as he called it, more people would probably die needlessly. More suspects would bite the dust before the MPs would get the chance to question them about their motives, their feelings, their own superstitions about fate and death in the street.

Stryker slid the jeep sideways several yards in front of the suspect—before the caped figure could react, even though he or she had to have seen the approaching flash of o.d. green out of the corner of his or her eye.

Both MPs jumped out the left side of the jeep and crouched down behind the vehicle's engine block, and Nilmes yelled, "Freeze, or your ass is all mine . . . we're U.S. MPs, honey." The last word in his directive came across more as bored sarcasm than any kind of sexual innuendo.

Though both policemen had their automatics braced across the hood of the jeep, safeties off, ready for action, neither really expected the suspect, caught out in the open, without any cover whatsoever, to resist detention.

Even before Nilmes could bring his pistol's trigger back, the suspect flung his poncho open and showered the jeep with a long, drawn-out burst of tracer fire from an AK-47 automatic rifle.

One of the first rounds slammed into Nilmes's forehead, somersaulting him back end over end across the asphalt behind the patrol vehicle. Stryker had already jerked off eight hollow-points at the silhouette twenty yards in front of him, but the flash of yellow and white light from the rifle muzzle of the person standing across from him prevented him from seeing if any of the rounds found their mark.

The caped figure emitted a low groan as two of the MP's bullets punched him in the belly like a sledgehammer, doubling him over while at the same time throwing him off his feet. As he went down, still firing, several glowing green tracers arced up into the thick, humid night and disappeared into the rain clouds as they burned themselves out against the heavy mist.

Stryker went down on one knee, pinched the ejector button on the left side of his pistol, and felt the sickest feeling his gut had experienced in years when the empty clip failed to slide free. His senses—he was in phase red now—told him the suspect was even then vaulting up over the jeep . . . would have his head in a matter of seconds if he didn't get that fresh magazine of seven hollow-points up into the butt of the .45. There was that ominous shifting of air all around, a change in his surroundings that signaled the animal deep within him that danger was driving him into a corner he'd be unable to escape. A dark, lonely place for lost souls he'd never be able to fight his way out of.

Over and over a sensation that the unknown was slamming a bayonet down into the back of his neck swept over Stryker, but the sergeant remained down on one knee, allowing just one more microsecond for the ejector to function properly . . . otherwise it would be hand-to-hand. Again.

As flashbacks of distant events flooded his mind and he began to see the gloomy afternoon he had fought to the death a North Vietnamese lieutenant on a plateau outside Duc Co, the air around him became suddenly alive with flashing red lights and wailing sirens. He felt the empty clip finally slide free, realized his rock-steady hand had already slammed the new magazine in, locking it tightly against the chamber. Had flipped down the rocker that let the locked-back slide fall forward, chambering the hot load.

He watched himself rising off one knee—was seeing himself from far off. In slow motion.

Damned if it hadn't happened again. What seemed to take an eternity flashed past him, uncaring, in mere seconds. Moments so crammed with action and emotions that time had refused to accept them. At least that's how Sgt. Mark Stryker interpreted what had just happened to him.

Richards's Decoy Squad had arrived in all its glory—was already deploying . . . two men dashing off down a side alley to the left. Richards and his senior man rushing up toward

27

the ex-Green Beret's bullet-riddled unit.

"You okay, Stryk?" Richards was asking.

"Jesus, sarge! What the fuck happened here?" He could hear Broox yelling the question at him, but the words were bouncing away, against a din that made all noise around him sound filtered, muffled.

Richards and Broox were now running over to the aid of Nilmes, who was still lying on his back, half in the small stream now flooding the filthy gutter, one hand against the scalp wound, blood gushing through his fingers as he slowly shook his head from side to side in pain.

Stryker's eyes were drawn like a magnet around to the right side of the jeep—to where the suspect would be lying on the street, also sprawled out on his back.

But the phantomlike figure was gone.

Stryker was automatically reaching for the mike on the dashboard. The thought racing through his mind just then was a question as to whether the radio was still operable. His eyes refused to inspect the inside of the jeep for damage, however—they were locked on the stretch of ground where the suspect had been standing, now seeking out any sign of a solid hit . . . a puddle of blood streaked with rainwater, a hand or jaw severed by the exploding impact of one of the hollow-points.

"Waco, this is Tango-six," he heard himself saying, sirens still bouncing off the tenements that rose up all around as more units loaded down with trigger-happy MPs coasted up on the scene. "We have a chopper-go this location . . . intersection of Hai Ba Trung and Tran Cao Van . . . we have shots fired, an MP down . . . repeating, I need a Dust-Off at this location, ASAP. . . ."

"Tango-six, roger your last . . . medevac en route . . . can you give Waco disposition on suspect, over. . . ."

Stryker started to depress the mike button, not sure—for the first time in years—what he was going to say over the air, and hesitated at the last moment.

Just as Spec4 Tim Bryant came over the air, cutting him

off. "Suspect described as five-feet-five, slender build—" The transmission broke off in a garbled surge of static.

"Male or female?" the dispatcher at headquarters broke squelch.

"Unknown, Waco," came a distant, metallic reply, once again coated over with static and crackling surges each time lightning cut across the monsoon-swollen blanket of black overhead. The thunder was incredible.

"Race? Gimme a race, soldier . . . Caucasian, Negro, PR, Victor-November?"

"Unknown, Waco." The voice on the other end of the transmission was strained, sounded out of breath. The tone was fluctuating, and it was apparent to everyone listening that the MP was still running at top speed, .45 in one hand, portable radio in the other.

"Soldier on foot pursuit, identify, over." The master sergeant at PMO had taken over the radio, irritation in his voice. None of this was making sense to the cops miles away from the action.

"Suspect wearing an army-issue poncho liner, Waco," Private Anthony Thomas cut in, saving valuable air time. "Possibly armed with an automatic weapon . . . AK-47 or Russian SKS . . . approach Code Zero at this time, over. . . ."

Stryker was ignoring the radio traffic; fought off the urge to join in on the chase—which direction would he go? He knew in the back of his mind that none of the men from Decoy had seen the suspect flee either. He shook off the explanation that they had shot it out with a ghost—that was what Lai would say. *Vietnam was crawling with ghosts*, she had always said. The most superstitious woman he had ever known. But that was ages ago, and hundreds of miles north, in Pleiku, where the weekly atrocities guaranteed there was a restless haunting waiting behind every tree. *God I miss her!* He heard himself calling her name over and over in his mind as he started over to his partner.

Richards had slipped his hand between the back of

Nilmes's head and the abrasive blacktop, was now leaning over the private, applying the bandage from his web-belt pouch as Stryker rushed up.

Nilmes refused to cry out, though the intense pain was etched across his features. His eyes stared straight up, avoiding his fellow MPs, choosing instead to follow a brightly burning flare as it floated along on the night breeze, quickly carried away across the edge of Saigon, hardly shedding any light across the intersection where he was sure he would die. Men just did not survive things so painful.

"Carl . . . hey, buddy." He could hear his partner, Sergeant Stryker, whispering to him, but he couldn't take his eyes off the flare. He knew in his gut that when the flare faded against the dark, he too would die, yet there was no fear in him, only a rush of security, now that he was surrounded by men he worked with. ". . . We're gonna get that bastard, Carl," he could hear the big MP promising. "We're gonna turn this town inside out until we nail his ass to a cross . . . you can bank on it."

"How 'bout a little code, boss-man?" The words came out of Nilmes's mouth barely audible, dry. Weak, like a heartbeat just before death.

"Got ya covered, honcho." Stryker smiled for the first time, remembering their first patrols together.

"Got ya covered, honcho. . . ."

A grin formed across Nilmes's face too, lingered for a moment, but vanished as another wave of thunder rolled down across the city, smothering out the last of the flares.

Stryker felt Richards pulling him gently to his feet, away from the MP private drifting off into deep shock, and both NCOs stepped off away from Nilmes as another soldier moved in to hold the injured man's head out of the water. "What the fuck happened here, Mark?" Sergeant Richards was asking, an incredulous look still chiseled across his face. "I've never known a man to act cooler under pressure than you—what went down here before we arrived?"

In the distance, the dull rhythmic beating of sharp rotors

against the hot night air was coming to them slowly across waves of windswept rain and cannonlike thunder. Its lights extinguished since lifting off from Tan Son Nhut airport, the Dust-Off's red cross and tail outline were still visible on the dark horizon. There was an electrifying intensity about Saigon that seemed to radiate against the night even on these moonless evenings, and the powerful Huey slic was caught in the middle of it, just like everyone else, a victim, whether innocent or not, cooperative or unwilling, silhouetted against the glow of the jungle on the outskirts of the city, vulnerable even now to those solitary rockets launched by elusive enemies of the people.

Pvt. Michael Broox went down on one knee and stopped just short of picking up the flattened .45 caliber slug lying on the other side of Stryker's jeep. CID will need pictures—right where it's at, he thought to himself, restraining the natural curiosity that urged him to also pick up the second slug lying a few feet away. Instead, he shone his kel-light down at it, illuminating the misshapen hollow-point, revealing no sign of blood anywhere on it. The final resting place . . .

Another MP was stooping over his shoulder, taking in the two rounds visually, as if he'd never seen thousands of them on the firing range before. "Motherfucker musta been wearin' a flak jacket or body armor," he decided, "judging from the way them dum dums were flattened out on impact."

"Yah, hopefully a couple are lodged in between the plates—that'd leave a hellacious bruise on the bastard," Broox smiled up at his fellow private.

"Shit, *hopefully* the rounds drilled the son-of-a-bitch *in between* his bulletproof vest and his belt line. Now *that* would be hard to explain to mama!"

"That's a rog . . . problem is," Broox's smile faded to his usual frown, "there's no blood trail. I doubt our man sustained more than a mean bruise to his belly."

"Maybe next time, bro . . . maybe next time."

The chopper had now passed low overhead, its rotors

beating down at the shifting layer of thick air above the men on the street with an angry vengeance.

"Set her down in between the two units with the park lights blinking; over. . . ." another MP was directing the Huey over the radio. "Broox!" he turned to the young private on the other side of Stryker's unit. "Get the red lights doused on all the jeeps here . . . I don't want the pilot blinded by all the Hollywood dramatics."

"The headlights, too!" Richards called over to him, taking his eyes away from Stryker's for the first time.

". . . Settin' her down between the bubble gum machines. . . ." The chopper pilot's voice came over the dozen jeep radios crammed around the intersection with a droning, inhuman quality that echoed off the tenement walls and added an eerie shade to all that had already befallen that block this night.

". . . We'll be popping *no* smoke this trip, copy?" the MP handling the ground contact advised the pilot. "Repeat, *no* smoke . . . you've got zero wind at this time and a cold LZ . . . eyeball the power line to your whiskey, between the hotel and the police kiosk, and the rest is wide open; over."

Seconds after the helicopter's tail dipped in preparation for setting down, garbage and papers lining the gutters were whipped into a powerful whirlwind that set off wildly down the street, and the Huey touched down without further incident.

"We better decide right now how the report's going to read, Stryker." The older buck sergeant was getting down to business. But Stryker didn't really hear him. Instead, he was seeing Lai's youthful, taunting face and reliving the events that had come together just that week. . . .

She had been his woman in Pleiku, while he was with the Special Forces in the Central Highlands. During the days he coordinated missions for the local strike force teams outside Duc Co, while she polished the teakwood floor of their bungalow-on-stilts and spent hours preparing the Asian meals he so loved. At night, during those weeks he was not out roaming the jungles, seeking out the Cong, she would place a tiny candle in the window, a sign he was to wake her—no matter how later the hour—for a little extra-curricular activity . . . one *had* to stay in shape, being a Green Beret's woman. Having been born Montagnarde, she not only accepted the fact that his first love was the mission, but understood it.

Hadn't she been raised among warriors all her life, and come to respect the contribution they made to her hamlet's safety? Lai couldn't imagine living with a man who did not make "chasing the VC" the main pastime of his life. She would not have been able to comprehend a land where the men of "the village" went off to work in three-piece suits and returned *every* evening before sunset!

Stryker did not notice the grin streaking his face as he recalled the day he had come in drunk from a three-week mission into Laos. It had been such a success—they had located and "liberated" seven American prisoners of war— with no friendly casualties, that the men had raided a side-street liquor cache in a village along the border and celebrated nonstop until the extraction chopper had arrived and carried them out, in more ways than one. Once back at Pleiku, a highly horny Sergeant Stryker had traded the village chieftain at the housing project, where he kept a modest home-away-from-home, an old bicycle, a beat-up AM radio and a plastic wristwatch, for the most beautiful eighteen-year-old Yarde he had ever seen.

At first, Lai had been wild and hard to tame—even months later she still had the tendency to butterfly on him when he was out in the boonies—but Stryker's fierce reputation was well known among the young bucks in the strike force compound, and Lai was steadfastly avoided for fear of a later confrontation with the legendary Green Beret.

Then the atrocities had hit the region, one after another— always at villages Stryker's A Team had just visited, and when it came time to extend his Vietnam tour, the disenchanted soldier had left the Special Forces and accepted employment as a private investigator for a wealthy Frenchman down in Saigon.

Lai, like most hill people, had never really considered Saigon part of her homeland. In fact, she detested—or was it feared?—everything connected with the huge metropolis she had never seen.

On the night he revealed to her that the time had come to pack up and leave Pleiku, they had argued, and she had run off into the night, naked beneath the shimmering rain, never to be seen again.

Stryker had moved half his belongings south to the capital, and when he returned weeks later to try again at sweet-talking Lai into joining him, he had found his bungalow occupied by another family, his property neatly packed away in a duffel bag and abandoned at the U.S. headquarters compound in Pleiku, and his woman still missing.

For days one of his close friends had questioned the villagers in the area about Lai, but none of them knew her whereabouts. And in the bottom of the duffel bag Stryker found the small photo album with the dragon and phoenix on the cover . . . Lai had gone through and removed all her pictures, and those of the two of them posing together. She had gone through his address book—the seal had been carefully jimmied—but he had no way of knowing what, if any, information she had copied down.

More weeks had passed without any word from her, and he had finally allowed one of the semiretired bar girls hanging out in the Miramar lobby to move in with him. This new pastime was known for her ability to interpret the fortune-telling tarot cards, and she was a hit with all the MPs. More than once, Stryker had come home from a graveyard shift to find several privates lounging on his couch, the girl reading their fortunes . . . for a price.

So long as she was not selling anything *else*, he remained

fairly happy, but it finally got so bad Stryker had to put out the word that his room at the Tu Do Street hotel was off limits to all Americans, friend or foe.

The girl never said anything about the painting on Stryker's wall—the self-portrait of Lai, done in bright oils on black felt, one of the few things she had neglected to remove from their bungalow in Pleiku. It showed her standing before a field of bamboo, naked from the waist up, her dark, almond eyes barely visible below the rim of a straw conical hat. No, the tarot reader had never said anything, thinking the painting to be typical of the oversexed MPs she had come to know and love, hate and love again over the years. Just another wall decoration from the endless displays of identical "tapestries" lining the streets along the riverbanks. Until the letter arrived.

Kim rarely opened his mail, usually only when she was feeling mischievous. But the U.S. postage stamp and the obvious feminine handwriting was more than she could resist.

It was from his sister, though Kim would take days to believe *that*. When Stryker finally recovered the letter, he felt an uneasiness settle in the pit of his stomach when he read the part toward the end.

And I received this letter just the other day, Mark. From a Co Muan Lai, if that means anything to you. Says she desperately needs to talk to you, and "are you still in Vietnam?" What should I tell her? You're always so damn secretive . . . I'll never forget the way you chewed me out for giving out your address to that girl from Taejon. . . .

Stryker was convinced his sister had sawdust for brains. "Why couldn't she have enclosed the letter?" he asked himself out loud as the girl throwing a temper tantrum beside him threatened to break a *ba-muoi-ba* bottle over his head. "Or at least write down something about her address."

That was the information Lai had taken from his address book!

He had immediately cabled her to send further details, but more than a week passed without any reply.

Then the photo plastered across Page 1 appeared in the *Vietnam Guardian*. The one depicting seven Asian women flat on their backs, dead. Alleged VC agents. Killed by a crack ARVN anti-terror team outside Pleiku. Men Stryker had probably trained himself.

And in the middle of the mangled, bullet-riddled corpses, a youthful-looking woman with pronounced, beautiful features identical to Lai's.

That had been only yesterday.

The battalion commander was sitting on his request for an immediate compassionate leave north, so that he could view the body, *her body*. The thought made him shudder. *After all these months, for it to end this way.*

But even now, he could not believe that Lai would have shifted to the communist cause, regardless of what had happened between the two of them. Hadn't the Arvins made mistakes before? Both sides had accidentally slaughtered civilians in the past, and made a big play for the exploitative news media in the end, hoping for the best of a bad situation.

And now, as he felt the blast of air from the helicopter touching down in the middle of the intersection, Stryker could not believe that he had allowed the situation with Lai to interfere with how he responded on the street, either. Sure, Nilmes was lying on his back several feet away, and the suspect had escaped. But hadn't he done all that was humanly possible? Hadn't he emptied a full clip in the face of heavy automatic weapons fire, ignoring his own safety as he confronted the suspect with only a handgun? The only thing racing through his mind during the shootout was whether or not he'd be able to reload before the man charged to finish him—he had never even imagined the suspect would flee when the odds had so mysteriously shifted to his side.

"Stryker, gimme a hand over here!"

MPs were fanning out all around the helicopter, its rotors still flapping around at a fast idle, kicking up dust as the medical team rushed off. The MPs took up defensive positions behind cement lampposts and parked cars—the crafty VC would like nothing more than to blow up an American Huey in the middle of downtown Saigon. The fireball alone would set several blocks ablaze—and each man held his M16 out at the dark.

"Whatta we got here?" One of the soldiers dashed up from under the prop-blast, still bent over at the waist, out of habit—nobody wanted to lose his head to a chopper rotor in the 'Nam. That would be a waste, carelessness pure and simple, when there were so many other honorable ways to die.

"Head wound," Richards muttered, switching hands with the MP who had been keeping Nilmes's head out of the gutter water. He glanced up at the corpsman. "Why, Egor!" a smile creased his grim features, "Welcome back to Saigontown!"

Sgt. Tommy "Egor" Johnson ignored the pleasantries and set about examining the wounded military policeman immediately. "Lotta blood," he decided. "But looks worse than it is. . . ."

"He'll live?" Stryker asked hopefully, quickly regretting the question as he noticed Nilmes's eyes now darting about at all the activity around him.

"He'll live. . . ."

"Mark, I want you to meet Egor Johnson," Richards said eagerly as the men from the chopper worked quickly and competently to stabilize their patient. "He's with the Fifty-seventh Medical Detachment—the original Dust-Offs, as a matter of fact. . . ."

Stryker held out a hand, still dazed himself, but Johnson never looked up from the task before him.

"Egor was flying slicks all over the 'Nam back in sixty-five and sixty-six," Richards continued, "but I didn't know they sent him back to ole Saigontown so soon. . . ."

"I was ridin' medevacs the whole time, Gary," Johnson corrected him. "There's a difference. Joyboys fly the *slicks* and gunships, pal. You're talkin' glory-tunes there! But medevacs are numba ten, brother. We lose a lotta good men. . . ." He said all this without once looking up.

"But very few *patients*, right *amigo*?" Richards added for Nilmes's benefit.

"Haven't lost a *patient* yet," Johnson replied, smiling for the first time, and Pvt. Carl Nilmes sighed and slowly closed his eyes in mild relief, confident he might wake up from this nightmare, after all.

As they gently lifted him aboard a stretcher and started over toward the chopper, he saw this giant they called Egor give Stryker and Richards the thumbs-up, then they were clambering aboard all over each other—a sudden crack from the rooftops announced the snipers had set up shop.

As the rotors picked up speed and the powerful engine began to vibrate the thin skin of the craft, he could see out of the corner of his eye—as they strapped him in atop several flak jackets—his men returning fire from behind their jeeps, ignoring him now as they concentrated on the lone Victor Charlie five floors up.

The intense pain over his left eye subsided, and the sudden rush of adrenaline and emptiness in his gut signaled the helicopter was ascending. Within seconds the raging fire fight was left far below, in the street where it belonged, and his eyes rested on the new string of flares the gunships had dropped along the edges of Saigon.

When he painfully turned to look out the opposite hatch and saw the soldier they called Egor balanced precariously across one of the chopper's landing skids, stuffing rags into the bullet-peppered fuel tanks like there was no tomorrow, he just smiled and closed his eyes tightly again, certain the blur of activity outside the craft and a thousand feet above the highest rooftop in Vietnam was all just part of his private little nightmare.

2. BLOOD ON THE BLADE

Sergeant Stryker stood at parade-rest in front of the Bravo Company commander's desk. It was a casual parade-rest— men were seldom held at attention or harassed in the 'Nam, but he hadn't been invited to sit, either. Stryker had that sort of problem with captains. He made them uneasy, and they didn't want him getting too comfortable off the street, in their offices—in *their* territory.

"Sergeant Stryker," the officer with the flat-top haircut took his black, thick-framed glasses off, set them across the ceramic "Buffy" elephant on his desk, and commenced rubbing his eyes as if the army didn't pay him enough to review an ex-Green Beret's personnel folder, "let's go over it one more time—*your* version of what went down last night. . . ."

"Is this a disciplinary hearing, captain?" Stryker kept his eyes on the officer's, and the pale, overweight man began drawing rockets over and over on an orange and black MACV memo pad.

"No, no . . . of course not. It's just that rumor control—"

"Rumor control, sir? I'm curious . . . does 'rumor control' have a name?"

"That's not important, sergeant—"

"How is Private Nilmes doing, sir?"

39

"He'll recover. The slug took a sliver of bone off the top of his skull, but no permanent damage. A couple months of light duty and we'll probably put him out on a static post until he DEROSes."

Stryker knew better than to ask about the suspect. Bryant and Thomas had chased shadows for an hour and come up with nothing. It took half that time to take out the sniper atop the Bamboo Surf Hotel, and even *he* had turned out to be just an old, half-blind *papa-san*, drunk and angry at the Americans for retiring him from the embassy militia force.

"Now about last night, Mark. . . ."

"It's all in my report, cap. We intercepted the suspect and before we could take him down, he showered us with automatic weapons fire. We returned fire, and it was such a clusterfuck I didn't even know whether the suspect was hit or not. After I reloaded, the cavalry arrived, and the caped desperado had vanished without a trace. I couldn't very well go racing off down any of a half-dozen dark alleys just to put on a show when I didn't even know which way the son-of-a-bitch rabbited."

"That makes sense . . . now isn't this easy—discussing it calmly, unemotionally, like an after-action report in Pleiku?" The captain was doing his best to break the ice. To show Stryker he was an all right guy. A commander the men could come to without fear of being tape recorded or belittled.

Stryker changed the subject. "About my request for compassionate leave of absence, sir . . ."

"Unfortunately, I can't spare you right now, sergeant, and I—"

"Captain, we're talking about the possible death of someone very close to me here. . . ."

"A woman you were shacking up with in Pleiku, from what I hear."

"You're telling me that *you* haven't got someone stashed downtown to cheer you up at night after the PM tears a bite out of your ass?"

"You already know the answer to that, sergeant." The smile left the officer's face and matched the grim, no-nonsense mask Stryker had created.

"From who? *Rumor control*? The grunt grapevine? I've never asked you about your sex life, *sir*." Stryker didn't enjoy arguing or playing games with the officers of the 716th. He had a great deal of respect for all of them—hell, they were all cops, and *had* to stick together, or their chances of surviving the Tour 365 were diminished considerably.

"Oh, come on, Sergeant Stryker!" The captain wiped his brow with an o.d. green handkerchief, noticeably drained. "Everyone at Puzzle Palace knows you NCOs that have been in the 'Nam since Day One keep secret little files on all of us—just in case you need a little leverage in the future. . . ."

Stryker was surprised by the captain's use of the term "Puzzle Palace." It was used to refer to anything from the MACV Headquarters Command, to the embassy in Saigon, to even the Pentagon back in The World, and was a taboo term utilized liberally by the enlisted men but forbidden in general conversation between officers and most career NCOs. The captain's use of it had taken the ex-Green Beret by surprise, and he had missed most of what the officer alleged afterwards. "Leverage, sir?"

"*Blackmail*, you son-of-a-bitch! If you weren't a Saigon Commando after my own heart—I like your arrest stats—I'd detail the Decoy Squad to tear all your bungalows downtown apart until they located these legendary records of yours, and then I'd have *all* you hotdogs out of my hair . . . permanently!"

"Aw, gimme a break, cap. Everybody keeps notes on everybody else around here . . . it's called CYA—cover your ass. . . ."

"I'm familiar with the term."

"You know how it all develops then, cap. We start off as nervous NCOs fresh off the assembly line, brand new E-five

41

chevrons on our arms. Brainwashed about priorities and responsibilities to the point we begin actually believing that *we* are responsible for even the most unpredictable screw-ups of our enlisted men. We begin jotting down little notes when we have to give the privates oral reprimands about sleeping on duty or leaving their rifle unattended in the back of their jeep, or coming to work with the slightest odor of booze on their breath—even though they just put in eighteen hours the night before.

"Nothing usually ever comes of the notes. Just a date, time . . . the man's name and the circumstances. Just a few facts here and there to fill up a pocket notebook, in case the kid turns into a bad cop and we gotta burn him later—then we've got all the evidence semidocumented right here," and Stryker smiled and patted the small notebook tucked away in his breast pocket.

"Then, eventually, the NCO completes his Vietnam tour, and for one reason or another extends for another year . . . becomes a seasoned vet . . . an old Asian hand, as those jerk-off foreign correspondents up on the terrace of the Continental Hotel so aptly coined the phrase. And he eventually discovers that the little fuck-ups and games of the enlisted men he's been documenting for the last year don't seem all that important after all.

"And he begins keeping tabs on the officers above him instead—the big fish. The policymakers whose 'little games' sometimes get the naive, well-intentioned and sometimes gung-ho privates killed just so the men with scrambled eggs on their hat can climb that military ladder of promotions and success—"

"Now hold on just a moment, Stryker—"

But the buck sergeant held up his own hand to silence the officer. "Now don't get me wrong—I haven't seen any incompetence here at the Seven-sixteenth like I saw up in Pleiku. . . ."

"But you're just playing it safe." The slightest hint of a grin returned to the captain's face.

"It's my job, honcho-*san*, to uphold the UCMJ and document any and all other infractions . . . regardless of who the perpetrator might be. Especially when evidence points to the eventual possibility one of my Mike-Papas might become the victim somewhere down the road. . . ."

The captain held up his hands in resignation.

"It's my duty as a Ninety-five Bravo," Stryker smiled back at the reference to his MOS code (military occupational specialty). "And if it's any consolation to you, cap . . . I don't have any files on you, or even," and he patted his breast pocket again, "pocket notebooks."

"That's a relief, sergeant. If I can believe you." The smile remained, but he began running the handkerchief across his bushy eyebrows.

"*You* got something to feel guilty about, sir? *You?*" Stryker asked in mock surprise.

"Let's just change the subject, my friend. Now about your request to take a hop up to Pleiku," and he began skimming the clipboard hanging on the wall next to the mounted teakwood cross-pistols, one of the MP insignias. "You're due to work the graveyard shift again tonight, eleven P.M. to eleven A.M., with confinement to the area tomorrow till twenty-one hundred hours for alert status. Now how do you expect—"

"Richards said he'd work my shift, cap," Stryker cut in.

"Richards *volunteered* to work your shift?" the officer asked incredulously. "He hasn't been in uniform for a couple wars."

"It cost me twenty for the nightwatch, and another ten to hang around for the Alert duty."

"No can do," the captain said seriously. "I've got Sergeant Richards and his Decoy Squad working Cholon tonight. He doesn't know it yet."

"Sir?"

"Yah, while you guys were confined to headquarters

completing paperwork on the shooting, another torch went down."

"Two in one night!?" Stryker became visibly upset. They had not even been told about it while in the back rooms of PMO, downing cupfuls of army coffee and using up black inked pens until well into the noon hour. And *that* was unusual—for word of something hot going down on the street not to reach the ears of every MP inside headquarters at the time.

"Same M.O. and same suspect description."

"We've got a witness?"

"*Had* a witness." The captain began pouring his favorite buck sergeant another cup of jet-black coffee. It smelled burnt to Stryker, but he drank the top half anyway. The adrenaline was still flowing from the fire fight of nine hours earlier, and he'd never be able to sleep this afternoon anyway. Too hot out, and too many aftershocks gnawing at his mind's eye.

"*Had* a witness, cap?"

"A *canh-sat*. Actually saw the suspect douse a gutter drunk with gasoline and light 'im up! Even exchanged shots with the man."

"Outfuckinstanding, sir . . ."

"Unfortunately, the Saigon policeman caught an AK round in the throat. He died three hours ago."

"Of all the luck."

"Yah. The round took his vertebrae right out the back of his neck and broke the window behind him with it."

"Christ . . ."

"Yah, total bummer."

"I guess I can see your position, cap. We gotta get this dirtball off the streets. Did the *canh-sat* leave any more clues on the suspect?"

"He couldn't talk—like I said, the bullet took out half his—"

"I mean . . . did he write anything down—"

44

"How could he? The poor man was paralyzed from the neck down."

"Oh yah . . . of course . . ." Stryker sat down, shaken by the news of a fellow cop's death. Few of the MPs degraded the Saigon policemen like the news media or called them "white mice" because of their white uniforms. Too many of the Americans owed their lives to the smaller *canh-sats*. Stryker wondered if the dead officer was anyone he knew. Some his fondest memories of true back-alley police work were with the combined police patrols—the Canh Luc Hon Hop.

Now that the buck sergeant had come around to seeing things from his perspective, the captain had a sudden change of heart. He picked a steno pad up off his desk, in between the grenade cigarette lighter and the ivory dragon statue, and scanned a short list of names. "Perhaps we can come to a compromise regarding your Pleiku request, Mark. . . ."

"I don't want any special treatment, cap." Stryker was beginning to realize his problems could not even compare to what the dead cop's widow was now facing, and he began to scold himself mentally, embarrassed and somewhat ashamed.

"And I wasn't planning on dishing out favors, either. I'll tell you what. There's no way I can spare you tonight, but Brickmann is due back in from that MPI class in Tokyo tomorrow morning. I had him and Raunchy Raul scheduled off-duty the next forty-eight hours, but if he won't mind—"

"He'll understand. And he *owes* me," Stryker grinned, recalling some past escapade the two had weathered together—the kind of misadventure you didn't tell the brass about. And on another note, "You actually sent that dastardly Ron Brickmann and shady Schultz to the land of the Geisha *together*?" Stryker folded his massive forearms across his chest and let out a heavy sigh.

"Yah, well, we all cram it up and break it off even at the best of times, smart-ass."

Stryker tried to resist the temptation, but the devil in him won out, and he patted the pocket notebook inside his breast pocket with an open palm. "Sounds like something that oughta go down in my secret files," he smiled.

The MP captain ignored the jest and flipped over a couple pages on the pad in his hands. "Got a new man in today, Mark. Been in-country fifteen months already, but it was up in Danang—been in the corps now nearly nine years, so he knows the ropes. I just want him to ride with you a couple nights till he gets to know his way around Saigon's major arteries."

"An NCO, cap?" Stryker subconsciously brushed the layer of soot and smog off his combat ribbons—he often judged an MP's experience and time in-country by the amount of pollution discoloring the Vietnam service ribbons over his left chest pocket of the khaki uniform. At night, the class-A's were usually left in the barracks and the men wore subdued fatigues, from which it was harder to tell how long the man had been stationed in Southeast Asia—you had to look at the shade of green on the jungle cammies. Dark green meant newbie, or FNG. Worn-out, lighter shades meant the man had been around awhile.

"Correct, a buck sergeant. One Cob Carmosino. Has seen some fireworks, according to his two-oh-one file. Two Silver Stars and a pocketful of ArComs. You're gonna love his Brooklyn accent, Stryker."

"Hey, no sweat, cap. We need more combat-tested NCOs. I'm all for it. I'll give him the blue-star tour of ole Saigontown, and—"

"All I ask that you do, Mark, is make sure he survives his first night with the Seven-sixteenth. I don't want to see another . . ."

Stryker shot the officer a cold sparkle out of the corner of his eyes, and the senior MP fell silent.

"You needn't lose any sleep over it, sir," Stryker muttered.

"I don't intend to lose any sleep over it, sergeant. I've

squashed the gossip here about last night—set 'em all straight. . . ."

"That wasn't necessary, sir. I can handle any—"

"But it *is* important, Stryker. Much as I hate to admit it, you've got a tough, solid reputation around here. The rookies look up to you, some even idolize you, I think—from what I've heard mingling with the troops out on the street . . . 'Sergeant Stryker this, and Sergeant Stryker that.' Get my drift?

"You're a charm. And I know you know what I'm talking about. The kids fight over the chance to ride a shift with you, hoping some of your street sense and lady luck will rub off on them. It's no different from the grunts in the boonies . . . one of 'em survives a claymore blast unscathed, or a tank backs over him without breaking a single bone—and the men get real damn superstitious, thinking if they stick with a man with such good luck, they too will survive their year in the 'Nam.

"It's no different in law enforcement. The men respect and trust you. They'll go where you tell 'em, do what you tell 'em to do, regardless how bad the situation looks. 'Cause they know you wouldn't order them to do something you wouldn't undertake yourself first.

"So now some loudmouth at PMO with a hard-on for you starts badmouthing your rep over this thing last night, and maybe some of the men—the ones who don't know how to judge the facts for themselves and need to be led over to the little boys' room—start shying away from you for no good reason. They start hanging around the hotdogs with a file full of DRs or article fifteens, and that's not what I need. What I need is for my smooth-running operation here in the capital of South Vietnam to continue rolling along smooth as a whore's ass. Is that understood, sergeant?"

Stryker shook his head slightly in mock amazement and saluted.

The captain resumed scanning the names on his duty

roster and refused to look up or return the salute. "Dismissed."

Stryker's flak jacket was beginning to feel like it was permanently attached to his skin. Both MP sergeants had discarded the green sweat-encrusted T-shirts hours earlier, but there seemed to be nothing available to combat the intense heat wave that had rolled in across Saigon.

"I can't remember it ever being this damn hot in Danang." Sergeant Carmosino finally broke the tense silence that had lingered between the soldiers the first four hours of the nightwatch.

"It's not usually this humid," Stryker smiled over at the NCO on his right. "I'm no weather forecaster, but I'd venture a guess it has something to do with the blanket of storm clouds that advanced down off the highlands this morning."

"Naw, I heard that the more clouds covering the earth, the colder it gets. . . ."

"Whatever . . ." Stryker knew he could eventually prove his new partner wrong, but he didn't feel like arguing the matter. And he hadn't been being difficult earlier in the shift—it was just that his mind was on Lai and what he'd find in the Pleiku morgue in the morning. He just wasn't in the mood for conversation.

Stryker suddenly jammed down on the brakes, and as the jeep slid to a stop, Carmosino's helmet flew off and clattered across the blacktop. "Did you hear that?" the ex-Green Beret whispered, instantly realizing he should have slowed to a stop instead of creating so much commotion—but the streets remained deserted and the alley they were in showed no signs of curious tenement dwellers looking down on them through steel-shuttered windows or bamboo-balcony drapes.

Carmosino strained to pick out the noises of the night, but a thousand crickets made the task impossible. "Hear what?"

Without answering, Stryker rammed the gears into

reverse and squealed the tires fifty feet back up the block, coming to a sudden stop at the entrance to a smaller back alley where all the street lights had been shot out years earlier and never replaced.

"I can't say as I really heard anything, Stryk—" the new man started to say, worrying more about the abandoned helmet liner now out of sight behind them—MP helmets were a treasured souvenir in the 'Nam, not only the source of endless fabricated war stories about how brave marines "liberated" them from their owners, but coveted keepsakes of many a feisty prostitute, some of whom nurtured precious memories from a time in their past when the MPs weren't harassing them but, perhaps, supporting them.

Carmosino wanted to remark about the way the heavy cloud cover the last few days gave Saigon an eerie appearance, especially at dusk. A surrealistic twilight that made a man wish he could call in sick and return to fight the citizens another day. In fact, he had a lot he wanted to say to this old Asian hand beside him—so many thoughts were racing through his mind about the intensity of the city, the mystery of the underworld Stryker had taken him through, that they became fused into a sensation that could be only described as awe. And Sgt. Cob Carmosino had never been impressed by a mere city. *This was amazing . . . unreal. . . .*

"It was down this part of the maze," Stryker revealed, as he started to unlatch his M16 from the MG support bar in the back of the vehicle. "I'm positive I heard a—"

A young woman's scream sliced through the stillness, and both MPs automatically drew their .45s, jumped from the jeep, and bolted down the dark, narrow passageway.

Every dozen feet or so they would trade the lead, the rear man covering the advancing MP with a straight-armed fanning motion of his weapon, and Stryker found himself in this position as they came upon a movement in the darkness, thirty feet ahead.

The crescent moon Stryker had seen for a few minutes just

after dusk refused to reappear during those rare interludes when the blanket of clouds parted on their shifting travels south toward the Mekong Delta, but he could see his partner in the dim light radiating from a score of distant flares as they drifted beyond the edge of the city. Carmosino was waving the ex-Green Beret up to his position.

Separated by an arm's length, they slowly advanced on the four American GIs who had torn the clothes off a young Vietnamese woman and had her pinned to the ground. Struggling violently—her legs kicking wildly in the air—she was still no match for them.

"Okay comrades!" Carmosino yelled as they charged the group, "The show's over!"

Stryker switched on his flashlight, and both MPs grabbed the nearest head of hair and jerked its owner to his feet, then sent him crashing against the tin walls of the tenements that rose up all around them. One of the soldiers started yelling warnings in the form of animallike grunts, the way contestants sometimes do in karate tournaments, and Carmosino responded by smashing his nightstick down onto the GI's forehead. The infantryman sank to the ground unconscious.

The fourth man rose to his feet and tried to run, but the pants tangled below his knees sent him flopping back to the dirt. Stryker and his partner quickly frisked the first two GIs, handcuffed their right ankles together, then radioed for a Vietnamese police jeep.

Carmosino took out his pocket notebook and army-issue pen, but found it hard to start his report as he stared down at the woman lying motionless at his feet. She was half on the pavement and half in the dirt, and as blood slowly trickled down from the corners of her mouth, her eyes remained fixed on the angry sky, mesmerized by the fury of the spider-weblike lightning bolts.

Stryker finally draped a blanket over her naked, shivering body. He asked her for some ID, but her face was a mask of shock and horror, and she could not even move her lips to speak. She only whimpered slightly, like a baby cat accidentally left out in the rain all night, and her body refused to stop trembling as she clutched the blanket up to her chin.

Carmosino folded his arms across his chest and leaned back against an abandoned vendor's wagon, eyeing his partner. He looked down at the girl—she couldn't have been more than nineteen or twenty—then back at Stryker, and slowly shook his head from side to side.

Stryker didn't react to the sign language. Disgust and misery were often a way of life in the city of sorrows. He couldn't get an ulcer over every victim they came across in the street.

An hour later they had resumed patrol, Stryker still behind the wheel. "I usually let the new man take the wheel his first week out in Saigon, Cob, but if you don't mind, I need something to occupy my mind—"

"Yah, same with me—I usually let the rooks get behind the wheel as soon as possible . . . makes 'em learn the streets and the emergency routes quicker, but I understand. Problems of the female persuasion?"

"What else could it be?" Stryker grinned sarcastically, not really wanting to get into it. *Women*, he thought as they turned down another dark alley behind Tu Do Street, *You can't live with 'em, you can't live without 'em. . . .*

"Wanna talk about it?" Carmosino began rubbing his temples.

Stryker didn't feel the need to open up to a fellow cop just then. He had had woman problems before. They usually did their best to come between him and the job. There were times he even considered the possibility one or two women rated a spot right up there next to his badge, but he couldn't remember the last time that had happened.

51

Except for Lai. Her face flashed in front of his mind's eye again.

When he was on the street, patroling, Stryker was convinced there was no greater love in his heart than for the beat. Especially when he was in the midst of his fellow brother cops—they all laughed about the women in their lives. Called them *insufferable cunts.* Always bitching about the night hours and the vice arrests. Yes, the men all laughed about the women in their lives, constantly referring to them as though they were nothing more than an irritant men let into their personal lives during weaker moments.

Stick with the whores, Perkins up in Pleiku had always said. *They'll never break your heart, you'll never break theirs, and they'll walk on your back all month for peanuts.*

But Stryker knew that was all brave talk and nothing more—a plastic front erected by tough men who melted the minute they walked through the doorway of that bungalow downtown.

Let a Vietnamese woman cry in your arms after an argument . . . let her tears touch your skin, and you fall under her exotic oriental spell from that moment on . . . you'll never escape her after that, another Green Beret had told him. *Her image will be etched in your mind the rest of your life. Even putting an entire ocean between you won't help. I know—I've tried. It doesn't help . . . I always come back. . . .*

"Want a bread roll?" Carmosino asked again, intruding into his partner's thoughts. He pulled a thin buttered roll out of his empty canteen holder. "Still warm . . . and fresh. . . ."

Stryker accepted the food without more than a slight nod, and Carmosino then tossed his helmet in the back seat of the jeep and peeled off his flak jacket. He folded it up like a bulky cardboard pillow and propped it up against his seat, then lay back and closed his eyes, smiling at the hot breeze that swept the tingling rain in over them—it was a refreshing sensation he had never felt anywhere outside of

Southeast Asia.

"Hey, hero." Stryker tried to sound as mellow and low key as he could. "Why don't you put some of that stuff back on— the war's far from over, you know. Just because we got fifty MP patrols supplementing the *canh-sats* in this town don't mean Charlie's too scared to venture out onto his rooftops to take pot shots at us every now and then."

"Gimme a break, Stryker," and the other buck sergeant let out an exaggerated yawn.

"Here it is only halfway through nineteen-sixty-seven and already we've lost eight MPs." The ex-Green Beret tried offering some stats to emphasize his point.

Carmosino muttered something about ". . . damn Saigon Commandos . . ." and Stryker responded

"Look at it this way . . . there's over four million Vietnamese in this town. . . ."

"*Big city* police work." The MP from Danang wasn't impressed.

"That means at least forty thousand VC, using a conservative estimate," Stryker continued. "Now they'll give you fuckin' better odds than that in Vegas, of all places!"

Carmosino opened his eyes and glanced over at his partner, then reached back and grabbed his helmet.

"Happy now?" he asked as he pulled it down over his eyes.

"Yeah, thanks . . . and what about your—" A small motorscooter had pulled up beside them as they left the maze of alleys and turned onto the normally festive street of banners, Tu Do. It was now deserted because of the curfew, except for a police checkpoint at the intersection of Le Loi, several blocks away. Stryker slowed the jeep to a crawl, eyeballing the two slender women on the Honda, their shapely legs balanced delicately over the left side.

Carmosino sensed their body language and looked up just as both girls flipped them the finger, sped up ahead of the jeep and turned right at the first intersection.

"Did you get that license number?" Carmosino had

53

bounced bolt upright at the obscene gestures. "If they wanna talk fuck, I'll cram my nightstick up their—"

"Don't worry about it," Stryker answered calmly. "This is Saigontown, brother. We get that kinda crap all the time—it's just their way of flirting. . . ."

"It's after curfew, Stryker. Them whores gotta play the game by the rules or face the consequences. I say let's stick 'em, *partner*," and he drew his .45 and chambered a round, then reholstered it.

"They were just looking for a little action, for Christ's sake," Stryker waved his suggestion off. "You probably would have just stacked us up anyway in a chase, and I'm getting too old for that crap, you *bic*, GI?"

Stryker turned down the opposite direction when he came to the next intersection, and they maneuvered down a narrow driveway between twelve-foot-high cement fences with broken bottles built into the tops, and came out in the midst of an all-night thieves' bazaar where vendors were peddling everything from stolen stereos to high school cherry girls eager to prove their worth in exchange for a gentle foreigner with a fat bankroll.

Stryker pulled up in front of a leaning table piled high with pineapples and coconuts, and he spoke briefly with the Chinese owner. Her teeth black with betel nut and her eyes dazed from the weak narcotic of the juice, she spoke proudly of her three daughters who "worked downtown, as civil servants." She was an old lady from Cholon, whose sons had all died in the war, and Stryker knew her daughters were really prostitutes working the bars of Truman Key, but he didn't say anything. He never had in the past, only purchased a small plastic bag of steaming sugarcane cubes, covered with salt and stuck strategically with toothpicks for easier handling. They were the only treats Stryker allowed his sweet tooth.

The latest directives at the guardmount briefings had been to "mingle with the Vietnamese. Get to know the shop owners, and frequent the sidewalk vendors. Give the citizens something to remember us by besides a nightstick scar—a few kind words, a generous tip will go a long way at the end of each war."

Stryker knew any MP worth his weight in salt didn't need orders to "mingle with the people." That was the great thing about Saigon. There were few stereotypes—each Vietnamese was a book and photo album unto himself. There were days Stryker couldn't believe the army actually *paid* him to walk his beat through Cholon, *mingling with the people*.

So Carmosino complimented the old lady behind the vendor's wagon on her small slabs of baked dog meat, and after washing them down with year-old Coca Cola, both MPs resumed patrol, seemingly oblivious to the hostility in the eyes of some of the younger male vendors nearby and the manner in which everyone else went about business as usual, as if the police had long ago been bribed not to bust this particular midnight market.

It wasn't long before Stryker noticed the Honda that had been following them for the last few blocks—emerging from a dark side street seconds after they left the bazaar.

He leaned over and motioned to Carmosino, but before they could formulate a risk-free plan of action, the sputtering cycle pulled up alongside them.

It was the two girls again, and just as Stryker caught the evil gleam in their eyes, the long, slender flash of cold steel descended on his partner's right leg. As the switchblade penetrated his trousers just above the knee, the other woman snatched the watch right off his wrist. The driver pulled up abruptly on the brakes, then darted off down another side alley.

Stryker brought his right hand up to keep the fountain of

blood out of his eyes as it spurted from his partner's wound. He flinched in preparation for the scream, but it never came. "Well, what the hell you waitin' for, Stryk?" Cob yelled with eyes wide in anger, "Let's get them whores!"

Stryker jammed all his weight down on the brakes, forced the jeep into reverse, and backed up to the alley. After hitting the red lights and siren, he reached down under the driver's seat for the small first-aid kit, but Carmosino had already emptied an M16 bandolier of its clips and was wrapping it around his leg.

The chase proceeded down through a maze of dilapidated tenements and ended abruptly at the intersection of Nguyen Hue and Le Loi when they caught up with the Honda.

It lay abandoned on its side at the entrance to another alley.

"You want me to get an ambulance in here, Cob?" Stryker asked, picking up the microphone, but it appeared obvious the Man From Danang was all psyched-up to play hero again. He drew his pistol, then slowly dismounted from the jeep, carefully testing his right leg as it touched solid ground. A grimace flashed across his face as he realized the knife had sliced deep into the muscle, but he brought out the other leg and started down the alley.

"You take that side," he directed, pointing at the far side of the twisting lane. Stryker complied, refusing to pull rank on a wounded man so long as the instructions remained rational.

They hadn't gotten even a dozen feet, when a large trash can, filled with bricks, came crashing down on Carmosino from a second floor balcony. Except for the noise that echoed up and down the alley, it was all over in a couple of seconds. Somehow he had managed to duck under the nearest doorway in time, yet a few bricks had found their mark.

After the dust settled, Stryker found him squatting up against the door, a dazed look on his face. His left shoulder was completely soaked with blood, and Stryker's stomach turned slightly when he located a piece of bone protruding from where a brick had fractured his partner's shoulder blade.

"No arguments—I'm gonna radio in a Dust-Off for you!" Stryker said, but as he turned to run back to the jeep, he was grabbed by the front of the shirt and jerked to the ground next to the injured MP.

"What you better *get* are those fuckin' broads!" he corrected the big man in charge of the shift. "They're makin' us look bad, *amigo!*" And though Carmosino's words hit him right between the eyes, the MP with the Brooklyn accent continued to stare down at the dirt.

Stryker spent nearly an hour searching the area, and after five units arrived to assist, all eleven MPs conducted a loft-to-loft search of the immediate neighborhood, but met with negative results. When Stryker returned to his partner, two Vietnamese policemen were lifting him into an ambulance. Carmosino managed a smile after his friends apologized for losing the suspects in the maze of alleys at the bottom of the hill they now overlooked. An eerie blue mist had settled over the housing project as the rains receded, and the warm breezes off the Saigon River rushed in to swirl it all about beneath the zodiacal glow of light from above.

"I better get a fuckin' Purple Heart outta this!" The injured sergeant smacked Stryker roughly against his upper arm, and the big MP grinned back a forced expression of pity and friendship.

"You know they don't give Purple Hearts to MPs, Cob. . . ."

"Why couldn't this have happened six months ago?" Carmosino yelled as the ambulance began its climb up the rain-slick hill in the direction of 3rd Field Hospital, lights flashing lazily but siren off. "I coulda used the R&R!"

Stryker gave a halfhearted wave to the departing ambulance, its dual strobes now sending shafts of crimson light slicing through the creeping mist. But his plastic smile faded as he thought about the chewing out his captain back at headquarters would reserve for him after *this* night's work.

He could always go AWOL, live off Kim's whoring money, the p she made when he was working the night shift . . . when she *thought* he was patroling the other side of town. The thought made him smile again, and he decided it was time to draw up another dozen or so phony assignment rosters, which he'd leave lying around the room—it was always best to keep that woman guessing.

Stryker walked back to the abandoned Honda and jotted down the license plate number, then ran a landline check with the *canh-sats*.

The reply came back almost immediately, followed by several clicks over the radio net acknowledging the disappointment of the entire nightwatch: It had been stolen from a traffic cop two days earlier while he was on his coffee break at the Xin Loi bar.

3. KINGDOM OF FILTH

The young girl was twelve, thirteen at the outside, but the naive twinkle of awe in her narrow almond eyes as she took in all the pretty sparkling chandoliers bathed in multicolored light across the ceiling made her look half her age, an innocent waif.

She stood atop a bamboo crate, in the middle of a sunken stage that might have reminded a newcomer of some pit in a slaughterhouse where animals were shot in the temple or had their heads lopped off entirely with a machete. The girl wore only a gray, loose-fitting sarong, and she was barefoot.

Behind her, in the shadows outside the spray of bright lights, stood several other young girls similarly clad—all under the impression they were being judged in a screening session. The finalists would go on to an actual beauty contest in Hong Kong. Whatever that was. And wherever Hong Kong was. All they knew was that a large meal of lobster and pork ribs awaited completion of the formalities, so long as the girls ceased whining and crying for their mothers. Clouds of blue cigarette smoke filled the huge arena.

Ten rows of bleachers, filled to overflowing with the most despicable collection of pimps and perverts, rose up to surround the girl on three sides, but she couldn't see any of them because of the bright, steaming spotlights, and when a loud voice from the dark calling out a price in Chinese followed the sudden striking of a small gong, the girl was so startled she almost fell off the crate.

A dark Indian wearing a silver-blue turban appeared almost magically beside her, and the girl decided then and there that something about this "contest" was not right. The halfbreed running his fingers through her long hair must have been twice her size.

The Indian made the girl's waist-length hair fan out in his broad palm so that the strands of jet black appeared to sparkle like fine silk under the hot lights. He yelled out something in Chinese and motioned toward the girl's cheekbones with his free hand, and several more voices called out numbers in the thousands, followed by the word 'piaster.'

The Indian was suddenly prying her lips apart, showing the audience her straight, slightly yellowed teeth, and when she began to struggle, he slapped her viciously, bringing a wave of stars and tears to her eyes.

Across the arena, in the fifth row, center section, U.S. Army deserter Julian Ramirez scanned the xeroxed program booklet in his dirty palms and decided *this* girl was not in the advertisements—had to be a last-minute addition. He carefully pulled the roll of piasters, MPC, and greenbacks halfway out of his jeans pocket and decided he just might be able to bluff past the Chinese bidders seated above and to the left of him.

The Indian made the young girl turn her back to the audience, and he slipped her sarong down a few inches, revealing broad, sturdy shoulders that would be able to carry baskets or parcel-poles for years to come.

Ramirez called out a bid, but his voice was drowned out by the din of numbers that erupted in the vast room when the Indian made the girl raise up the bottoms of her feet and it was learned they were soft and uncalloused, unlike the harsh soles of the peasant girls the men were used to bidding on.

The young girl in the center of the spotlights fought back the tears, but the rush of memories flooded down on her as she thought back to events of only a day ago. Her parents had dressed her up in a new sarong and allowed her to ride the train with them all the way north from the tiny village of Cho Gao. It was the first time she had ever seen the legendary city of Saigon, or at least the western edge of it: Cholon.

Her parents had even taken her to a Chinese cinema on a paved street, Tran Hung Dao, and afterwards treated her to a platter of boiled chicken—the closest thing to meat she had eaten for as long as she could remember.

Then they were met by a bent-over, sleazy-looking man in an alley off the exit ramps of an open-air cafe, and she was turned over to him by her tearful mother with the explanation that the man was a distant uncle who was going to escort her to a beauty contest—the kind that could get her picture on the front of those fancy magazines from Hong Kong. Whatever a magazine was.

She had not made the connection when several thousand piasters exchanged hands after the tearful farewell, though the sight of so many pink and blue bills had made her eyes wide with surprise—they had always been so poor. But so had been most of the other village people, so she didn't really have anything to compare her miserable existence with.

After a pedicab had taken her mother and father out of sight—she could still hear her mother crying in the night as it rushed away—the little girl had smiled up at this long-lost uncle and had begun to greet him properly when she was jerked off her feet and roughly dumped in an empty rice sack, only to appear hours later in a basement cellar with several other bewildered girls her same age.

She was now beginning to feel the aches and pains from the numerous bruises inflicted on her during the transfer to this deserted warehouse at the edge of the city, and she was beginning to wonder if this was any way to run a "contest," and if it was really worth a lobster dinner. Whatever a lobster was.

Army deserter Julian Ramirez scratched at his belly vigorously, pulled a couple hairs out, ignoring the slight sting, and raised them up to the spotlights in the ceiling for inspection. He muttered a curse at the sight of the small "crab" clinging to the shaft's end and dropped the hairs down between his boots and made to kick them away between the bleacher planks, never noticing the Chinese on either side of him were brushing themselves off with alarm and scooting as far away as the cramped space would permit.

The Indian standing beside the girl below him pulled the girl's forearms out beneath the harsh light to show they were clean and free of syringe marks, and Ramirez called out in pidgin Vietnamese for him to bare the entire package for inspection.

Though several drunken cheers followed this suggestion, many of the men in the bleachers turned to look up at Ramirez with nothing but contempt and disgust in their eyes.

The Indian immediately tore the girl's one-piece sarong free with one powerful jerk, and she fell to the floor, curling up in the fetal position, suddenly sick to her stomach at her nakedness and frightened beyond comprehension at her vulnerability before so many invisible eyes inspecting her every curve and thought. Her ears were filled with the rush of inaudible, unintelligible bids flooding down to the Indian in a collage of grunts and half-sentences, and her eyes were tightly closed against the nightmare suddenly developing around her.

Ramirez stood up and called out a high number, surprised at how physically developed such a girl who claimed to be her age appeared—she would make a fine addition to his harem of child pornography models, whether she co-operated or not. He just *had* to have her.

The big Indian smiled up at Ramirez and raised two fingers in a casual salute acknowledging his generous bid, and at that moment both side doors burst open and the arena was filled with shrill whistles and bullhorn directives as a squad of Vietnamese national police rushed in, shotguns and revolvers at the ready.

Several groans of resignation filled the businessmen all around Ramirez, but only one man on a bottom bleacher near the door made a move to escape, and he was quickly butt-stroked by an observant *canh-sat* and knocked to the ground, senseless.

Two uniformed policewomen walked in after the sergeant-in-charge ran a torrent of instructions through the bullhorn in rapid Vietnamese, and they began rounding up the girls and escorting them out to a police van while the *canh-sats* kept their weapons trained on the spectators. The sergeant with the bullhorn took off his rainjacket and draped it over the tiny child from Cho Gao—he was a big man, and the garment fell to her ankles. The sergeant then carried her out to the van, brushing her tears away with his lead-laced gloves and bringing a relieved warmth to her with his reassuring smile and fatherly eyes.

When the sergeant returned to the arena, he slammed the nearest bidder on the nose with his fist and began yelling down at him as he kicked him in the side, demanding his national ID card. More policemen were filing into the warehouse, loaded down with handcuffs and ankle chains.

Ramirez decided then and there—at the sight of the thick saps coming out—that it was time to make a hasty exit. He casually started down the closest bench-steps, ignoring a young police private who yelled up at him to resume his seat. As he gained the ground and was almost to the door, the sergeant grabbed him by the arm and swung him around. "Maybe you do not understand Vietnamese," the *canh-sat* yelled, 'So I explain to you in English: This building under arrest! You must—"

The police sergeant did not know why a broad smile flashed across the American's face just then. He did not know if it was because of his English, or because the deserter did not fear the police, but what caused the *canh-sat* to stop in midsentence was the large automatic the tall Mexican produced from within his long trenchcoat.

Ramirez jerked off two rounds in rapid succession even before he had the .45 planted firmly against the policeman's forehead, and the rounds split the man's skull partially right at the nose—spraying blood out from between his eyes across the Chinese seated in the bottom rows as the sergeant whirled around and tumbled, dead before his body struck the dirt floor of the arena face first.

A young police private several feet away leveled his 12-gauge Ithica shotgun at the fleeing American, but jerked the load of double .0 buckshot up into the ceiling at the last moment when one of the policewomen from outside appeared directly behind the deserter.

Julian Ramirez almost stumbled over the slender police-woman in his haste to clear the doorway before it was saturated with shotgun blasts. He could tell instantly that the woman in the beige uniform was unarmed, but as he brushed against her he rammed the barrel of the automatic in between the slight swell of strapped-down breasts beneath the unflattering tunic and jerked the trigger in three times, showering himself with more blood as the young, lifeless body was catapulted backwards, away from him, by the impact of the soft-nosed slugs.

He brought the pistol out at arm's length and fired off another bullet at the second policewoman emerging from the mint-green van, but she ducked back in between the doors, screaming as she dove for the floor of the vehicle. Grinning demonically, Ramirez fired his last two rounds into the side of the van, reveling in the sound of the slugs punching through the metal . . . slapping with pounding force against the unprotected bodies of the girls huddled inside.

The young *canh-sat* who had pulled up short of firing through the tempting doorway now dashed out into the street, but the American had vanished—could have escaped down any of five dimly lit streets running down from the rear of the boxlike warehouse.

He ran over to the police jeep parked in front of the van and yelled his plea for additional assistance over the microphone dangling from the radio on a short cord. Then he opened the rear doors to the van from which the screams were pouring and looked inside, his first-aid packet already in his hands. But the inside of the van had been turned into a horror show merely by two bullets' bouncing about inside, and he backed away from the vehicle in an awkward stagger, his evening's meal of rice and fish heads spewing forth before he could hide his shock behind the nearest tree.

Sgt. Mark Stryker peered out the open hatch as the helicopter began its spiral descent down toward the airbase. A vast panorama of varying shades of green stretched out for several miles in one direction—rice paddies. They gave way to what appeared, from the air, to be an impenetrable blanket of jungle, but what Stryker knew was an intricate network of camouflaged trails and encampments. Along one edge of the treeline began a sparse maze of huts and then whole hamlets with circles of shiny concertina around them. And then a spiderweb layout of boulevards and buildings that spelled home to him.

Pleiku.

The doorgunner sprayed an area along the western outskirts of the city with machine gun fire, and as Stryker watched the tracers burn down through the intermittent cloud cover and kick up paddy water and muck, he asked the Spec4 behind the M60 what he was shooting at.

The doorgunner gave Stryker a cursory inspection with grim, hate-filled eyes, noticed the buck sergeant's deep tan and chestload of combat ribbons across the tailored khakis, and changed his attitude. "Haven't seen the cotton this low in a long time," he muttered, spitting a wad of chewing tobacco out the hatch as he referred to the wisps of cloud here and there. "I like the way the red tracers look as they sizzle down through them. . . ."

His last sentence was uttered more as a challenge than fact, but Stryker wasn't in the mood to argue or reprimand. He didn't have the energy to lecture the twenty-year-old about the innocent farmers he was endangering, or the water buffalo that was more important to a Vietnamese family down there than both the family cars back in hometown U.S.A.

It didn't really matter to him anymore—now that it looked like Lai was dead. No one else mattered to him in Pleiku, and as the chopper began its swift landing maneuvers designed to discourage snipers, the ex-Green Beret found himself studying the monkeys racing about in the treetops and wondering why it felt so good to be back in the Central Highlands of South Vietnam when this should probably be the saddest day of his life.

No military vehicles met him at the airport.

He hadn't arranged for transportation ahead of time, but there was always that chance that word would reach his old Special Forces buddies that he was coming home, and they'd have a jeep and a half dozen of the old troopers there to meet him.

Stryker spent several minutes waiting beside the baggage terminal, out of habit, for his duffel bag. Then, when it didn't arrive, he remembered he was traveling with only the AWOL bag grasped firmly in his fist, and he hadn't even taken a plane here, but a helicopter hop from Saigon. He frowned and shook off the daze, embarrassed that his fatigue was winning out.

Stryker bought a small plastic baggie of iced coffee from a filthy, barefoot teenage girl who had a stand set up by the main terminal corridor. Then he started through the exit lanes and caught the stare of a tall, slender woman in a tight halter-top and silk miniskirt leaning against a mailbox, smooth sleek legs displayed provocatively.

"Maybe you buy me sand*weech*, mista?" she asked in a light singsong voice, shifting her ample chest about to provide him a generous view as he walked past her.

"Sorry dear," and he pulled his empty front pockets inside out in a casual manner that betrayed he was much practiced in deceit. "No money, no honey. . . ." and he walked on without looking back, the fires of passion hardly more than smoldering coal.

"Son-of-a-*beetch*," she muttered in a French accent Stryker saw clean through, and she turned to an Australian behind the ex-Green Beret and bent over to whisper a suggestive phrase into his ear. The Australian turned red, grabbed his suitcase with both arms, and hustled past Stryker.

Outside, several pedicab drivers competed to relieve the big sergeant of his AWOL overnight bag, but he held on to it tightly and began bargaining for a one-way trip to the Special Forces installation.

"Mark!" a male voice with a heavy Vietnamese accent called out behind him. "Don't deal with those bloodsuckers! We're better late than never, can't you agree?"

Stryker recognized the voice long before he turned around and saw the jeepload of Montagnarde strike force members and "Kiet," behind the steering wheel—one of the Luc Luong Dac Biet sergeants who had practically deserted the Arvins to fight alongside the Yardes.

"Why, Kiet!" Stryker floated across the half-dozen yards to the curb and embraced the Vietnamese in a hearty bear hug. "You son of a buck!"

"What brings you back to Pleiku, I should ask?" smiled Kiet, with his peculiar phrasing. It brought back a flood of memories to Stryker—the middle-aged stocky soldier used the same sentence structure whether they were trying to outdrink the bar girls downtown or on a LRRP mission deep behind enemy lines. Kiet tugged at Stryker's collar and motioned for the other strikers to check out the gleaming brass that identified him as a Military Policeman. "I didn't believe it when they told me you actually became a Saigon Commando." And he burst out laughing with the other four men who understood English. "Getting soft in your old age?"

"Saigon's where the real action is, Kiet." Stryker's eyes grew serious, and the smiles faded from the faces of the men around him. "Street action, brother. Nine-to-five combat, where you can shoot up Cholon, then go home to mama . . . know what I mean?" He allowed himself a grin, and the Yardes all smiled along in unison with the tainted humor.

"Aw, yes . . ." a soldier in the back grumbled good-naturedly. "Lotta cherry girls in Saigon. . . ."

"Bookoo pussy!" a second warrior put the thoughts of every man there into words.

Stryker laughed along with them and climbed into the back of the jeep. "Yah, buddy, gettin' tired of jumpin' out of perfectly good airplanes, you know? I'm almost halfway to retirement, my friend. . . ." And he patted a rock-hard belly, still flat as a drum. "Time to sit back and start enjoying life . . . watch the girls drifting past on the warm Saigon breeze in their sheer *ao dais*. . . ."

"Ah, Saigon . . ." Kiet mused loudly, stretching his arms out dramatically, even though he had never been to the capital.

"Yes, Saigon . . ."

Kiet slipped in behind the steering wheel, and in a few minutes they were in front of the hospital—the Yardes knew Stryker wasn't really in the mood to socialize just then with his old Green Beret buddies. They had learned, somehow, that Lai was rumored to have been gunned down while running the highlands with a band of renegade VC, and Stryker had come home to identify and claim her body.

The American buck sergeant felt tears welling up in the

corners of his eyes as the jeep circled around to the back emergency entrance, where the morgue was located. He got out of the jeep slowly, feeling an unsettling fear in the pit of his gut, and started toward the sentry gate without speaking another word to the Yards. They waited a respectful few seconds, then backed up slowly and drove off, and he vaguely could hear the jeep's motor purring as it disappeared down the dirty pathway behind the hospital.

Stryker began to produce his ID card, fell in line behind Vietnamese employees waiting to sign onto the installation, but the guard on duty focused weary eyes on his name tag, stopped what he was doing, and rushed over to the MP sergeant. "If you'll follow me, buddy . . . I'll get ya past all the red tape and chair-borne warriors inside. . . ."

Stryker noticed the Spec5 chevrons on the man's uniform—rank equivalent to his own. *That's the only reason he called me buddy.* . . . He followed the specialist in through the tall doors, wondering what the medic had done to warrant being placed on gate duty.

"The MPs are all out chasin' the VC this morning, pal," he answered Stryker's thoughts with excited words that conveyed he had also recognized the collar brass. "Got mortared again this morning right at dawn, and them MPs saddled up on their V100s and rode off into the sunrise. Takin' real heavy casualties . . . even had to pull the newbie off this static post to help man the assault tanks . . . case you were wondering. . . ."

Sporadic machine gun fire could be heard beyond the city's edge, in the direction the helicopter doorgunner had been spraying the jungle earlier, and soon after both men disappeared within the walls of the hospital, a heavy pall of black, oily smoke began to drift over the city, signaling a fuel tank somewhere had gone up.

Stryker was led through a room where bodies were arranged in various stages of autopsy—the physicians on duty that morning had been called away to the emergency

69

room to treat the wounded MPs coming in from the fire fight between Pleiku and the airbase—and his guide stopped before a clipboard on a desk outside a sealed room.

"Want me to sign in, *buddy*?" Stryker asked in an emotionless tone, searching his breast pocket absent-mindedly for a pen.

"Are you serious, pal?" the medic turned around, all smiles. "If we can't trust the police, who can we—"

Stryker shot the man an icy stare, cutting him short. *He* didn't trust people who were so cheerful or sociable, especially on a day they were apparently under enemy attack.

As if on cue, the medic took on a somber look and led Stryker into a small, cement-walled cubicle about the size of the poolroom back at headquarters. It was cool inside, but not icy as it should be—two air-conditioners were laboring noisily along the far wall, the holes cut through the concrete expressly for them . . . there were no windows.

In the walls on either side of him Stryker saw small, numbered doors about two feet by three feet in size, with the kind of spring-latch handles that could be found in meat storage lockers or cooling bins. "She's in number fourteen, sergeant." The medic produced his most respectful tone, then quietly left the room after saying, "I'm sorry for you, buddy. . . ."

Stryker grabbed onto the latch and recoiled as the icy steel bit into his moist palms. He held on to it again, pulled it free, and watched the small door spring open slowly by itself.

Inside, there was a smaller handle, attached to a long, narrow metal drawer on rollers, and on the card taped above the handle were the words:

UNIDENTIFIED VIETNAMESE NATIONAL FEMALE,

20s.

KIA 30 JUNE 1967 GSW   CASE 67-22,714
HOLD FOR POSITIVE IDENTIFICATION & NONOK

Stryker felt the tears coming on again as he reread the tiny, stained index card. *So impersonal . . . so cold . . .* his right hand curled up in a fist as he grabbed onto the handle with the other. *She doesn't deserve this. . . .* But he began thinking back to the hundreds of autopsies he had witnessed as a cop, where they tape recorded every move that was made, described every wound that was found . . . for court later, and he marveled at how he had sat through all of them without being the least bit affected, the least bit repulsed.

Now, as he was pulling the drawer slowly out of the wall—the temporary crypt—he found he was praying to a god he believed had forsaken him long ago . . . was pleading with him they had not cut into her like all the rest.

The woman in the container was lying on her back, totally naked, arms at her sides, breasts still giving off the slightest amber shade, but smooth and lifeless, relaxed, ascetic in death.

She should be covered, his thoughts cried out at him, and Stryker looked around the room without moving, but saw no sheets or blankets.

He forced himself to look at her face, and his eyes fell to the long, silky black hair draped across her shoulders, now breathing life into the icy room, or so he imagined.

He had sat up so many nights, just staring down at her tranquil, precisely chiseled features when they were living together so many months ago—her high cheekbones and the mischievous gleam in her eyes were what had set her off from the other women of the area, but now the lids were closed forever and the cheekbones had lost their color. The nostrils still had that defiant flare, inbred in her hill people even in their most docile and submissive moods, and—

And then he noticed it.

Or the lack of it. Lai had had a small razorline scar running just below her right eye. Something you'd never notice unless you *knew* about it, or had slept with the woman for years, examining, probing, gently kissing every curve and feature by candlelight as she slept, exhausted after the hours of anxious, almost desperate lovemaking.

He took the woman's wrist in his hand, felt his stomach start to turn as his mind screeched at him for handling the dead—he had carried so many fallen soldiers back to shelter in the past, had piled up hundreds of dead VC without ever thinking about it twice. Why did this bother him so, now?

Stryker examined the inside of the wrist, where it met the woman's hand. The small birthmark, shaped like a flower, half the size of a dime, was not there.

He stood back, stared down at her face again, and sighed heavily at the uncanny resemblance. And then he let the tears flow freely.

This woman was not Muan Lai.

Julian Ramirez toyed with his Pancho Villa mustache, watching intently as the video tape came to its conclusion and the young girl barely out of puberty was gang-raped by several adult males, then thrown out a second-story window, right in front of a speeding lorry. It was his favorite part—already he had reviewed the reel four times.

"I'll take one hundred copies, to start," he told the Indian sitting across from him in the tiny back room adjacent to the gambling den in Cholon. "Payment on delivery . . . and delivery no later than Friday. . . ."

"And if payment is not in cash—" the Indian was about the explain how the price would escalate.

"It will be. And if delivery is not on time, the price drops fifty percent. My clients are hungry for—"

"I guarantee delivery Friday, noon." The Indian bit the toothpick in half and began chewing on it. "You are an ice cube, Mr. Ramirez. You are cold as the devil is red-hot."

"I did not ask for your—" Ramirez's rush of excitement over the profits the video tapes would bring changed to hostility without any warning, but the Indian, still wearing the blue-silver turban fashioned in his home town of Calcutta, cut him short.

"Stay seated, Mr. Ramirez," he said matter-of-factly, one hand hidden from view, and Julian knew a weapon of some sort lay nestled beneath the man's shawl. "I must say I do not enjoy doing business with you—"

"*You* are the one peddling the smut, pal—" Ramirez interrupted.

"Aw, but *I* do this to support my family . . . and you . . . *you* are engaged in nothing but *this*—you soak it up, frolic in it like a filthy hog in a pig sty."

"And why should that bother an old, experienced merchant like you? Surely you have been cheating and dealing with foreigners since the French were here. Hell, I don't know why I'm trying to reason with you . . . you're a fuckin' foreigner yourself. . . ."

"I saw the look in your eye. When you killed that *canh-sat*. It was a look of defiance and adventure. Not the look a man has on his face—in his eyes, when he is running for his life! You are a demon, Mr. Ramirez. I am convinced of it . . . *a demon*!" And as if the power of his own words might make the American pounce on him like a monster, the Indian gathered up his samples and wares and rushed out of the room.

Ramirez emitted a roaring laugh. "Friday, Mohammad, you motherfucker! Have the goods here, Friday! Or I'll cast a Long Ju Ju curse on you!" and he continued laughing as he gathered up his multicolored silk scarves and began wrapping them around his throat.

The army deserter stepped out the back door of the gambling den and took in a deep breath, only to let it back out with a painful cough, doubling over slightly as he cursed. "Damn humidity. I should've skipped out on Uncle Sammy when I was in Korea. . . ."

He flagged down a three-wheeled cyclo and settled himself

down with much irritation in the benchseat positioned over the two front wheels.

"Where you go?" the cycle driver leaned over and a wave of rice wine odor settled across the passenger.

"I'll give you directions," Ramirez snapped, always careful about letting *anyone* know his destination. It was the way you led your life if you wanted to stay free. Out of the stockade. Ahead of them crafty MP-sons-of-bitches. Sometimes he even switched cycles or taxis if there was a longer than usual distance to traverse. And he always got out a dozen blocks away from his apartment and walked in, using a different route whenever time permitted. "Just head east on Hong Thap Tu!"

"Okay, okay boss. You GI? Maybe you want boom-boom tonight? I give you special price—" the forty-year-old war veteran with one leg missing bent his grizzled chin down toward Ramirez's ear again.

"Cut the crap, pops!" the deserter interrupted. "Just drive this crate and save the welcome-wagon bullshit. . . ." But Ramirez allowed himself a smile at the amazement this cyclo clown would show if he were ever invited to one of *Ramirez's* boom-boom sessions, where there was always wall-to-wall cunt.

A few minutes later, the cyclo pulled over at the intersection of Hai Ba Trung and Han Thuyen, and the deserter hoisted his slender frame out of the greasy contraption and brought a one hundred-piaster note (about twenty cents) out of his back pocket. "Oh no, no, no . . ." the cyclo driver shook his head back and forth dramatically. "Three hundred p this trip!"

"Who you trying to con, asshole?" Ramirez jammed the soiled note into the driver's grubby paw. "You only took me twenty blocks—that's a penny a block, that comes to—"

"How long you stay Veeyet-Nommm?" the bent-over veteran asked indignantly, brushing the piasters away again.

"Long enough to know an amateurish con job when I get

hit with it, motherfucker," Ramirez looked the shorter man straight in the eye. "Now do you want this play money, or do I give it to the Arvin Old Soldiers' Home?" He forced the note out again, and this time the driver slapped it loose, causing it to flutter away on the evening breeze. Several gutter children, begging on the nearest corner, chased after the bill, then began fighting amongst themselves when a tiny boy jumped up and snatched it out of a blue cloud of bus exhaust.

"Three hundred p," the driver repeated, deciding then and there he had had enough of American arrogance—*these* round-eyes were beginning to get worse than the French bastards.

"Aw, go screw yourself," Ramirez muttered, turning to walk off, but the driver grabbed his arm and pulled hard, repeating his demand for a higher fare.

When the U.S. Army deserter was jerked back around, he had the stolen .45 in his hand, and he extended his arm out until the edge of the barrel was seated firmly against the driver's adam's apple. The man didn't even have time to cry out or allow his eyes to fly wide with the fear Ramirez so loved seeing.

The large round exploded through the back of the man's neck and slammed into a business woman dressed in a fancy *cheong-sam* who was passing behind him. The bullet threw her against the plate glass window of the French bakery that ran half the length of that block, passed through her body, exiting out the right side, and came to rest in the face of a youngster eating a buttered almond croissant, killing the six-year-old instantly.

In the time it took the cyclo driver's nearly severed head to impact against the cracks in the sidewalk, and in the time it took the well-built Eurasian businesswoman to realize half her breast had been painfully torn free from the rest of her chest, Julian Ramirez had disappeared from sight.

4. GRIPE SESSION, SAIGON STYLE

Stryker saw the paper airplane coming even before it left the private's hand. Instead of ducking, he waited until the last second, then batted it down with a lightning-fast swing of his nightstick. Just as quickly, the baton had been returned to its holder, and the MP sergeant was sifting through the pile of papers on the podium as if nothing had happened.

"Ooooohhhh . . . crash landing!" someone from the back of the room called out dramatically after the projectile flattened across the teakwood floor. A few chuckles broke the unusual silence in the large, top-floor barracks briefing room.

"Okay, let me have a small percentage of your attention, please." Stryker held up his right hand slightly but kept his eyes on the topmost paper.

"Where's our favorite lieutenant, sarge?" another anonymous voice sounded in the back row of the fifty or so men.

"Don't tell me *you* are in charge of the guardmount this afternoon," a third jokester called out sarcastically.

"The Lou is takin' one of his seldom-used sick days," Stryker explained. "Therefore, the honors are all mine."

"The ol' black syph finally draggin' him down, eh?" More laughter, a little heartier this time.

"Naw, I get the impression he's having woman problems

off post," Stryker looked up for the first time and allowed himself a grin. "But that's just between me and our little private group here." In reply, the fifty black helmets with white lettering bobbed up and down slightly, in the affirmative.

"Like I said," the private in the back of the room kept it up, "*Woman problems.*"

The grin faded from Stryker's face, and, as if on cue, the youthful cops fell silent. Secreted in the distant corner of the room, a burping water cooler made the only noise now, and, after a particularly lengthy release of gurgling bubbles from it, an MP nearby muttered, "Ahhhhh . . . I needed that."

"About this complaint from the ambassador." Stryker waved an official-looking document in the air between him and the soldiers.

"Who's the ambassador *this* month?" a buck sergeant in the middle of the group grumbled without raising his eyes above the brim of his helmet liner—it was tilted at just the right angle across his brow and rested on the edge of his nose. Stryker had assumed the man to be sleeping all along. He ignored him now, as if he actually still was.

"Now I realize you fellas got a million busy-work chores on your checklist you gotta complete before you can resume cruising the nightclub district or taking it easy out along Plantation Road, but this is bitch number four from the old man: The marine security detachment at the ambassador's residence is finding discarded prophylactics under the tamarind trees along the east wall of their compound—"

"Discarded *what*?" A corporal in the front row turned to the NCO seated beside him.

"Condoms," he whispered back.

"What?" The corporal was maintaining he still wasn't familiar with the word. The sergeant turned the other way and spoke a few sentences into the ear of the private on his right.

Several MPs in the second and third rows of folding chairs

leaned forward out of habit, but they could not hear what their beloved line sergeant, Raunchy-Raul Schultz, was saying or suggesting.

"So since you already got a million and one b.s. items to check off on your clipboards," Stryker continued, "You'll hardly notice one more little—"

"What do the chair-borne warriors at Puzzle Palace suggest we do?" A stocky PFC remained seated, but the tone of his voice made it sound like he had just stood up. "Stake out the tamarind trees over on Phung Khac Khoan till we make a vice arrest?"

"Sounds like a job for CID," another disenchanted trooper muttered.

"Or MPI."

"It's probably the damn marines themselves goofing off with those housegirls of Bunker's," the same MP who had mentioned the officers at MACV Headquarters spoke up again. "Who else could get past their sentries?"

"Aw, knock it off, Bryant," a weary-looking man in civilian clothing raised his voice slightly. "He's just tellin' you guys all this for your own safety."

"Sergeant Richards is right," Stryker acknowledged the Decoy Squad leader's remark with the slightest tip of his helmet. "We know you got better things to do, but *if*, and I only say 'if' with the slightest suspicions, mind you . . . but if any of you clowns are involved in the extracurricular activities beneath the tamarind trees—"

"Surely you jest," another man in the front row said incredulously, motioning at his own chest with the fingers from both raised hands.

"We happen to know some of you guys got a thing going with the embassy marines," Richards revealed for the first time. "Your patrols stop by there on graveyards now and then when the ambassador's out of town. The guards let you sample the tangerines the old man gets shipped in from Bangkok every morning, fresh, in return for small 'favors' on the street downtown whenever a leatherneck from the Saigon detachment has a little too much to drink and tears down a bar or something. . . ."

"It's only natural you'd cave in under the temptation and also 'sample' some of that dark meat under the sarongs snoozing in the maid's quarters," Stryker added.

"It's happened before." Richards stood up and turned to face the men in response to their growing crescendo of grumbled protests. The sergeant raised both his hands in a futile attempt to quell the clamor. "No, seriously. That's why the Don Juans around here are still wearing E-five chevrons after so many years—not speaking from personal experience, of course. . . ."

There were several more "of courses" tossed back at him than he cared to hear.

"So anyway," Stryker resumed, chasing control of the briefing. "We just thought we'd pass the word: The jarhead's got 'imself a new gunnysack in charge of the consular patrols and executive protection. I hear he's a real bad ass when it comes to regs and S.O.P."

"In other words," Richards took his seat seconds before the paper airplane violated *his* space, "*if* you guys are pumping the housegirls for information, better keep your ass low, because this new leatherneck just might tattoo it with a load of double-ought buck. . . . Is that a roger?"

"Shee-it . . ." came a sigh of disappointment from the middle of the room. Stryker raised himself slightly on the toes of his jump boots but did not spot the disgruntled soldier who had reacted to the news. No sweat, he thought to himself. If they keep it up, it's only a matter of time before I'm visiting gunshot victims at the 3rd Field ER ward. . . .

"Now, on to regular business." Stryker checked his watch. It was almost 1730 hours. This relief shift was due out on the street in fifteen minutes to supplement the regular eleven-to-eleven twelve-hour shifts. He doubted he'd be able to conclude the briefing in that amount of time. "Private

Nilmes is recovering at Seventeenth Field Army Hospital," he said. "Like in the movies, just a scalp wound. The man was damn lucky. Now, you've all got the description of the suspect, and I realize it's not much to go on: long rain poncho and an AK-forty-seven." He paused briefly, then said sarcastically, "Shouldn't be hard to spot. And, off the record, use your own discretion on probable cause to stop-and-detain. If you get a gut feeling about someone on the street—and if it relates to a cop-shooting—screw his rights. You let me and the PM worry about repercussions—that's what we're here for. Just use common sense, during the hours of daylight, that is. If it's past curfew . . . well, you know the rules of engagement in a town under martial law. Right? If the son-of-a-bitch gives you any flak, paste his balls to the cobblestones, then and there!"

"Is Carl taking visitors?" Anthony Thomas in the front row beside Bryant spoke for the first time that afternoon.

"We tried to smuggle a bar girl up to his room last night," Schultz volunteered this latest revelation. "But some goon in a WAC nurse's uniform caught us in the stairwell, between floors. It was considerably disheartening," he grinned, "and a bit hard to explain."

"Yes, I can imagine."

All eyes turned to the back of the room.

Where Lieutenant Slipka stood in the shadows of the doorway, hands on his hips, grinning eyes telling you he had just caught you red-handed again.

"Attention!" one of the NCOs in the back of the room shouted, but before the enlisted men could snap to their feet, Slipka was walking up toward the podium, waving his hands out as if to keep everyone seated. "At ease, at ease," he muttered. "As you were."

Stryker watched with guarded affection as his favorite officer bounded up the steps in front of him. Short-cropped blond hair made the sparkle of his eyes stand out, even past the blue-tint sunglasses. The man radiated confidence. The men liked him too, which was all-important in a combat zone, even Saigon.

Especially Saigon, Stryker thought.

Slipka slipped the small red notebook from his shirt pocket and made as if to scribble a few hastily observed reminders down in it as he passed Schultz on the right. Schultz slowly sank down in his chair, blushing. The lieutenant grinned demonically, as if he finally had the man by the balls and was ready to pin him to the mat. The men loved it—they clapped Slipka's little good-humor skit and all order in the room evaporated. They could all see his left eye hugging the outside crack of its socket as it stayed glued on Schultz while his boots carried him past.

"Pardon my interruption." Slipka nodded to Stryker then consulted a separate set of notes from another pocket. "Gentlemen, Nilmes *is* being allowed visitors starting tomorrow, and I'd like a couple dozen of you down at the hospital at sixteen hundred hours sharp to witness the PM's presentation of the Purple Heart. . . ."

"I thought they didn't give MPs Purple Hearts," Bryant whispered over to Richards, but the Decoy Squad sergeant remained silent.

"Also, we got a new buck sergeant in the Seven-sixteenth this week," and Slipka's smile faded slightly as he glanced back at Stryker. The sergeant's eyes, however, remained locked on his clipboard in thought. "Unfortunately, Sergeant Carmosino is 'billeted' right down the hall from Nilmes—recuperating from a knife wound to the thigh . . . I'm sure you've all already heard secondhand stories about the incident from the midnight shift. What I'm getting at is this: Be sure you stop by and welcome Carmosino to the Seven-sixteenth while you're down at the hospital. And treat him with a little respect—he's not a newbie, for Christsake, like the rest of us. The man's fresh down from rocket resort, Danang."

"Stabbed his first night out?" Mike Broox folded his arms

across his chest in resignation. "Musta been riding patrol with Stryker."

"Tomorrow," the lieutenant continued, "The National Police are holding a mass for the *canh-sat* killed by our torch suspect—you've all read the front-page newspaper stories on that one, I'm sure. We're not making it mandatory, but I'm convinced the family would appreciate the presence of some MP uniforms at a time like—"

"Say no more," Stryker spoke up. "We'll be there, Lou." He forced a tight grin. "You'll find every man in the battalion looks upon *canh-sats* killed in the line of duty as brothers-in-arms. We've already sent contributions to the man's wife, and Drake is putting together a real nice obit to put into the brigade newsmagazine—for what it's worth."

"Excellent, excellent." Slipka slapped his notebook back in his pocket. "In that case, I'll be returning the guardmount to you, sergeant . . . unless, of course, the men feel in the mood for a little uniform inspection to brighten up all the bad news."

The barrage of retorts the men would have unleashed on the easygoing sergeant failed to answer this fairly new officer. Though he had already been tested in combat, a lot of the men were unsure how to classify Slipka. He seemed friendly enough, and not one private could complain with any justification that the Lou had written him up for anything, yet there was that strange 'something' in the man's expression that constantly kept the MPs of Bravo Company on edge: not so much suspicious, but uneasy. Perhaps it would just take time. And perhaps Richards and Stryker could get that new NCO, Schultz, drunk at Mimi's Bar. He had supposedly shipped over to the 'Nam with Slipka, and the two of them had worked together back at Fort Carson, but Raunchy Raul was having his own problems lately and rarely seemed in the mood for his legendary off-duty escapades. Then again, the owner of Mimi's, a notorious "persuader" in her own right, just might possess what it took

82

to loosen the cynical New Yorker up a little.

Stryker made a production of checking his watch and comparing its face with the clock glowing on the far wall, under the huge plaque bearing names of military policemen who had died in Saigon. "Well, actually sir . . . it's getting late, and we've still got a lot to cover. . . ."

"Of course . . . of course," Slipka was already excusing himself from the room, shooting Schultz a wary eye on his way toward the door. Moments later, he was gone.

"I want you to be on the lookout for this creep." Stryker taped a large file photo of a Latino on the bulletin board behind the podium. "He's a first-class scumbag who I want snatched off the street as soon as possible. And the first man to nab his ass gets a week off in the port of his choice: either Hong Kong or Bangkok." Men who had never taken notes in their life began reaching for their pens and pads.

"I've seen that ugly mug somewhere before," Bryant nodded to Thomas.

"Ramirez, Julian . . ." Stryker read his rap sheet off without looking up. "Served in Korea as a finance specialist and courier. He's now classified deserter, and specializes in child pornography. He sports a Pancho Villa mustache these days, and has been seen wearing multicolored scarves or long trenchcoats. And I repeat: *trench*coats, not rain ponchos like our torch. Use caution if you come across him in the streets—he's armed with at least a forty-five automatic, minimum. Hell only knows what he's got stashed under his coat."

"Wears a trenchcoat in this heat?" Schultz was wiping sweat from his forehead with an o.d. green handkerchief.

"We believe he's shackin' somewhere in the vicinity of Hai Ba Trung and Han Thuyen," Stryker continued.

"What's the BOLO for?" Thomas asked, well aware the sergeant was just about to tell them. It was his way of participating in job-oriented discussions, which had their own little slot on the employee efficiency reports the army was coming out with lately. Even in Vietnam, MPs dreaded paperwork more than any sniper's random bullet.

"You've read about the shootout in Cholon the other day?" Stryker waited for a certain number of helmets to bob up and down before he continued. "Where the two *canh-sats* were gunned down at a police raid on a child auction?" More bobbing.

"*He's* our man?" Richards looked genuinely interested for the first time that afternoon. Both sergeants knew his Decoy Squad often got the task of solving crimes the uniformed men couldn't get close to.

"As far as we can tell. Policewoman who survived the shootout picked him out of a VNP mugbook. Could be a real bad ass, gentlemen."

"Shee-it." The same man who had voiced his displeasure at having his extracurricular activities on Phung Khac Khoan street curtailed now groaned at the improbability of any hoodlum's scaring him. Stryker just smiled inwardly. He knew the feeling. After a year or two in Southeast Asia, the men often fell into a mode of thinking that left them believing nothing could ever compare to their experience working the toughest beat in the world. Talk of a hardened criminal or notorious street gang only made them laugh. Months of patroling the back alleys of the capital and policing the denizens of the human underworld hardened them into a protective shell of deceptive confidence that made them see their squads as bordering on indestructible. That was why so many of them couldn't adapt to civilian policework back in The World, Stryker mused as he let his eyes roam the collage of grim faces beneath the black helmets before him. After Saigon, the rules changed. It was difficut for the MPs to conform to their new environment. Actually, Stryker knew, the streets remained the same across the globe. You just couldn't use the same tactics and policies in London or L.A. that had been automatic, conditioned reflex in Saigon. He often found himself wondering where men like that would eventually end up. After Saigon. Guatemala? Lebanon?

"And speaking of the torch," Stryker allowed the men ample time to exhale their frustrations, then continued with the briefing, "we still don't have much on him—"

"Or her," Bryant added.

"Or her," Stryker conceded, frowning as he nodded his head.

"Damn women's libber," Thomas elbowed the Spec4 in the ribs.

"Probably his old lady," Broox suggested. "I've seen Chean when she gets in a bad mood—hotter than a hornet!" A few men on either side contributed the mandatory chuckles, then Stryker interrupted the verbal horseplay.

"All I'm saying is watch your back out there. We've already surpassed our quota of KIAs this year, and I'm getting tired of making visits down to the hospital. Granted, there are several instances when you'll be unable to alter fate and circumstances, but a little caution never hurt anybody. I don't wanna see none of my men getting apathetic on me. . . ."

"Apa-*what*?" the same MP who had claimed he didn't know what a condom was was feigning bewilderment again. The man beside Schultz handed the sergeant a small rectangular packet, and moments later Raunchy Raul had the elastic balloon stretched to its limits and was aiming it like a rubberband at the heckler's ear. The condom snapped, however, before he could shoot it, and went cartwheeling through the air between the podium and the front row, spraying lubrication gel in its wake. Schultz farted with his lips. "Aw, fuck," the man who got struck just beneath the rim of the helmet liner muttered as he cupped the back of his head with his hand.

"Raunchy Raul strikes again," a corporal in the last row mumbled, and several wads of paper arced out toward the sergeant from the middle of the assemblage.

"So beat it." Stryker waved them toward the door, and soon forty-some pairs of jungle boots were shuffling out into the red dust where a line of parked MP jeeps stretched toward the perimeter, several hundred yards distant. "And the first man to chalk up five AWOLs by midnight rates a roast beef sandwich at the Tan Son Nhut USO," he added.

Several men responded with eager grins and the thumbs-up sign. Moments later, the air was alive with two dozen sirens, as they ran a spot check on each patrol unit's emergency equipment and field radio. On a barracks stairwell two stories above the troopers, five housegirls clustered along the railing as they did every afternoon, abandoning the laundry and piles of GI boots awaiting a spitshine, to watch the brief display of revolving lights and flashing strobes, and to clap after the MPs from 4th squad spent thirty or forty seconds playing music with their sirens—a strange sort of private competition that only cops of the street could understand and appreciate.

"Hey *manoi*! Come on down for a ride!" Thomas called up to the youngest housegirl. She was dark as a mahogany tree, barely four and a half feet tall, with bare feet that boasted bottoms rough as sandpaper, but the girl possessed a chest that could put many a barracks pinup bunny to shame. The men showered the teenager with compliments and lewd proposals, but the older housegirls kept her protectively under wing, and Stryker doubted she had even lost her cherry yet—despite the worn-out saying he heard everyday: There's no such thing as a virgin in Saigon.

"Awright, knock off the chatter!" he said, moving out onto the barracks porch overlooking the jeeps. "The women there got their job to do, and you clowns got yours, so move it! Leave Dang alone for a change."

The housegirl, Dang, smiled shyly down at the men, ignoring their patrol sergeant, and swished her hips about for a second until the men erupted into a chorus of howls and barks. But the sound of several powerful motors turning

86

over soon drowned out the Americans, and, as unit after unit rolled out the compound gate, the housegirls hustled Dang from view.

Stryker could hear them scolding her in Vietnamese. *Dang*, he laughed at the name as he walked back into the shaded patio toward the watercooler. They shoulda named her *Damn* for all the hard-ons she causes around here.

"I heard Brickmann's getting into her pants." The captain had appeared out of nowhere and stood in the doorway, frowning.

"Naw, I doubt it," Stryker replied, acknowledging the officer's presence with a dip of the chin, but he did not salute since they were under cover of the roof overhang. "The Brick's got more class than to go around bangin' jailbait, and besides, I'd bet a month's pay young Dang there really *is* still a cherry girl, despite her provocative smile."

"A month's pay?" The officer seemed doubtful.

"Sure, cap. Don't you notice how that old *mama-san* with the black smile guards her like an attack dog? Hell, no way a guy could get past her!"

"Yah, the old hen *is* quite an obstacle," the captain laughed, folding his arms across his chest as he turned to watch two patrol jeeps loaded down with an entire squad of MPs rumbling onto the installation from airport duty out at Fort Hustler.

"Speaking from personal experience, sir?" Stryker baited the company commander with a wry smile and unblinking eyes.

"Unfortunately, yes." His own grin faded and he began nervously fidgeting with his wedding ring.

"Yeah, me too," Stryker muttered under his breath in a condoling tone as he downed the paper cone of water and hopped over the railing into his jeep. "Me too . . ."

"I see you're without a partner today." The officer with three years' worth of campaign stars on his Vietnam service ribbon forced his gaze from the rowdy group of MPs dragging their gear from the jeeps into their quarters.

"I guess nobody felt lucky today," Stryker said, unchaining the steering wheel. He pumped the gas pedal a couple times, then twisted the starter toggle. The souped-up engine under the hood rumbled to life. He gunned the accelerator three times, creating a swirl of smoke and dust beneath the exhaust pipe as he "blew out the cobwebs."

"I thought you always had a waiting list of volunteers ready to accompany you on your nightly rounds."

"I guess the men figure three strikes—"

"And you're out," said the captain.

"Roger that. Can't really blame them, though. Some of the guys used to consider me a charm . . . you know how it goes. We've discussed it a million times. Somehow I always bump into felons loitering on street corners, and the kids working patrol and bucking for a super-cop arrest record figure some of ol' lady luck'll rub off on them. But lately I've had this run of *bad* luck, and superstitious as these guys are, I'd be lucky if they don't bar me from their private little choir practices down on Tu Do."

"I read somewhere bad luck runs in cycles." The captain gazed out at the smoky horizon and paused. Stryker's ears seemed to twitch forward, like a suspicious horse annoyed with its master's tricks, and he braced himself for the unmistakable twirling whiz of an incoming rocket. But the air remained calm. Unshifting, stagnant—even oppressive, but there was no sudden change or threatening vibration that always seemed to precede a surprise attack. "I believe it was back when I was a line lieutenant at Fort Carson—yah, that was it. There was this radio station psychic who did a weekly program . . . damn, what was her name."

"Lou Wright." Stryker quickly flipped through his memory bank and her name sprang forth like a Halloween trick-or-treater hiding behind bushes.

"That's it!" the captain was amazed Stryker had remembered the woman. "You listened to her too?"

"Didn't everybody?" Stryker shifted the jeep into neutral and let it idle. "Graveyards were always shorter when you could tune into her Denver talk show."

"Shit." It was the first time Stryker ever heard the officer utter a profanity. "And I thought I was the only cop ever crazy enough to tune into a show like that," the captain laughed.

"Cops, on the whole, are a suspicious breed," Stryker smiled, producing the tiger claw necklace around his neck. He shifted the gold clasp around so that it sparkled against the sun's hot rays. "I don't think I ever met a street MP who didn't have his little hang-ups about avoiding a certain patrol unit, or wearing his good luck ring, or substituting a chrome clip for the black ones the armorers issue—stuff like that."

"Well I'll be doggoned." The officer sounded suddenly like a Nebraska farmboy. "And I thought I was the only one around here who insisted on never leaving my hooch without my Fraternal Order of Police ring."

"Rest easy, sir." Stryker lifted his fist up so the captain could inspect the ring on his right hand. It too was an FOP ring cast in silver with a police-blue stone. "Never travel anywhere without it."

"Hell, I thought you'd have a Special Forces ring or something. Maybe an arm band or one of them Montagnarde bracelets with a Green Beret flash on it."

Stryker's features went somber and his grin lost some of its sincerity. "Those days are long gone, cap." His thoughts shifted to Lai and he saw her face in the clouds clear as if she were floating in front of him. "I'm back to being just a simple street cop."

"There's no such thing as a simple street cop," the captain said.

"No more jumping out of perfectly good airplanes."

"It takes pride, integrity, and guts to be a good policeman these days."

89

"No dreams of seeing my future son at the position of attention, receiving silver jump wings on his chest." Stryker sighed dramatically.

"Yes, I firmly believe a street cop deserves ten times the salary society pays him. . . ."

"No more Green Berets tilted at just the right angle . . . no more cigars hanging strategically from lower lips at airport bars while surveying the round-eyes walking past, searching out their brave paratrooper-for-a-night. . . ."

"If I was God . . . if *I* had the power to decide who got paid what, you can bet your beret my street cops would get the highest salaries on the scale. You ever see one of them Wall Street executives volunteer to ride along on a single eight-hour shift with the N.Y.P.D. just to see, as a private citizen, of course, what it's really like for the men on the block—the cops who maintain law and order in an otherwise lawless society . . . the urban warriors who so unselfishly serve and protect so the streets will remain passable and the egomaniac execs can make it to the office every morning at nine o'clock? *Fuck no!*"

"An infantry point man probably hauls in two hundred bucks after taxes each month." Stryker was more talking to himself than the captain now. "For putting his life on the line twelve hours a day, in a foreign jungle crowded with commies anxious to cancel his ticket. Would you ever see a politician volunteering to trade places with him for even an hour?"

"Or a politician's son . . ." the captain added.

"Fuck no," Stryker answered himself at the same time the captain spoke. "A point man should be the highest-paid professional in American society, but he makes less than some jock scrubbing mud off cars at a carwash back in The World—"

"Where there's more cunt behind the wheel than one man could handle."

"And do you see any pussy around here?" Stryker raised

90

both arms out to encompass the compound.

The captain started to offer his reply when a private in khakis stepped out of a taxi at the main gate with two grinning, buxom women hanging on his arms. They headed for the outdoor theater after the off-duty MP signed the Vietnamese onto the installation.

Stryker immediately amended his question. "And do you see any *clean* pussy around here?" The captain let out a hearty laugh and doubled over, holding his gut.

The private gave him a casual salute, and though he was without his hat, neither Stryker nor the officer said anything. "Evening sirs." The private was all smiles as he spoke the confident greeting. Stryker envisioned the three of them— one whore sitting on the kid's face and the other with her head bobbing up and down over his crotch—entangled across the sweat-slick sheets of a one-man cot up in a dark barracks somewhere after the movie. Stryker glanced over at the cinema sign and grinned. Appropriately enough, the new James Bond movie was playing: *Thunderball*.

"You think you can handle them?" Stryker called out to the private.

"Gee, sarge," the private feigned total innocence in his reply, "I'm just takin' these ladies to the flick. The only way *this* hero is gettin' sticky tonight is holdin' a jumbo bucket of buttered popcorn!"

Stryker shot him a who-you-trying-to-kid look but didn't say anything.

"Ladies of questionable virtue," the captain muttered, not loud enough for the private to hear. The kid was soon beyond the sapper barriers and quickly disappeared from sight.

"Anyway, as I was saying," the captain continued. "This talk-show psychic claimed bad luck runs in cycles— sometimes years at a time."

"Years?" Stryker's face snapped back toward the officer. In the distance, a fierce exchange of automatic weapons fire suddenly broke the afternoon calm, then just as quickly

91

ceased, the echoes fading with the breeze.

"Yah. As I recall, seven- and nine-year cycles were the most frequently revealed time periods, Lou's callers were told. Then again, there were those who she felt were only going through a few months of Murphy's Law syndrome and would fall back in grace with the odds game anytime soon." The captain's eyes were intently scanning the distant horizon again, perhaps seeking out some spiral of smoke in the direction of the shooting, while his concentration remained on the subject at hand. "I seem to have been the victim of some indiscriminate bad-luck cycles myself in the past," he admitted. "I once considered trying to match it all up with my star charts and crap like that but never had the time to spare. . . ." He was beginning to sound like the conversation would flow along these lines for more time than Stryker had on his hands, but the MP sergeant was suddenly not in the mood to drive away. The prospect of being burdened with a nine-year bad-luck cycle just seemed a bit unfair.

Then again, maybe he'd climb out of it soon—maybe he was just caught up in the shorter, monthly series of depressing events. Maybe . . .

"Waco, this is Car Thirty-six Delta!" A young, excited voice broke through the static on the radio band of his jeep monitor. "We have a Ten-one hundred, Repeat: Ten-one hundred at—" A surge of static covered the MP's transmission, drowning out the sound of weapons discharging in the background.

"Your location, Thirty-six Delta, over . . ." the dispatcher came over the air calm as lagoon waters. "Gimme your location, bud. . . ."

More static . . . then, "Repeat . . . MP needs help! Corner of . . ." Then total fade-out and other units crowding the net with unnecessary transmissions.

"Waco, this is Car Fifteen-Alpha . . . what was his location?"

"Waco, Car Twelve is at Tu Do and Lo Loi . . . what was

that Ten-one hundred?"

"All units!" the more powerful base station wiped the mobile uits off the air. "Code One! Repeat. Stay off the air unless emergency traffic . . . Thirty-six Delta's in a dead zone. . . ."

Stryker and the captain just stared at the huge radio bolted to the back seat, unmoving. Without a location, there wasn't much anybody could do. Thirty-six Delta was a courier unit that was authorized to roam the entire city, delivering sensitive paperwork to various American and Vietnamese agencies across Saigon.

"Car Thirty-six Delta," the dispatcher sounded much older than his forty-some years. "Try again, son . . . you're still broken . . . gimme your location, MP . . . Waco over. . . ."

". . . 'ceiving sniper fire . . . 'ner of Le Van Duyet and Hien Vuong . . . do you copy, Waco? Partner's got a bad belly wound . . . will be running him Code to Third Field; over. . . ."

Stryker grabbed the mike from its dashboard clip and depressed the plastic transmission lever. "That's negative, Thirty-six Delta!" He didn't waste time identifying himself —every MP in the 716th Battalion recognized *that* voice. "Remain at that location until we get additional units there to take out the sniper. . . . Do you copy my last? We'll get a Dust-Off out to pick up your partner as soon as possible!"

"Too late for that, sarge!" came the reply. A siren was growing fast in the distance. "We're already halfway to the hospital. Car Twenty-two Echo is on scene, though—he's got the sniper pinned down. . . ."

The unit with the wounded man aboard could already be seen approaching the International Hotel compound, where the MPs were billeted.

Stryker ran the unit designation through his mental filebox: 22-Echo. That would be the gung-ho private with the alphabet for a last name. . . .

"Awright, disregard proceeding to the hospital!" Stryker cut in just as the patrol jeep was on the verge of screaming past down the crowded avenue outside the compound walls. "Bring it in here and we'll utilize the colonel's bird on the roof—traffic's too congested for you to proceed on the ground." The jeep was already cutting across lanes to make it into the maze of roadblocks outside the main gate. "Now gimme a description on that sniper, and his exact location. . . ."

A confident if not somewhat cocky voice came over the air in a bored tone just then. Stryker had to lean closer to the radio speaker just to hear it. "Waco, this is Twenty-two Echo at Le Van Duyet and Hien Vuong . . . you can cancel all Mike-Papas responding my location . . . and you can cancel one rooftop Victor Charlie; over. . . ."

Upon hearing the voice, Stryker connected it with a name on his hundred-man roster: Uhernik. *Goddamned Hungarian*, he smiled his thoughts up at the bewildered captain. Didn't even call in on scene. "Confirming you're a solo unit, Twenty-two Echo?" Stryker talked to his microphone again. "One confirmed kill, this location, Car Niner." The soldier from Czechoslovakia dodged the question with a play on words.

"Copy your last, Twenty-two Echo," Stryker added, a tint of irritation to his tone. "But are there any other Mike-Papas at your location?"

"Negative," the dry reply came back barely breaking squelch.

"And you're a solo unit?"

A moment of dead silence, then, "One Victor-November policewoman aboard," came the hesitant answer. Several clicks from mikes in other MP units broke static—it was the men's way of snickering over the air without actually laughing.

"Confirming you're a *Canh Luc Hon Hop* unit?" Stryker's icy tone showed no hint of the smile on his face. He already knew the answer to his question, but one of his favorite pastimes was making MP privates who were goofing off squirm for the minimum tense half minute. A *Canh Luc Hon Hop* unit was a combined American-Vietnamese police patrol, and he knew Uhernik hadn't ridden with one in over a week.

"Car Niner, this is Twenty-two Echo," the words came across slow—radio formalities always allowed MPs on the line those precious few seconds to come up with an alibi or excuse for whatever they had been caught red-handed at. ". . . this Mike-Papa was in the process of relaying her to PMO for interpreter duties when the Ten-one hundred went down. . . ."

The lengthy explanation continued to drag on over the net, but Stryker wasn't paying attenton anymore. He knew it was nothing to get an ulcer over. If the kid *had* been up to something, he'd have never admitted over the air that a policewoman was in his unit in the first place. Stryker'd probably end up writing him up for a medal or something anyway—but for now it was time to concentrate on the MP unit skidding up to them through the compound's main gate.

Stryker's eyes shifted from the terrified expression on the driver's face to the look of intense pain on the man's partner's features—from chin to eyebrows he seemed one complex contortion of agony. Both of them were buck private—unusual, for most MPs received their PFC stripes upon landing in the 'Nam—and the man with the belly wound sat straight up in the passenger seat, his shoulders forcing the cushion back to its limit as both hands kept the sheet of plastic pressed against the pile of intestines oozing down through his fingers and onto his lap. The jeep had come to a stop but the siren was still winding down as Stryker yelled for the gate sentries to phone up to the rooftop MP. "Tell him the chopper's to be ready ASAP!" He was pulling out his own first-aid packet now. "I wanna be airborne in zero-five, got that?"

The Spec4 in the white kiosk waved an acknowledgment —he was already busy on the field phone, with his free hand cupping one ear against the roar of Saigon traffic outside the installation. Above, the slow, double-swish of Huey rotors being set into motion filtered down through the thick, muggy air from the rooftop.

"This really sucks, Sergeant Stryker," the man with the gut injury found the energy to smile as the husky NCO and the captain began lifting him onto a stretcher.

"That's why they call it a sucking chest wound," Stryker grinned back, ignoring the inaccuracy of his curbside diagnosis—the concerned look in his eyes was so alien to the grin on his lips, the MP in his arms felt a wave of relief settle over him.

"And I just paid the rent on my hooch downtown, sarge." He couldn't have been twenty years old at the most. "Can you believe that run of luck? Can you?"

Stryker and the captain exchanged knowing glances, but the sergeant replied to the gate MP who was assisting them instead. "Hustle it up, trooper! We wanna get him in out of the dust before that gunship topside starts throwing rotorblast down at us—with this kind of wound, keeping it clean is the most important thing . . . infection now will ruin this man's whole day. . . ."

The last sentence was whispered, but the injured MP wouldn't have heard anything even if it had been screamed at him. He was drifting into a delirious shock. "Twenty lousy bucks, and now I can't even enjoy it," he was saying, his speech slurred like a drunkard's now. "And it's the first time I ever paid on the first of the month . . . I'm always a day or two late, you know sarge? *Always* . . ."

"But you got your woman to think of, right?" Stryker was bending low now as they entered the hotel lobby. "She's gotta stay somewhere, eh?"

"Aw . . . yah, roger-that, sarge . . . aw man, she's really gonna have a case of the ass at me over this one. I was supposed to take her to the Caravelle tonight . . . aw man, she's gonna be real pissed off. Ya think you could smooth it over for me, Sergeant Stryker?" He grimaced at a bolt of pain lancing down through his bowels. "Hell, I musta taken a bazooka round, sarge. I can't feel nothing anymore but the pain. Nothin', sarge . . . I'm not gonna make it, am I?"

His face seemed to grow calm, even relaxed, very suddenly, and Stryker searched for the right words as the stress lines faded from around the man's eyes. Behind them, doormen in black slacks and wine-colored jackets were rushing to get the elevator open, automatically knowing the Americans' destination. Vietnamese girls in tight white maid outfits shuffled out of the way or stood behind the check-in counter, eyes wide and delicate hands across gaping mouths, displaying just the right amount of shock and compassion. The MPs had been using the Internation Hotel as their street headquarters for some time now, but the employees had yet to grow accustomed to all the excitement and action connected with police "stationhouses" across the globe.

Stryker did not say to the wounded MP what he wanted to. He did not tell the man he'd be fine, and wait till he saw the nurses at 3rd Field Army Hospital. Instead, he remarked, "You still shackin' with that cute girl runs the pizza stand at the bowling alley?"

"Same—same," the private's face transformed in front of their eyes to one of intense pleasure as the memories flooded back to him. "Ain't she a doll, Stryk?"

"Definitely a real looker, bud. I've always wondered what she looks like with her hair down. I could never get close to her . . . after *you* hustled her out from under the rest of us." They were squeezing into the elevator now. At first it appeared the stretcher would be too long, but somehow they got it in and the doors were sliding shut.

"Ah . . . her hair . . ." the private's mind drifted back to the last moment he had spent with his Vietnamese girlfriend—perhaps just that morning, on the street corner below their apartment balcony, where she kissed him with a bird peck on the cheek as he settled in on the back seat of the Honda that was hired on a weekly basis to race him back to the barracks after the curfew was lifted with the rising sun. "But you should see her thighs, sarge. Magic thighs, I calls them: *magic thighs* . . ." The elevator began its jerky ascent toward the roof, and though the MPs standing were nearly thrown off balance by the jolt, the injured private didn't seem to notice.

Stryker glanced at the wound though his instincts told him to look away. Already they were discolored, and losing their elasticity. The life, like a garden hose disconnected in preparation for the coming fall freeze, was slowly draining from his intestines.

"She's always got a bowl of that shrimp soup waiting for me, sarge, when I get off duty—you know the kind. . . ." Stryker knew. It was a Vietnamese specialty. All the MPs knew. "Do you think I'll be getting off duty today."

Stryker bit his lower lip, trying to come up with the best response. Wondering if the man would even understand what was being said between the two of them.

"Do you think I'll ever see her again?" They were rushing across the rooftop now, lifting the stretcher onto the skid straps. The colonel himself was aboard, waving them closer. "She's saucy as some of them Thai women, sarge . . . I don't think she'll wait. . . ."

"She'll wait for you, brother." Stryker was suddenly busy making sure the bonds were secure—already the Huey's rotors were invisible overhead, and the skids seemed to be trying to lift off right in front of him. "She'll wait for you!" he was yelling now, in competition with the rotors' roar. "I'll see to it, mister—I guarantee it!"

"She won't wait for me, sarge!" Tears were streaming down the man's face now. The captain had scampered aboard the helicopter, and Stryker could see that, as usual, the cargo compartment was crammed full of psy-ops equipment—room for just one more crouching man straddling the open hatch.

Stryker leaped up over the MP on the stretcher and was caught by the two military police officers—each grabbed an upper arm and fought to steady him as the chopper lifted off and was banking away from the building. Stryker whirled around and was quickly leaning across the injured man's face. The captain, behind him, held onto Stryker's web gear. Below, ninety feet of dead space separated the doorway from the rows of sand-filled petrol-tank barriers and the maze of sparkling concertina spread across the ground.

"You're gonna be okay, trooper," Stryker was holding the improvised shield over the man's belly wound, fighting to keep the smog from getting at it. "Before you know it we'll be spiraling down onto that big red cross at—"

"She won't wait for me, sarge!" They were reading each other's lips now against the din of flapping rotors a few feet above. "It's in their blood . . . they don't like to sleep alone after dark!" and he tilted his face away, scanning the blackened tenement rooftops racing past in a blur below. "She won't wait. . . ."

Stryker watched the private's eyes roll back before the lids fluttered against the wind and fought to stay open. "She'll wait for you man! You've got my word on it!" But already the MP's grip on Stryker's wrist had fallen limp and his smile fell apart except for the downblast trying to force the edges of his lips back.

"She'll wait for you, brother," Stryker said, glancing down at the man's bloodied name tag. "I'll see to it," and he closed his eyes tightly, knowing the woman would not wait long. Her man was dead.

5. HONORABLE INTENTIONS

"Some more coffee?"

The stewardess could not remember when a mere soldier had so interested her before. He sat by the window, light brown hair cropped close to the skin. Face clean-shaven in contrast to the thick, jet-black brows. *Makes him look like an owl*, she smiled to herself as she leaned over the sleeping soldier near the aisle and tapped the "owl" on the shoulder.

"Yes sir?" he whirled around, nearly upsetting the tray. "Uh . . . ma'am?"

"Coffee, soldier?" she asked in her most seductive voice, careful to display her chest at its most strategic angle. She smiled, and he had no way of knowing she smiled because she had kept herself from saying *coffee, tea, or me?*

"Uh . . . no ma'am . . . no thank you . . ." And he turned back to stare out the window at the depressing sheet of gray slapping at the plane. They were descending into another monsoon storm front on their approach to Saigon's Tan Son Nhut airport. It was as if he had never even looked at her—was still seeing some ghost of a face beyond the window glass, out in that depressing wall of clouds.

"How about some orange juice?" she persisted, beginning to wonder now why she even cared that this soldier seemed different than all the rest. "Or a candy bar?"

He didn't even answer her this time. Just kept staring out that damn window at the layers of rain pounding the outer skin of the plane.

A massive hand had cupped the right cheek of her buttocks, and the Pan Am stewardess whirled around herself this time as the meaty master sergeant lying across three seats behind her answered her scowl with an ear-to-ear grin. "How 'bout a see-gar, honey?" he reached out for her again, but she slapped the ridge of hairy knuckles and scurried behind the rolling table piled high with ice and liquor bottles.

"I'll see what I can come up with." She forced a smile, instantly regretting her choice of words. But it was too late—half the sergeant's side of the plane had heard and were now answering her comment with obscene murmurs and lewd proposals. The sergeant hugged his pillow, ecstatic.

She expertly retreated to the steward's station however, and commenced watching the private glued to his window. A mere private, she mentally reprimanded herself. Mesmerized by a mere private . . .

But there *was* something different about the kid, she decided. And it wasn't connected with the somberness and soul-searching many a recruit resorted to at the last minute as they approached their generation's combat zone. He wasn't biting his fingernails like the eighteen-year-olds. And he wasn't bragging about war stories like the NCOs. He looked more like a man on a private mission. A mission the importance of which transcended any mandatory obligations the military expected of him.

She had managed to get a look at his right shoulder—there was no combat patch sewn on it, so it wasn't as if he was some veteran warrior returning to a savage woman he had finally come to terms with. The patch on his left shoulder was vaguely familiar: a training command somewhere. Georgia? These men were all dressed in fatigue uniforms so she couldn't glance at their collar brass and hazard an educated guess. Some of the veteran NCOs on the private's side of the plane were wearing the verticle dagger flanked by two battle axes. She knew that made them military policemen. The little group on the opposite side appeared to be slick-sleeved, or without combat experience. Including the sergeant who had grabbed her. *Engineers!* She knew she could have his lousy stripes if she wanted to press the issue, but Christ—these men *were* headed for war. Some of them would not be boarding their freedom flight in a year's time.

She spent a moment recalling the faces that got back on the craft after their Tour 365. Dazed, glassy-eyed, unsmiling most of them. Then there were the REMFs who had spent their year in the rear, bartending in the clubs or filing the KIA reports—they always clapped uproariously when the plane's wheels finally lifted off the runway tarmac. She wondered which group her little soldier would be in and why she even cared. She had boyfriends in every port—Paris, Singapore, San Francisco. But none of them were men.

Private Greg Marsh stared out at the silver sheets of rain obscuring the cloudbank, but his mind's eye saw an American soldier far below, in some steaming jungle outside Saigon, bringing up the tail end of an infantry patrol that was coming in from the field after five days without enemy contact.

"Let me be the first to welcome you to South Vietnam. . . ." A metallic voice was trilling over the plane's intercom, but it came to him dreamlike, a world away, and he did not feel the stewardess pulling his seatbelt tight.

As the plane descended down through the last of the looming, fantasyland clouds, he was not seeing the gray, billowing blanket of mist and swamp vapor, but the platoon of grunts outside of Gia Dinh.

Greg did not realize he was biting his lower lip as his mind anticipated the ambush that would wipe out half the squad, but even as the blood began to trickle down his chin the enemy failed to spring forth and the platoon straggled into camp unscathed. . . .

But minus one man.

He thought back to that first telegram from the government. His mother had almost suffered a heart attack over it. His younger brother had put his fist through the apartment wall, furious—helpless. Greg still carried the original cable in his pocket, but he didn't need to pull it out now. He had it memorized.

WESTERN UNION TELEGRAM
1021A EDT FEB 14 67 =WASHINGTON DC 1014P EDT
XV GOVT CAS PDB= CONSTANCE MARSH
714 STATE STREET RM. 2811 CHICAGO
DONT PHONE DONT DELIVER BETWEEN
10PM AND 6AM
THE SECRETARY OF THE ARMY HAS ASKED ME TO EXPRESS HIS DEEP REGRET THAT YOUR SON, SGT. NATHAN MARSH, IS MISS-IN ACTION, THE REPUBLIC OF VIETNAM AS OF 11 FEB 67 IN THE VICINITY GIA DINH/SIAGON. ANY STATUS CHANGE REGARDING YOUR SON'S UNWITNESSED DISAPPEAR-ANCE AT A TIME HIS COMPANY WAS NOT EXPERIENCING CONTACT WITH HOSTILE FORCES WILL BE DULY REPORTED TO YOU. PLEASE ACCEPT MY DEEPEST SYMPATHY. THIS CONFIRMS PERSONAL NOTIFICATION MADE BY A REPRESENTATIVE OF THE SECRETARY OF THE ARMY.
PATTERSON MICHAELS
MAJOR GENERAL, USA, Z98
THE ADJUTANT GENERAL

Two months later the midnight police raids had started. That was after the men in his brother's squad signed sworn

103

statements that none of them had witnessed Nathan's disappearance, and that the platoon had encountered no hostilities whatsoever during the entire weeklong patrol. Of course, it was possible the veteran buck sergeant, who had been the last man in the spread-out formation, had stumbled into a tiger pit or *punji* trap—perhaps some wily VC had even reached out and snatched off his head when no one was looking, but everyone seemed to agree all that was unlikely.

Greg even had a pocketful of letters from his brother's closest friend, but they contained nothing comforting—only detailed accounts of some of the patrols the two of them had gone out on together. The man claimed he knew nothing about Nathan's mysterious disappearance, and after several subsequent letters suggesting Greg was wasting his time (". . . let Uncle Sam find your brother . . . if Nate even wants to be found. . . ."), the infantryman had broken off all contact with the Marsh family.

Greg's younger brother, Franky, had been arrested by the police during one of the last middle-of-the-night raids. After the door crashed in and the combined patrol of MPs and Chicago's Finest failed to find Nathan hiding in any of the closets or under the bed, the usual apologies were extended to their mother and the officers began their retreat toward the stairwell. But Franky had reached the breaking point, and the cops' explanations (". . . Sorry, but it's all routine follow-up after a wartime desertion, ma'am. . . .") did not serve to restrain him this time. Greg, who had wanted to wear the silver Chicago star ever since he could remember, rushed across the room to tackle his brother, but he was not fast enough, and the kid had jumped on one of the MP's backs.

And was promptly clubbed to the ground.

Greg had pleaded with the men. He would control his temperamental brother—he'd sign any waiver the officers wanted to produce. Just leave Franky to him, and it would never happen again. But they had taken the teenager away, and the judge had decided, in all his wisdom, that their mother, a widow ten years now, was unable to control her unruly son and he would, henceforth, be confined to the juvenile delinquent detention center at the Cook County jail.

Ten days later, young Franky, who had no previous arrest record and had never even been reprimanded by his teachers in school, waited until the ten o'clock lights-out whistle, then quietly climbed up to the iron grill across the ventilation shaft in the ceiling and draped the torn towel through it.

Then hung himself.

Greg Marsh watched the ground slowly rising to meet him outside the plane's window. He watched the long lines of concrete hangers passing by, and the countless guard towers and parked tanks that were positioned strategically between them every few hundred feet. He watched the scattered groups of Vietnamese in black pajamas and torn fatigue shirts pull their conical straw hats down over their faces to shield them from the swirling sand as the jet airliner roared past the bomb craters they were repairing in the rain.

Greg watched the thick sheets of water slam down on the little people as they raced about dragging debris off the runway or reinforcing sagging coils of endless concertina wire. But his mind's eye was seeing his mother back in Chicago. She had worked several jobs for years so that he, her number two son, could attend college and pull the family out of their South Side slum. Her knee money (that's what she called the meager wages she earned scrubbing floors and mopping hallways after the sun went down), combined with the monthly allotments Nate had sent home from Asia had been just enough to see him off to college. But then the army had advised them Nathan was missing, and, weeks later, labeled AWOL—Absent Without Leave. The news brought disgrace and embarrassment to the family—especially after the first police raid. The walls were tissue-thin as it was, and word traveled fast: the March family had a deserter son in its ranks. Soon the walls in the laundry and the lobby were covered with graffiti claiming Nathan was a coward who didn't deserve to ever return to the land of the red, white, and blue, and though the Marsh family vowed never to lose faith in their soldier-son, life in that overcrowded tenement had chilled to an uncomfortable low.

Greg Marsh was arriving in Saigon during one of the heaviest monsoons the South Vietnamese capital had ever seen, but he had no way of knowing that. Even the pilot of their long, sleek 727 made no mention of the weather—he seemed too busy persuading the craft's controls to guide the airliner in and out of the rocket craters left over from the morning's surprise barrage. Through weary eyes, Greg watched the distant treeline rushing past in a multihued green blur, but he was not seeing the guerrilla-infested palms the other passengers were worried about. He didn't notice the security jeeps cruising the flight line either, or the SPs with their dog teams, walking among the Vietnamese peasants who had been hired to repair the pockmarked runway. Instead, he was seeing his missing brother's face staring back at him through the gray mist. . . .

Sgt. Nathan Marsh had been drafted and sent to Vietnam three years earlier. And had stayed.

Greg had a hundred letters from his brother, telling about his Saigon romances, and his greater love for the engagements in the jungle. About how he had already extended his tour in Vietnam three times and planned to sign another waiver. *There was just nothing to compare with a jungle patrol at dusk.* . . . He had written it so many times.

That was why Greg could never believe his brother had deserted his fellow soldiers.

True, his letters those last few months had been filled with complaints about graft and corruption in the military hierarchy—both Vietnamese and American—and his final letter had hinted about some sort of bungled drug-running operation Nate had happened upon, but nothing so serious he would give up his stripes and shame his family back in The

106

World. And everyone in Nathan's unit had maintained they were not even encountering so much as sniper fire on that last mission. They could offer no explanation for their sergeant's disappearance.

Greg believed his brother was not a deserter. And he believed Nathan was not a casualty of the war either. He was, in fact, convinced his brother had been murdered by his own men, and that the mystery centered around the jigsaw puzzle of stories contained in the packet of letters at the bottom of Greg Marsh's duffel bag. The belly of the huge airliner now touching down across the rain-slick runway northwest of Saigon was crammed to the hilt with hundreds of identical canvas containers, but Greg felt his contained the key to solving a mystery that had held his family hostage for too many months already.

After several attempts at gaining a visa to South Vietnam had failed (he had met up with several roadblocks everywhere he turned—the U.S. and Vietnamese embassies . . . even the Post Office, where his passport application had been rejected), Greg had been amazed how easily the army allowed him into its ranks and eagerly approved his request for a Vietnam tour after he signed a contract guaranteeing him a slot in the next Military Police school cycle. His mother had been heartbroken, of course. Abandon his studies to go wandering off to war? Ridiculous!

But he had convinced her—or at least convinced himself—that under the circumstances there was no other course he could take. And why couldn't he, after this was all over and Nathan was back among them, return to his college classes or even apply for an officer's commission in the military? That would surely bring him closer to a job with Chicago's Finest in four or five years. He had always been so patient, waiting for Nate to get this, or do that. Surely he could wait a little longer for that law degree and silver badge.

Greg's father had died of stomach cancer nearly two decades earlier, and he couldn't remember the man's face except for the large black and white photo in that dark hallway back in Chicago, and his memories of his mother praying beside a skeletal, graying old man of thirty when Greg and Nathan were only children.

The plane was finished racing its reverse thrusters now, and as it began taxiing toward the distant terminal, Greg noticed, for the first time, the show of military force along both sides of the runway. Air force security police atop rumbling V100 assault tanks cruised back and forth in the warm drizzle, looking grim and businesslike. Gun jeeps with Hog-60s mounted between the front seats sat beside sandbagged bunkers every few hundred yards. He glanced down at the 201 personnel file in his lap. Assignment: the 716th Military Police Battalion of the 18th MP Brigade. The weathered old crow of a gunny sergeant who had been sitting beside him during the first leg of their flight between Oakland and Anchorage had noticed the military orders also, and Greg could clearly remember the polished look of irritation in his snarl when he muttered, "Another Saigon Commando, eh?" When the plane lifted off from Alaska, the marine found himself a different seat.

"Please remain seated until the aircraft comes to a complete stop. . . ." the copilot gave the usual terse directive over the intercom, and, seconds later, with the plane still rolling slowly toward a portable stairwell truck, an assortment of grizzled veterans were on their feet, pulling bags and briefcases out of the overhead compartments. *Briefcases!* Greg wondered incredulously to himself. *This is Vietnam?* He thought about his duffel bag in the belly of the craft and made a mental note not to forget it after they deplaned. The contents would help him somehow prove his brother was not a deserter, but had happened upon something so secret or too hot to handle that he had been eliminated by his own people. The thought began to scare Greg somewhat. He, a mere private, was planning on going up against men who had survived months in the jungles of

Indochina—had most probably killed more guerrillas than *he* had fingers!

Suddenly the plane jolted to an abrupt stop, and several of the men around his seat were thrown off balance. A briefcase fell from the overhead storage bin, and papers exploded into the aisle. The stewardess who had been so helpful earlier was bending over a few feet away now—helping to scoop the mess up as more and more soldiers began crowding into the aisle.

Up front, a side door opened, and along with a suffocating blast of tropical heat, a squad of Vietnamese policemen in white shirts and light blue pants rushed down the crowded aisle, scanning the few Asian faces suspiciously before returning to collect everyone's customs cards and disembarkation papers. Greg leaned out toward the aisle and peered up toward the front of the plane. It appeared none of the air policemen had boarded the craft with the angry-looking *canh-sat*s. He glanced back down at the runway through the rapidly fogging portal window and stared out at an American SP patrol. Blue jeep with white stars on the sides. Three men aboard, wearing camo fatigues and white helmets. Looking tough, hardened by the heat and sun. He noticed the tanned muscles rippling up at the planeload of fresh, pale-faced newbies. The shirts of the air policemen had been tailored skin-tight, with the sleeves rolled up high above the biceps. All three airmen were grinning up at the aircraft. How long did they have to go on their Vietnam tour, Greg wondered. Not very long, judging by the smirks on their faces. He wondered how they compared with the army MPs he'd soon be riding alongside. Or maybe they'd stick him in a guard tower somewhere, or one of them high-risk static posts, and he wouldn't see street patrol for months.

It didn't really matter, he knew. So long as he had made it to the 'Nam. And such luck . . . there it was right outside his window: Saigon.

"Oh! Excuse me. . . ." The pretty stewardess had backed

her shapely hips up into his row of triple seats to allow some impatient officers past in the aisle. She had bumped his elbow with her thigh and his last cup of water had spilled onto Greg's lap. She was suddenly busy trying to wipe the mess up; he was protesting mildly that it was no problem—it was just water . . . it would dry. No damage done.

Christ! he thought. She was practically giving him a massage with that damn towel. He could feel himself growing hard as the low-cut blouse jiggled from side to side in front of his eyes. "Really!" Greg smiled, feeling himself blushing. "It's okay, ma'am."

But now she was picking his customs packet off the floor . . . had he actually dropped it in the confusion, or did she knock it down there on purpose? And she was stuffing a napkin or something in between the papers. He started to tell her the folded napkin, or whatever it was, didn't belong to him, but the plane was quickly a bustle of impatient activity—a trio of loud sergeants had boarded and was shouting everyone off the plane—and after a wink and the slightest hint of a seductive smile, the woman with the swirl of reddish-gold hair pinned up on top of her head was gone.

"Army to the right! Air force to the left!" one of the NCOs was directing the passengers. "Navy and marines proceed through to the center. Let's hustle it, gentlemen! Charlie likes to hit us with mortars when it rains like this."

"We want you dispersed as soon as possible!" a second NCO bellowed. "Before Charlie can triangulate his mike-mikes on you. And there's to be no loitering on the airfield. If no one starts to lead you toward the terminal building ricky-tik, then by all means, take it upon *yourself* to exit from the kill zone before the Cong can get a sight picture on ya!"

"Horseshit . . ." a major behind Greg muttered under his breath. "Bunch of clowns . . . tryin' to scare the new-bies. . . ." Greg noticed he was wearing summer greens, and was one of those carrying a briefcase. The private tried to get a closer look at his collar brass—the insignia would reveal his army MOS—but when he finally spied the gleaming judge advocate symbol he was unfamiliar with which specialty it was attached to.

The drizzle lifted as Greg stuck his head out the doorway and started down the stairwell to the tarmac. Wide shafts of sunlight shot down through a break in the clouds, and within moments everything seemed to shrivel up under the increased heat. The smell in the thick air was of a thousand military uniforms drying in the breeze.

On his way down the steps Greg scanned the scattered military transports that had coasted up toward the impenetrable ring of security jeeps, and after he saw no HQ716 markings on any of the bumpers (a drill sergeant at The School had taught him that trick) he showed his papers to one of the *canh-sat*s and proceeded directly to the terminal.

Two-foot-tall cracked silver letters welcomed visitors and servicemen alike to TAN SON NHUT INTERNATIONAL AIRPORT, SAIGON. He smiled at the intensity of it all—the heat, the countless lines of conical straw hats working on the runways, the Phantom jet-fighters swooping down low over the guard towers on the perimeter waving their wings—and got in a formation of soldiers who appeared to be lining up for a customs inspection. It appeared none of the duffel bags were being opened, and, in lieu of passports, the GIs only had to flash their green ID cards to enter the country.

"They get you on the way out a year from now," a corporal with a First Division combat patch on his right shoulder turned back to smile at Greg, reading his thoughts. "No dope . . . no war trophies . . . no housegirls . . ." he laughed at his private little joke, "but they don't give a shit what you bring *into* the damn country."

The slow procession through the customs checkpoint was orderly for the most part, and quietly dull. The youthful-looking inspector routinely jerked Greg's paperwork from under his arm, glanced at his ID card without comparing the skinhead snapshot to his current likeness, and slapped a

111

PASSED CUSTOMS sticker emblazoned in black English and green Vietnamese across his duffel bag without opening it. But once past the customs station, the atmosphere of the terminal changed drastically.

There were no walls for the most part, and therefore none of the iron grilles and security personnel that had cluttered the runway side of the building. The ceiling was supported by thick beams, and the walls were not walls at all, but a fancy network of dull grilles that let the muggy Saigon air filter through with what little breeze happened by on that day. The change in architecture was also an open invitation to every form of lowlife and con man the South Vietnamese capital had to offer. They seemed to be gathered in restless groups just beyond the baggage terminal: pimps with painted bar girls dangling from each arm, greasy cyclo and hack drivers motioning passengers out toward their respective vehicles, con men selling blackmarket goods and tickets to the porno palaces downtown, beggar children and mangled cripples lined up strategically at the narrow exits— all ready, it appeared, to fight to the death over each new wave of naive soldier-boys. The noise was deafening.

Greg did not like the way the terminal interior was so dark. He couldn't see a light on anywhere, yet the city couldn't be suffering from a power blackout. An old woman was guarding a moaning soda machine, and, off in the distance, behind a postcard rack with two postcards left on it, a stereo speaker was blaring Vietnamese rock music. He had not been three seconds past the one-way exit gates when two dark-skinned boys in baggy GI shorts rushed up and ripped his duffel bag out of his grip. "I show you taxi stop, Joe!" one of them grinned eagerly, but the smile disappeared as the other youth tugged on the bag in the opposite direction, jerking him off his feet. The two began arguing in Vietnamese, and then the bag was abandoned and they were wrestling on the cool concrete floor.

An old man wearing filthy beachcomber pants, black tire-tread thongs and a red muscle shirt started over toward him, eyes hidden behind thick black sunglasses even in *this* dimly lit building, but Greg snatched up his duffel bag and continued on toward the shafts of sunlight that marked the corridor leading outside. The old man, his mouth filled with a huge, stubby cigar, grabbed Greg's arm and pointed toward a parked but sputtering three-wheeled cyclo. "Take you downtown, mister! Fifty p!"

"Uh . . . I believe I won't be going downtown just yet." Greg tried to remain polite. "But do you know where Camp Alpha is, perhaps?"

"Oh sure . . . sure," the man was pulling him over toward the long line of vehicles now. "Hotel Alfie . . . Tu Do Street . . ." The old man's eyes brightened. "Numba one! Lotsa girls at Hotel Alfie, Joe!"

"No . . . no," Greg frowned at the language barrier. And damned if his pocket dictionary wasn't at the bottom of his duffel bag. "Camp Alpha, *papa-san*. A . . . l . . . p . . . h . . . a . . ." he slowly spelled it out and showed him a copy of his assignment orders. Alpha was circled in red.

The old man frowned back and scrunched his eyelids up in feigned concentration as he examined the sheet of paper more closely, snatching it from Greg's hand. Behind him, someone else was cupping their hand around his waist, and he turned to see a slender woman in hot pants and a bulging halter top smiling up at him. Despite the thick coat of makeup, she was still very attractive, and Greg was taken aback by the length of her hair. Jet black, it seemed to fall down past her hips, and he even made a slight attempt to look past her shoulders to see just how long it really was. "Maybe you need place stay tonight?" she asked in a soft voice that seemed to sing the words up at him. Greg failed to see the desperation in her eyes. That would take time, and a few months on the street. In a patrol jeep.

"Why, I . . . I don't know. . . ." He was beginning to feel strange inside. Hypnotized. Like he was, of all the crazy

113

things, falling under her spell. Those eyes . . .

"I take you home, okay?" She had already wrapped her arms around one of his, was gently pulling him away from the cyclo driver. The old man held on, tugging back slightly, and she threw a glare at him and jerked Greg free. Started leading him out into the bright sunlight and the street, cluttered with smog-poisoned tamarinds. "I take you home . . . cook for you . . . give you numba one massage . . . maybe you like I do that for you?" She gave him a bright smile, and Greg marveled at how straight her teeth were. And white. The DIs back at the academy had always laughed and told him Vietnamese women had black teeth coated with the narcotic betel nut juice. Even now, he could hear that crazy Kip Mather giggling about how the Yardes up in the Highlands even filed their teeth down sometimes—considered it a mark of beauty or something. But you could never tell about the instructors back at Gordon . . . even everyone's favorite, Kip. After all, he *had* gone and married that Vietnamese girl despite all his own war stories and warnings, hadn't he?

"What's your name?" the girl was asking him now, her smile back. She seemed genuinely interested, and Greg was actually feeling refreshed by her refusal to call him Joe like everyone else at the airport.

"Greg," he said, but before he could ask hers, her smile exploded in recognition of some sort.

"Gregory!" she nodded her head up and down in obvious approval. "Same-same Gregory Peck!"

"Ah . . . yes, Gregory Peck." He was beginning to miss out on her sudden enthusiasm.

"Movie star!" she beamed, pointing to the huge, colorful posters glued like wallpaper to the cement slabs rising all around them. The posters depicted Chinese and Vietnamese actors dressed in ancient battle garb and engaging in bloody conflict. Above the vivid scenes were words Greg found intriguing. Vietnamese. But he could read it. Or at least he

114

could recognize the script. The characters were Roman, just like the American alphabet, but everywhere dots, dashes and an abundance of slashes and curves were added for some sort of accent he was convinced would take years to learn.

The girl started running her slender fingers through the hair on his arm. "You are very beautiful," Greg said in an almost apologetic tone, "but I'm afraid I can't go anywhere with you today, my dear." The smile evaporated from her face and she eyed him coldly, anticipating his next words. "I just arrived here today. This is my first time in your country . . . I'm afraid I—"

The smile flashed back across the girl's face. Greg decided she must be about nineteen or twenty, the makeup aside. "Oh," she said with relief in her eyes. "A *newbie!*" And she laughed at her stupidity.

"Yes." He frowned at the descriptive title. It seemed to leave a bad taste in his mouth. ". . . a newbie. They tell me I have to go through—"

"Camp Alfie," she interrupted him. "Process . . . process." She feigned mock irritation, "All the time process . . ."

Greg nodded his head, smiling too now. He was amazed he could so quickly come to enjoy the company of one who was obviously nothing more than a common whore, and though somewhere in the back of his mind a nagging voice was wondering how many drunk soldiers she had had between her legs in her lifetime, his devilish side was trying to peek down her blouse as they sauntered down the sidewalk arm in arm.

"I take you to Camp Alfie," she decided, stopping beside a vendor's stand where sugarcane cubes sat steaming in an old aquarium filled with boiling water. "Then when you get out next week, you come stay with me, okay Gregory?" She said it all matter-of-factly and didn't even bother to check his eyes but concentrated on fishing through her tiny purse for some toylike dong coins. A few seconds later, she had handed five piasters over to the smiling *mama-san* behind the counter and was picking up two plastic baggies filled with the sweet cubes. "I be good woman for you, Gregory," she said seriously, like they had known each other for years and were just now contemplating marriage. "I never butterfly on you . . . you bic? I never butterfly on you, ching-ching. . . ."

"Butterfly?" Greg showed his innocence with his naive expression.

"Butterfly. You know," and she made her arms slowly imitate a graceful butterfly. "No flutter from man to man behind your back. Only be true to you. . . ."

Only be true to you. The words made him think of a song from his childhood, but he couldn't remember the artist or the title.

"Do you have pen?" she asked after taking one of the sugarcane cubes with her slender, amber fingers and plopping it carefully onto his tongue. "Pen and paper?"

"A pen and paper?" He was suddenly unable to concentrate on what she was saying. He had never tasted anything so good. In comparison to oatmeal for breakfast and meat and potatos for supper all his life, these steaming cubes of sugarcane slapped his taste buds awake as though they had been in a coma all these years.

"Pen . . . or pencil," she said, deciding to pull some paper from her own purse. "I write my address. When you fini camp process, you show to taxi and he take you see me. . . ."

Greg started to go through his pockets with one hand, trying to hold on to the sugarcane and all his paperwork with the other at the same time. He found a pen finally, but in the process, a sheaf of papers fell to the ground at his feet. He quickly stooped down to gather them up before the breeze could snatch anything away, and he noticed the napkin the stewardess had folded up and stuffed down between the 201 file and his *Time* magazine. While the girl started to scribble an address down, he unfolded the napkin and felt himself blushing again as he read the words that flashed out at him.

Welcome to Saigon, soldier-boy! I suggest you stay away from the local girls. Are you lonely in the big city? Come see Sharon and I'll treat you to dinner.
Room 313, the Caravelle. 23 Lam Son.

Greg didn't notice he was shaking his head from side to side in disbelief. You didn't even read about things like this happening in fantasy novels anymore.

"Something the matter?" the girl was up close to him again, pushing the piece of paper down into his pants pocket. Again, he felt himself growing hard against her touch. Christ, he started to think, they never told me the life of a soldier would be so . . .

But he said, "Uh . . . no. No problem," and he glanced down at the red outline of lipstick the stewardess had left between the words "I'll treat you" and the hotel address. She had curved her lips into a circle so that the impression of red across the napkin was physical proof her methods of making soldiers feel good were very openminded. He found himself suddenly laughing—the woman had practically left him a measuring gauge. He mentally calculated shapes and sizes and shook his head again, still giggling, and stuffed the napkin back down into his pocket on top of the note the prostitute had given him.

"My name Judy!" She decided the time was right to spring it on him.

"Judy?"

"Yes . . . you like?" She appeared concerned about his approval.

"Sure . . . sure, but what's your Vietnamese name?"

"You could not pronounce it," she frowned. Remembering some time in her past perhaps? When a cruel GI had made fun of it?

"Try me." Greg watched two MP jeeps scream past several intersections down the road, lights flashing and sirens blaring, in pursuit of a taxicab loaded down with belligerent

117

soldiers who were leaning out the window and directing obscene gestures at their pursuers.

"Ngoc Nga," she said slowly, her voice sounding like another person entirely when she switched from the unexciting English to her own singsong language.

"Say again?" Greg found himself reverting back to the radio slang they had instilled in him back at The School.

"See!" she seemed now on the verge of pouting. "I knew you would make fun—"

"No . . . no," Greg protested mildly, raising a hand to silence her. "Just repeat it for me again. And slowly . . ." he leaned closer to her, breathing in the exotic French perfume, moving his ear next to her lips. "Slowly."

"Nyaaa-nyaeee," she pronounced it for him as though she were trying to say her name in English.

Greg concentrated intently on the way she made the syllables rise and fall like notes on a musical scale, but he knew he'd be unable to mimic her. Unwilling to insult the first Vietnamese he had ever met on an intimate basis, he held out his hand as if ready to shake hers. "Happy to meet you, *Judy*!"

The innocent-eyes game worked, and she smiled back, tilting her head to the side so that all movement of her body was an extension of her childlike personality.

Greg started to ask her how far away she lived when the bright smile vanished from her face and she pulled her arms free from him and darted to the side, eyes searching frantically for something—an escape route?

Greg looked up to see an army military police jeep coasting up to them. A husky buck sergeant in his early thirties, arms rippling with finely toned muscles, leaned out the side of the jeep slightly and snarled something at the girl in Vietnamese and she disappeared into the shadows of a side alley without a word of reply. Marsh felt like he had just missed something very important—like he had been dozing back in UCMJ class and one of the drill sergeants was about to bop him up side the head with an open palm. But for the life of him he wasn't sure what had just happened.

"Was she bothering you?" the MP sergeant cut off the ignition and hopped out of the jeep even before the powerful rumbling engine choked itself dead. His hair, light brown and close-cropped beneath the black helmet, appeared almost bleached blond from the tropical sun. A neatly trimmed mustache enhanced his rough but handsome features. *And was that a bullet hole in his earlobe? Jesus H!*

"Uh . . . no, sergeant," he sputtered like the hundreds of Hondas cruising past them just then. "I guess you could say she was just welcoming me to Sai—"

"Your papers," the NCO folded thick forearms across his chest, suddenly bored with an explanation he'd heard a thousand times.

"Huh?" Marsh slowly dropped his duffel bag to the ground.

"Let me see your ID, partner." The sergeant forced a polite smile. Marsh was in fatigues, and slick-sleeved at that. Fatigues bore no collar brass, and without combat experience and the unit patch that came with it, the MP had no way of knowing he was detaining a fellow military policeman.

Greg glanced over at the bumper on the patrol unit. The bright yellow digits 54HQB716 flashed back at him. He quickly produced his laminated ID card and orders assigning him to the MP Battalion at the International. "Just like your number there," he motioned toward the jeep's bumper as he handed the sergeant the papers. "I'm trying to find Camp Alfie . . . I mean Camp Alpha, but eventually I'll be assigned to the Seven-sixteenth, sarge. . . ."

"Ah, Marsh!" the MP's eyes lit up as he found the recruit's name on the poorly mimeographed sheet. "I was just on my way to Tan Son Nhut to pick you up, son. Welcome to the Pearl of the Orient!" and he held out a hand in front of the bright show of movie-star teeth.

Greg glanced at the black name tag on the man's khaki

shirt. The narrow white letters bristled back at him like a jungle cat yawning just to show its fangs: Stryker. Above the name tag were two unit awards in the form of small rectangular ribbons. He recognized the blue U.S. Presidential Unit decoration and the Vietnamese Cross of Gallantry citation with its three vertical gold stripes against a crimson field. The DIs back at Gordon made sure the rookies knew what all the fancy ribbons stood for.

"Mark Stryker," the sergeant introduced himself as they clasped hands. Greg had expected the mean-looking soldier to psyche him out with a bone-crushing handshake, but the man's greeting came across more as brotherly reunion where there was no need to impress anyone. Greg had shaken hands with pianists and professors—who were so gentle and weak he hated to move his own hand up and down. And he had shaken hands with construction workers—who did their best to imitate politicians and convey their self-confidence by outsqueezing your fingers. Marsh decided this Stryker character was somewhere in between, if he fitted into his scale of intimidation at all. Perhaps the man just felt no need to impress or provoke anybody one way or the other—an MP's abilities would be quickly judged by how they *hand*led themselves on the street, the sergeants back at The School had always told him, not how they shook hands.

Stryker checked his watch and quickly scanned the traffic already beginning to snarl the four-lane street that led down into the city a few miles to the southeast. "We better get a move-on before the afternoon siesta begins. . . ."

"You'll be taking me to Camp Alpha then?" Greg ran his eyes across the three rows of ribbons on the sergeant's left chest. He recognized a Bronze Star and Purple Heart above the usual Vietnam service and campaign ribbons. And though Stryker's khakis were unwrinkled and his jump boots shiny as mirrors, the ribbons seemed dull and lifeless in comparison, almost dusty. Smog-caked?

The private would soon learn the MPs of the 716th played

a private little game where you were judged by the amount of street smog coating your uniform ribbons more than by any handshake.

"We're gonna play hooky and bypass Alpha," Stryker grinned as he motioned the private into his jeep. In the back, the police net was crackling out unintelligible codes mixed with bursts of radio static. "We're running real low on manpower this month, and are gonna put you right to work, if that's all right with you. . . ."

Stryker shot him a judging glance out the corner of his eye. "Of course," Greg mumbled back without arguing. "The sooner I'm on the street, the better." Dual visions of both the airline stewardess and the Vietnamese hooker lying naked on a hotel bed, waiting for him, flashed in front of his mind's eye.

"Fine. We'll have Jake get your two-oh-one file over to Personnel tomorrow. He's the company clerk: Jake Drake. Keeps the unit's paperwork on track. Good man, all personality quirks aside—you'll like him."

"Personality quirks?" Greg really didn't want to know. Saigon was assaulting him on all sides: Stryker had pulled the jeep out into heavy traffic amid a screeching of sedan brakes and lorry horns. They entered a swarm of countless motorscooters, and the sidewalks everywhere were overflowing with throngs of pedestrians that made a game of darting in and out of the deafening traffic. Traffic cops on wooden boxes stood in the middle of it all, blowing their whistles and waving the trucks and cars through as if the drivers were actually paying attention to them.

"Jake's all right," Stryker decided as he twisted the steering wheel hard to the right and swerved expertly between two overloaded buses filled with cursing Orientals. Greg thought back to the two MP jeeps he had seen running lights-and-siren earlier, and the pursuit classes he had barely passed back at Gordon—where there wasn't a tenth this much traffic! He tried to envision himself racing code-Hot down into Saigon without killing himself or his partner. "It's just that he's got this pet rat," the sergeant continued.

"Rat?" Greg felt himself growing dizzy at the swirl of activity bombarding him on all sides . . . pressing down on him beneath the silver overcast.

"She's harmless, of course. He calls her Gertrude. Just wanted to warn you. . . ."

Greg swallowed hard as a fire truck, siren wailing loud as his sudden headache, appeared around a blind corner and nearly smashed into them head-on. Stryker carried on the conversation as if nothing out of the ordinary had happened. ". . . In case he's in-processing you at the Orderly Room tonight and Gertrude, who is trained to lay in wait across the curls on his head for newbies like yourself, makes a sudden appearance. It'd make my day if just once a new man didn't even flinch at the sight of that goofy rat standing up on her hind legs, leaning out to sniff at you. Yes, that'd be one to tell Richards about. . . ."

"Thanks," Greg said numbly. "I'll be sure to act like I don't even notice anything."

"Little things like that," Stryker smiled over at him as two girls on a Honda—one riding side-saddle with a miniskirt that failed to conceal a thing—cut them off at a major intersection and the sergeant was forced to brake hard for the first time, "are what keep the battalion running smoothly. You know . . . humorous little episodes to keep the troops giggling while they work. Also helps to keep your sanity if you can laugh about this job, Greg. Yes, Saigon can do a job on your head, if you don't watch her. . . ." Marsh glanced over at Stryker. The man was talking about the town as if it were a goddamned woman . . . and a cocktease at that.

Overhead, a fleet of gunships roared past only a few hundred yards above the blackened tenements rising up all around them. The already noisy air was suddenly filled with a chopping wop-wop-wop vibration that drowned out the sergeant's words for a few seconds. ". . . and it'll be my job to see to it you don't lose your marbles before your tour is up here in the 'Nam," Stryker said. "So if you got any problems bugging you after we get you settled in, don't hesitate to come talk to me. . . ." The helicopters quickly disappeared from sight, vanishing in the haze beyond the edge of the city . . . over the jungle somewhere. Their dull, flapping rotors could still be heard for several seconds afterward, however.

Greg realized he had been holding his breath for quite a while, and as the jeep was forced to slow for a traffic jam ahead, he gazed off to his right, hoping for a diversion—something to take his mind off this sergeant's display of defensive driving. Instead, both men noticed a crowd rushing like a moonlit tide toward something in the center of the avenue halfway down the side street jutting through the hill to their right. Despite the clamor of horns and disgruntled motorists ahead, both MPs could still hear the sudden muffled wave of gasps that rose from the restless crowd as a puff of smoke erupted within the circle of quickly growing pedestrians.

"What do you think the problem is?" Marsh almost had to yell to get his question across to the sergeant because of the noise.

Women in the crowd were beginning to scream now, and a slender *canh-sat* in his early twenties, on a foot beat in the area, began running toward the disturbance. Nuns in blue and white robes were falling to their knees on the outskirts of the now unruly mob, bowing their heads to the earth beneath clasped hands as the sickening stench of burnt flesh drifted up to assault the MPs' nostrils.

"Smells like another monk is barbecuing himself," Stryker said matter-of-factly. "And damned if I didn't leave my pocket camera back at the hotel again . . . never fails, ya know?"

"*Barbecuing* himself?" Marsh asked incredulously, sitting

123

up straight in his seat.

Stryker had intently scanned the edge of the crowd at the first sign of trouble, but when it appeared the human torch was in no way connected with their murder suspect but just another Buddhist protest against the Saigon government's alleged insensitivity toward the non-Catholic community, he made no move to get involved. "Now and then the bonzes douse themselves with gasoline and light up a Winston to make their political statements. . . ."

"What a town!" Marsh was tempted to stand up in the jeep to see if he could get a better view of the suicide. He wanted to ask the sergeant if he could go over for a look. "How often does it happen?"

"Every now and then," Stryker was noncommittal. He glanced over his right shoulder to gauge the traffic flow behind them, then jerked the wheel over and stomped down on the gas pedal. Tires spun, and the jeep roared down toward the circle of shocked and startled Asians. "Suppose you wanna check it out. . . ."

"Well, I gotta admit I can't remember the time I last saw someone torch themselves. . . ." Marsh's eyes were darting back and forth almost comically, like he was straining to miss nothing.

They pulled up along the edge of the crowd and Stryker cut the engine. "Be my guest," he motioned toward the wisps of blue smoke with his chin. "I'll stand by the jeep so nobody makes off with your duffel bag or *my* tires." Marsh hopped out and started into the mass of arms and elbows. "And Greg—"

"Yah, sarge?" he hesitated as he was plunging headlong into the crowd.

"Watch your ass in there. . . ."

"Sure sarge . . . sure." And he disappeared beyond the clusters of shorter college radicals who had positioned their placards and banners strategically around the rapidly charring corpse for the TV cameras being hastily set up across the street.

At the top of the street, two Vietnamese police jeeps slid around the corner on two wheels each, and, turning to watch their arrival, Stryker grinned at seeing a dark green MP jeep right behind them. All three vehicles had their red lights twirling and sirens screaming like wounded leopards.

Stryker let out his most hearty sigh as Tim Bryant and Anthony Thomas skidded up to his jeep and jumped out in their race to beat the *canh-sat*s to the scene. Both enlisted men slid to an embarrassed halt upon seeing the huge sergeant slowly folding his arms across his chest.

"Oh . . . hi, Mark!" Bryant called out with an ear-to-ear smile.

Stryker ignored the greeting and said, "I didn't hear you two call over the net and advise Waco you'd be running hot down through this part of town."

"I just got my *canh-sat* scanner hooked up this morning!" Thomas reached back into the jeep and pulled the small silver box from under the dashboard where it had been taped with fingerprint strips. "We just picked up their call down the street and intercepted these hotdogs," he pointed at the Vietnamese policemen, "a few seconds ago."

"I wasn't aware either of you could speak Vietnamese," Stryker challenged them.

The MPs glanced into the back seat, startled looks on both their faces, like they had lost something precious during the Code Three run. A grin immediately reappeared on Bryant's face, though, as Thomas reached in and helped up the Vietnamese policewoman who had been thrown to the floorboards somewhere during the last five or six blocks.

"You okay, Miss N-Win?" Thomas asked with concern in his eyes as he brushed the dust from the front of her mint-brown uniform. As his fingers got too close to her chest, she slapped them away and commenced trying to straighten out the leather strap that ran between her breasts from her shoulder to gunbelt.

125

"I'm OK!" she snapped back, her tone contrasting with the smile in her eyes.

Stryker didn't want to know what was going on.

One thing he *did* know was that Bryant and Thomas were not scheduled to have a policewoman riding with them, but so long as she still had her uniform on and the sun was above the horizon, he wouldn't press the issue. Until then, the three MPs had been ignoring the activity all around them. They did not see the orange flames turn bright yellow as they consumed the last of the monk sitting cross-legged a few dozen yards away; did not see him lose the last of his bonze-induced self-control and tumble onto his side.

They only heard the crowd moan loudly in confused and painful unison.

"Since you're here," Stryker said with only mild sarcasm, "why don't you go over and snap off some photos for Officer Toi," he told Bryant. "Got your Kodak, don't you?"

"Of course," Bryant slapped his bulging thigh pocket. "Never hit the streets without it." Thomas pinched his nostrils shut as he followed his partner into the crowd. The smell was becoming nauseating.

Officer Jon Toi was a Vietnamese policeman the MPs of the 716th had adopted recently as their human mascot. A large portion of his den, back at the government-financed housing project police families were provided rent-free, had its walls covered with street photos the men had contributed to the *canh-sat*'s collection. Stryker called it his ghoul's gallery. To him, the walls were plastered with a macabre collage of murder victims, missing persons, and suspects that police had killed in self-defense. Toi had invited him up there for a beer one time, and while the two cops cleaned their service weapons, Stryker couldn't help but feel haunted. Perhaps it was because he recognized many of the faces on Toi's notorious wall. Stryker had not paid the man a return visit in months, though a lot of the younger MPs made the pad their second home.

"Good afternoon, Sergeant Stryker." The policewoman was leaning against his side of the jeep now. She rested her elbow on the nightstick holder by his left leg, reminding him of a naive schoolgirl who wanted to play with his siren or something. She seemed to know him. Either that, or she was well aware of his reputation with the ladies.

"Hello there, Miss . . . Nguyen was it?" He flashed her his most sensual smile.

"Yes, but please call me Lai. I hope Tim and Anthony are not in trouble now because I was out riding with them. . . ."

But Stryker's smile had fallen apart like a mirror collapsing.

Lai? The name shot bouncing through his mind like the echoes of a pistol discharge fired in a tunnel. Flashbacks of Lai's face hit him from all sides.

"Sergeant? You are all right, sir?" she had placed her hand across his arm, and for the first time Stryker noticed how strikingly beautiful she was, despite the uniform.

"Your name is Lai?" He pulled his thoughts back from the memories, or tried to. Visions of the dead woman in the Pleiku morgue were flickering at him now. "Such a pretty name . . ."

"This is such a . . . disgusting scene." The policewoman motioned toward the disturbance breaking out among the four male *canh-sat*s and some of the students. "I'm sorry you Americans have to see my people acting this way—"

"I've been in Vietnam several years now, Miss Lai . . . I'm used to seeing—"

"But still," she held up a dainty hand, cutting short his own interruption. Stryker wondered how such a tiny woman would fare in a Tu Do Street bar fight. "There is no excuse for this kind of—"

"I take it you are a Catholic," Stryker grinned, glancing out at the crowd now and then, keeping his eye on the spot where the two black MP helmets were bobbing up and down. So long as he could see them, he wasn't worried.

127

When you lost sight of them, *then* you started to sweat: The guys were always losing their helmet liners during back alley brawls. The lightweight liners had no chin straps like the combat helmets or riot face shields.

"I was born Buddhist," she contradicted him, and a grin showed she was pleased with his surprise. "But after so many years in law enforcement, you tend to lose your religious convictions. . . ."

How many times had Stryker heard that one? "And how many years *have* you been working the street?" He bit his lower lip in anticipation, proud at how easily he had cornered her.

The woman moved her gun strap slightly to the right so Stryker could read her shield number. "August will mark my thirteenth year with the National Police."

Stryker almost fell out of his seat.

Thirteen *years*? He had guessed perhaps thirteen months, just off probation. That would make her at least thirty-one years old! And she looked like a high school kid. "Thirteen years?" he asked the question in Vietnamese to make sure they understood each other.

"Yes," she nodded her head slightly. "I started in nineteen fifty-four, working as a matron at the old Vo Thanh stationhouse, when I was eighteen."

"Christ," he set his mental calculator to buzzing. "You'll be eligible for retirement around nineteen seventy-four or five," he smiled. "Same time as me." It never ceased to amaze him how these Vietnamese women could look so young, when their ID cards would show they were actually ten . . . even twenty years older than they appeared. "Maybe we could meet then and set up house," he laughed.

"In nineteen seventy-four?" she gave him a please-don't-tease-me frown.

"We could combine our pensions, and live together like royalty."

Lai laughed louder than he had, and several of the

128

Buddhist monks kneeling at the edge of the crowd looked at them irritably. "In Vietnam nobody thinks about a pension, sergeant. How can we plan for the future when Saigon is constantly in such turmoil?" He was impressed with her knowledge of English. Maybe he could get her an interpreter assignment at PMO. "When the government changes hands with the seasons," she exaggerated slightly, "and we never really know if our pension deductions are really even being set aside for us, or just deposited in the commissioner's bank account."

An ambulance was rolling up to the scene now, though its driver was experiencing considerable difficulty making his way through the growing crowd. "Got some great shots, sarge!" Bryant and Thomas were climbing back into their jeep, and the policewoman took their return as a sign to leave Stryker's side. Moments later, Marsh had exited from the wall of Vietnamese, too, and smiled at the policewoman and let her pass in front of him before jumping onto the shotgun side of the watch commander's jeep.

"Good for you," Stryker flipped the starter switch over, and the souped-up cylinders beneath the hood rumbled to life like a growling attack dog on a leash. Bryant was expecting him to say something about getting Miss Lai back to the stationhouse, but instead Stryker just grinned and said, "Now get back over to your assigned precinct and stay out of trouble."

"It was nice finally meeting you, Sergeant Stryker!" Lai called out to him in a weak voice as she climbed into the back seat and the three of them were rolling away.

Stryker tipped his helmet to her and turned to start off in the opposite direction.

"Stop by the stationhouse some night, and I'll see to it you get some fresh coffee," she added before they were out of earshot. "*American* style!"

"You've got a deal!" Stryker waved at them without looking, but Lai was unable to hear him because of the roar

129

of the crowd. Additional police had arrived on the scene, and when they tried to smother the flames with a blanket, they were rushed by several of the students.

"Don't you think we should stay and help them?" Marsh asked, a look of deep concern creasing his features.

"The *canh-sat*s will be all right." Stryker pointed to a large truck, loaded down with several reinforcements, that was coasting up to the scene.

"If they need us, they'll call for us, right?" Marsh twisted his neck around to watch the baton-wielding officers charge into the crowd.

"Exactly," said Stryker. "If you happen onto a *canh-sat* having trouble in the street, then by all means give him a hand or stick around to make sure he's okay. But regarding these crazy bonze burnings, the PM would just as soon we didn't make much of an appearance unless things really get out of hand and the VNPs call for help. Otherwise, UPI photos of American MPs at the scene of this kind of trouble would only lend fuel to the commies' propaganda machine. Get my drift?"

"Sure . . . sure," Marsh shook his head from side to side in resignation. "I was just a little worried about those cops back there. . . ."

"Hey, listen: Bryant and Thomas are two of my biggest hotdogs, okay? If they had sensed anything big brewing back there, they'd have suggested we hang around. Believe me . . . they're not ones to miss out on the stick time, Greg."

"So tell me about the Seven-sixteenth." The private changed the subject. He straightened himself out in the seat and locked eyes with a prostitute on a street corner whose leg was cocked atop a cinderblock. Just the right amount of thigh flashed out at the newbie. "Christ . . . did you see that?"

"Friend, you'll see more cunt on this job than you could ever fit into your schedule," Stryker frowned. "I suggest you just keep your zipper up until you've worked the streets for a few months and get a feel for this town. It'll save you tons of grief down the line. . . ."

"Speaking from personal experience?" Marsh grinned at the wrong time.

Stryker began the routine rebuke but was interrupted by a young girl rushing out through traffic to flag down their jeep. "Baby come! Baby come!" she was yelling in English, arms waving back and forth frantically even after the jeep had skidded to a stop.

"Where?" he asked her in Vietnamese, and the girl pointed toward a line of dilapidated tenements leaning out from the bowels of a filthy side street. The girl was thirteen or fourteen, but her slender frame and short hair made her look younger. Her face was dirty, and tears had carved streaks down through the grit. She wore pink shorts, rubber thongs, and a thin T-shirt with the words YANKEE GO HOME stenciled across the front, and Marsh watched her under-developed breasts jiggle up and down beneath the fabric as she jumped around beside the jeep, waiting for them to dismount and follow her back.

Stryker frowned at their luck and quickly called in his location to the dispatcher. "And send me a Ten-fifty-two when you get a chance; over. . . ." he mumbled as an afterthought.

Marsh recognized the ambulance code from all the weeks of training at The School. "Ten-four, Car Niner. . . ." came the scratchy reply over the radio. "Waco out at seventeen-twenty hours."

"Don't name it after me," an anonymous voice broke squelch briefly, just before Stryker turned the radio off and started to chain the steering wheel and brake pedal together.

"Name it after Raunchy Raul!" Another private put forth his best effort at disguising his voice. He failed miserably, and numerous microphone clicks followed the weak transmission.

"Waco to all units! Cut the—" Stryker turned the radio off

131

just then and hopped out of the jeep.

"Grab that first-aid kit back there," Stryker told his "partner" as he followed the girl off the sizzling blacktop onto a crumbling sidewalk. Marsh noticed the man kept his fingers along the side of his holstered .45 with the crook of his thumb resting across the butt safety device. Marsh was thinking about other things, though. He was trying to remember what they had taught him in the childbirth classes. Hadn't they seen a no-holds-barred step-by-step training flick filmed right in an emergency room back at Fort Sam Houston?

He grabbed the converted ammo box with the large red cross painted on the top and both sides and rushed to catch up with Stryker.

When the sergeant held a poncho liner that had been nailed up to serve as a door aside, Marsh peeked into the dimly lit one-room dwelling to find a woman lying on her back. Though she was covered with a blanket, it was obvious her knees were bent, feet flat on the floor, legs spread wide underneath. A large bulge under the o.d. green GI blanket showed where her stomach was. Her face was drenched in sweat, and her eyes darted back and forth between her child's face and Stryker's. The MP helmets didn't seem to reassure her in the least.

Stryker perked his ears, hoping to hear a growing siren in the distance, but all he could hear was the child yelling "Baby come! Baby come!"

"I want some boiling water." He grabbed her and shook her silent. "Get me some boiling water, and a woman from one of these other apartments. And I need some rubber bands. And get me some—"

The woman on the floor began screaming in rapid Vietnamese, "He's coming! The baby is coming! I cannot wait any longer!"

Though he spoke little Vietnamese, Greg Marsh caught the drift of what was being said. "Oh my God . . ."

he groaned.

"Nobody told me there'd be days like this," Stryker began humming as he rolled his sleeves up further, clear to the tops of his shoulders. "Let's see . . ." Stryker's eyes rolled toward the ceiling as he began more mental calculations. "This will be number eleven." He went down on one knee and lifted up the blanket. "How does 'Mark Mekong' sound?" The joke was intended for both the woman and the private, but they only stared at him wide-eyed. "I've already christened them with 'Stryker-*san*' and 'Mike-Papa. . . .'"

The woman closed her eyes tightly and arced her head back as far as the skin would permit before emitting a long, drawn-out scream.

"Get on down here, Marsh," Stryker's smile faded. "That's the kid's head there." He pointed at the small ball of hair magically appearing beneath the blanket. Marsh felt the blood rushing to his head. "Now slip on them plastic gloves and cup your hands under *baby-san*'s head for support while I talk to *mama-san* here. . . ."

Marsh did as he was instructed, and after Stryker whispered some words into the woman's ears, he turned back to the private. "These childbirths are something you'll have to get used to, pal. Probably you'll only come across them two or three times during your tour. I just seem to have worse runs of luck than the other guys working the street. Usually the ambulance gets here long before now and you don't even have to examine the woman's snatch, but once in a while the odds catch up with you. . . . Ambulance is probably caught up in a traffic jam back at the barbecue down the street."

"Looks like the water sac has already burst," Marsh observed, trying to act a little more professional now. "Lucky for us . . ."

"When the kid makes his appearance we don't do nothing but wrap him up in clean sheets," Stryker reminded the rookie. "Leave the cleanup to the hospital people. If there's

133

lotsa bleeding, then go ahead and rubber band the umb-cord, but don't do no cuttin'. Even here in the 'Nam. Leave the cuttin' to the ambo-crews, unless the woman dies and you gotta separate them for whatever reason. Luckily that ain't never happened to me yet."

"I thought that little runt was gonna go get some help," Marsh said, breathing hard now as the adrenaline began to flow.

Stryker examined the infant again. It was certainly taking its time. "Might as well use this opportunity to continue my briefing on the Seven-sixteenth," Stryker said. Both MPs squatted unmoving between the woman's legs, the blanket draped across her knees now.

You gotta be kidding me! Marsh was thinking, but he just squatted there. What else was there to do except keep the kid's head up off the filthy tenement floor?

"We've got this suspect running around the area now dousing drunks with gasoline or bopping them up side the head with Molotov cocktails," Stryker muttered. "Blasted one of my partners in the head last week. We're still huntin' his ass. And we got a couple of Honda Honeys we're looking for too. Stabbed one of our new sergeants in the leg while we were on routine patrol. We got an asshole deserter peddlin' kiddy porn and dustin' *canh-sat*s with a large-caliber handgun to make matters worse, but I'll fill you in on all this in greater detail once we get back to the Orderly Room." The expression on Stryker's face told the private: At least *you're* still young enough to get into another line of work!

"Finally!" Marsh sighed as the sound of a siren in the distance became audible.

At the same moment, the door behind the two military policemen creaked slowly open, and a metallic object clattered across the ground between them. Private Greg Marsh's eyes locked onto the grenade rolling to rest under the baby's head at the same time the newborn child uttered its first piercing cries.

6. OMINOUS OMENS

Before Stryker or Marsh even began to react—either to dive for cover, or for the grenade—a booming voice followed the projectile through the door and the tension drained from the MP sergeant like juice from the coconuts the privates often lined up out on the firing range for target practice. "Got a light, Mark?" Stryker immediately recognized the husky voice of one of his fellow NCOs, Ron Brickmann. "I seem to have misplaced my devoted incendiary device. . . ." The Brick, as the men called him, had a passion for compiling syllables until his sentences were an abstract study in conversation at its most complex.

But the child ignored him, wailing on. The MPs on their knees just stayed where they were, eyes wide, mouths agape—though Stryker *was* beginning to narrow those eyes into an irritated scowl.

"Ah . . . *there* she be!" Brickmann was down on one knee between the two Americans, and had scooped up the "grenade" as the bewildered mother in front of him watched, a terrified mask across her features. Stryker could see that the old pineapple-style hand grenade still had its pin intact.

"What the hell's going on?" Greg Marsh tried to concentrate on keeping the baby's slick body off the floor as one nervous eye followed the huge buck sergeant's activities.

The Brick, probably the biggest NCO in the battalion, was now tugging on the grenade's pin.

"Brick—" Stryker started to call out, but he fell silent just as quickly when the narrow top flap of the device sprang open and a long flame shot up to bathe the dark room in flickering yellow light.

Brickmann had managed to keep a huge cigar dangling from his lower lip the last few minutes, and as he dipped his head and touched the flame of the gag novelty cigarette lighter to his Havana, Stryker let out a heavy sigh. "Why you son-of-a—"

"Got here as quick as I could," Sergeant Brickmann cut in, all smiles now as he sent a puff of inky smoke down at the set of legs spread wide before him. "What's the prognosis on the parturition?"

Greg Marsh eyeballed the cigarette lighter that had been converted from an old Korean War grenade. "You didn't happen to see an ambulance on your way over here, did ya?"

"I don't believe we've had the pleasure. . . ." The Brick held out his hand. As a reflex action, Marsh almost dropped the infant's head to reach for it. But he caught himself, and, instead, produced an intense frown.

"Meet Pvt. Greg Marsh," Stryker growled. The Brick nodded his head.

"And you must be the notorious Sergeant Brickmann," Marsh finally grinned wryly. "The drill sergeants back at The School warned us about you." His eyes focused on the NCO's name tag to confirm his suspicions.

"My friends call me Ron," The Brick reached out and patted Marsh on the shoulder, "But—"

"But I'm not your friend yet," Marsh had anticipated the play on words. The DIs back at Fort Gordon had told the few troops destined for the 716th that this Brickmann character was a real card. A man you definitely wanted to have on your side in a bar fight. But after tempers had cooled and hostilities were over, he became a trickster you had to keep your eye on. Treated you like an unworthy recruit until you proved yourself on the street in some crazy capacity, but the results were worth it: You were then placed on The Brick's invitation mailing list, and Sergeant Ron threw some of the best choir practices east of Cambodia.

An old beat-up Vietnamese ambulance had rolled up outside unnoticed, and soon two bored-looking men sauntered into the tiny cubicle, a stretcher rolled up between their arms. One glance at the scene unfolding before them and both men produced disgusted frowns and halted in the doorway.

"Knock off the bullshit and attend to this damsel in distress!" Brickmann turned, snapping like a whip. The Vietnamese paused to glance at each other as if debating the situation, but both rushed to the Americans' aid when The Brick yelled, *"Lie-day!"* which was irritated Arvin for "come here!"

A few minutes later, the military policemen were backing out the door, bowing to the new mother almost comically— she was all smiles now, jabbering at them in rapid Vietnamese to stay for some reason or other. But they had to go, Stryker told her in pidgin-Viet, pleased to meet you ma'am. . . . The woman blushed, remembering the way they *had* actually met, and she was, reluctantly, waving them out the door.

Having second thoughts, Brickmann reached into his fatigue pockets and came up with a business card packet. He produced a fancy laminated job that seemed coated with mother-of-pearl. The gleam caught Stryker's eye as The Brick handed the card to the new mother. "Just be sure and name him after ol' Ronny!" He flashed his teeth down at the woman.

"Ronnnnnee!" the woman imitated him as best she could, and she clutched the business card to her breast.

Stryker was hustling them out into the street. "Let me see those!" he latched onto the packet before Brickmann could

137

stuff it back down into his shirt pocket. He quickly scanned the bold type, and smiled. "I gotta give ya credit, Brick—ya got *class*!" He handed the card to Marsh.

TO SERVE AND PROTECT
Emergencies: 22211
Sgt. Ronald Brickmann
716th Military Police
INTERNATIONAL HOTEL
Saigon Vietnam

"Where can *I* get some of these printed up?" Marsh asked without taking his eyes from the card. The reflective coating made one want to latch onto the card and refuse to surrender it—as if it were worth more than a few cents.

Brickmann snatched the card back. "Professional secret," he muttered, hopping back into his jeep. In a puff of smoke he was gone, smiling in satisfaction like it was sunlight basking him. Marsh noticed the man was alone.

"He doesn't have a partner?" he asked.

"The Brick kinda just prowls around on his own," Stryker answered. "He's got free reign of the city. He just kinda shows up wherever trouble's brewing. . . ."

"What about them goofy business cards?"

"Some of the guys get 'em printed up downtown," Stryker replied. "They're not officially recognized, of course, so if you start passin' 'em around, refrain from letting any of the officers see them. It kinda gets under their skin, if you know what I mean."

"No, I don't think I do, to tell you the truth."

"Well, some of the guys get all kinds of bullcrap printed on them: 'Fuck the army' emblazoned across the top, or something like 'Have a nice day, asshole' across the bottom—but those are reserved for special occasions, of course."

"Of course."

Stryker hopped into his jeep, but in the right seat for a change. "You drive us to the International," he instructed.

"But—"

"I'll give you directions." Stryker held up a hand, allowing no room for argument. "No better way for a rook to learn the town than to get behind the steering wheel of a patrol jeep—and no better time to start than now."

"But—"

"Just start down that street there," Stryker ducked as a huge golden dragonfly swooped down and bounced off the top of his helmet. Marsh's eyes flew wide—the thing must have been nearly a foot long!

"But . . . the *International?*"

"It's a hotel downtown," Stryker smiled proudly, "on good ole Tran Hung Dao."

"But . . . a *hotel?* I was figuring on a barracks-type of environment, actually."

"Hey, don't buck it, private." Stryker's subtle retort was not given without his ever present grin. "Would you rather live with forty other GIs in an infantry-style flophouse, a lousy dorm . . . or is an inn, complete with housegirls and two-man rooms more your style?"

"Well . . ."

"Take a left here," Stryker said. He decided to change the subject before he forgot what was on his mind. "And another thing, bud. Getting back to those business cards. They're gonna run you five or ten bucks per thousand—if you use that fancy style The Brick had. So do us both a favor, and let me look the design you choose over before you give it to the back-alley artist downtown, okay?"

"Why, sarge? You worried about my judgment? I haven't even decided whether or not I'll get any of them goofy cards—"

"Oh, you'll get 'em," Stryker frowned, thinking about his own packet. His supply was getting low—he only had a dozen or so left, and *that* would only last him another three

139

or four days at the most. "Those cards are an . . . extension of your personality. The PMO issued authorized cards for the longest time—you know, the kind with a big blank for the individual patrolman to print his name in? But they were too plain for the guys—blahzey . . . boring. Some goof-off . . . I think it was Sergeant Richards, well, he got the bright idea to print off a stack of unique Gung Ho cards that nobody else had, and the scheme quickly spread until nearly everyone was competing to pass out a better, more outlandish business card."

"Gimme a little credit, okay sarge?"

"I just don't wanna see you getting into any trouble right off the bat, pal. You hafta understand. The men of the Seven-sixteenth are the finest bunch of cops you'd ever want to work with. Some of 'em are getting 'short,' and their attitudes have a lot to be desired. They're probably gonna ETS and return to the States to be super cops or something, which is fine.

"But what I'm getting at, is don't let their bad attitudes rub off on you. They're the minority. And they're the ones who are all cop at heart and soldiers last."

"Of The Troops And For The Troops," Marsh repeated the MP motto as it had been drilled into him back at The School.

"That's just what I'm getting at," Stryker frowned. "You're already sounding sarcastic about our mission. . . ."

"It's just that I joined this army to be a policeman," Greg said sheepishly. "A *cop.* I wasn't expecting all the GI bullshit that goes along with it. The guard duty, the barracks fire guards, all the boonies patrols with full combat gear—you'd have thought I was eleven-Foxtrot instead of Ninety-five Bravo. Christ, the week I spent at Oakland processing to come here to 'Nam was even worse than Boot Camp: six eighteen-hour days of KP, straight! Now that had nothing to do with law enforcement, Sergeant Stryker. . . ."

"Yah, I'd like to deck the asshole who came up with the

term 'Kitchen Police,'" Stryker laughed as he pointed down toward the next intersection, swollen with a hundred motorscooters and daredevil pedestrians stepping out in front of the bumper-to-bumper traffic. "Turn right here.

"I just want you to understand what our mission is all about," he continued. "Why we have to be soldiers as well as policemen in order to get the job done overseas."

Marsh wanted to tell Stryker why he had really come to Vietnam. He wanted to tell him about his brother Nathan. Wanted to drill him about the incident where the infantry sergeant had turned up missing on the outskirts of Saigon after an uneventful jungle patrol. Wanted to find out what Stryker knew. What the men of the 716th knew. Instead, he said, "I'll be okay, sarge. I just wanna be a good cop. Keep a low profile. Who knows, I might turn out to be a twenty-year man—make you proud!"

"I just want you to know things aren't so bad here in Saigon. In fact, we probably got it sacked here, as far as the Military Police Corps goes. We got the damned best provost marshal in the brigade right down the street there. And the company commanders are heaven-sent . . . real cops at heart. So long as you do your job, and don't get involved in dope or dames, you'll do fine.

"And as far as the business cards we were discussing . . ."

"Don't worry, sarge," Marsh smiled over at him as he carefully swerved in and out of traffic funneling tight to pass through a police checkpoint. "I won't have 'em put 'Fuck the army' on my cards. I just wanna put in my time so's I can get one of them Eighteenth Brigade combat patches sewn onto my right shoulder."

Stryker reached over and patted him on the shoulder. "You're okay, Marsh—I don't care *what* the women on Tu Do street are already saying about ya!" And he let out a hearty laugh that sent the bewildered Marsh to grinning. A woman standing on the curb a few feet away reached out and ran long slender fingers along his arm, accenting the gesture with a seductive smile and a wet kiss blown through the air at him.

The private automatically recoiled, glancing down at his wrist as he slowed the vehicle. His watch was still in place. Behind them, fading in the distance, the woman in the tight miniskirt and healthy halter top was calling out to him something about Saigon Tea.

Stryker laughed again at the private's anxiety-laced expression. "She just wanted to run her fingers through the hair on your arms," he said. "They're not used to monkeys like us foreigners. . . ."

"But I thought the prostitutes hated the MPs—"

"Oh, a lot of them do." Stryker nodded his head somberly in the affirmative. "With plenty of reason. But most of the hookers in this town are in love with us. It's hard to explain, and perhaps the best way is just to let you find out on your own . . . after a couple months on the street. . . ."

Suddenly there came a roaring of metal smacking upon metal off to their left, and Marsh brought the MP jeep to a halt as a convoy of rumbling Vietnamese tanks charged across the intersection directly in front of them. The convoy, led by QC gun jeeps, was several blocks in length, and, as the MPs waited patiently in the rising clouds of dust, several motorscooters coasted up on either side of them.

Marsh scanned the faces of the Arvins lounging on the smooth tops and sides of the monstrous tanks. Grim, youthful. Hardened, innocent. Tough and eager for conflict, frail and lusting for the girls on the street corners. The few that returned his stare waved and smile—not the glares of resentment he had expected. But most of the soldiers were drooling over the scantily clad women straddling the high-curbed gutters, paying little attention to the Americans. And then the convoy was gone, and they were waiting for the dust to clear.

Already several of the motorscooters were sputtering off into the foglike haze, and Marsh checked the expressions of those riders who were still parked on either side of him.

The Vietnamese seemed so skinny to him. He could not understand why the VC were such a formidable enemy in the bush, but then again, a rifle did even up the odds rather quickly. To his right, an entire family seemed balanced precariously atop a Honda-50. The mother and father shared the seat, while a young girl sat behind them, her arms tightly around her mother's waist. The sharp license plate over the rear bumper kept the child from sliding off. On the bar in front of the father, his young son was straddled, and across the handlebars a baby sat cross-legged, enjoying the rushing view and multitude of sensations. Behind the family on wheels another motorscooter was sputtering past. Two young men kept their eyes straight ahead as they passed the military policemen. Clothed in gray work coveralls and faded baseball caps, both wore dark sunglasses and sported scraggly mustaches that had yet to fill out. A youth on an ancient bicycle was suddenly clinging to the MP jeep as Marsh started off through the intersection. He held out a hand to Stryker, and, in a frowning businesslike tone, was demanding his daily quota of bubble gum.

Like a shopkeeper who was used to the street gangs and their extortion rackets, Stryker—to Marsh's surprise— handed over a brightly wrapped ball of gum, and the kid vanished in traffic without so much as a single word of thanks. Stryker just grinned, shaking his head slowly.

To his left, Marsh spotted three or four scooters loaded down with Vietnamese girls in their late teens. All wearing blue and white *ao dais*, they appeared to be on their way to or from school, or perhaps the Catholic youth group meetings he had read so much about in the orientation classes back in Oakland.

Some of the girls shot furtive glances over at the private, but others kept their narrow almond eyes on the road ahead, ignoring the MPs. Marsh was impressed with how they could ride side-saddle, looking so feminine and elegant, without falling right off the Hondas at every turn. He felt himself growing hard as the girl nearest him—her billowing silk pantaloons inches away and sheer as tissue—locked eyes with his, radiating a sophistication . . . a private little mystery she dared him to solve . . . to pursue. If he was man enough.

But Pvt. Greg Marsh hadn't even in-processed into the 716th yet. How could he be expected to chase after—

"'Course the Military Police Corps offers considerable opportunities." Stryker was breaking into his thoughts again as they merged with traffic and started down into the heart of the bustling city. "If you're like me, you'll probably keep extending over and over to remain in ol' Saigontown. But there's those of us who transfer off to Europe or the States for a couple years—just for the change of scenery, of course. But, eventually, they're always drawn back to the Pearl of the Orient," and Stryker smiled broadly as he surveyed the metropolis spreading out before them.

Marsh noticed how the pride in this sergeant's tone was contagious. Already he was sounding like Telly Savalas, when the TV cop swept his arms out to encompass the New York skyline and made some kind of dramatic remark about ". . . ridding *his* city of the scumbags preying on humanity . . ."

What bothered Marsh was that now *he* was finding Saigon beautiful too. It was almost scary, but there *was* something about this town that was dragging the skeptical Marsh under her spell! It made him uneasy, yet it made him feel good also . . . in a strange sort of way.

"And how long have you been patroling the 'Nam, Sergeant Stryker?" Marsh's question came across coated with awe and respect, which even startled the private, but instead of responding with carefully calculated words of wisdom, the MP sergeant's eyes had narrowed and he was shielding the sun overheard with a massive, raised hand. He frowned, contemplating. "What . . . what is it?" Marsh was almost afraid to ask.

"Appears we got a sun dog spying down on us," Stryker decided.

"I'm sorry, I didn't quite catch that—"

"Sun dogs, bud. See that ring of light around the sun, playing tricks with the haze? Shouldn't be up there, my friend . . . just shouldn't be present on a steaming afternoon like this. . . ."

Marsh, careful to gauge his speed against objects in the roadway up ahead, stole a glance skyward.

"It's a bad omen, my friend. Awful bad omen—should only be present on a shivering cold day when there's crystals floating up there between Mr. Sun and us. . . . Now who ever heard of ice crystals floatin' around over the *Veeyet*-Nam?"

Marsh returned his eyes to the road to make sure the path was still clear, then stared back up at the sun again. "Can't say as I've ever seen a sight quite like that before," he admitted, "except maybe a couple times back in Illinois, when it gets real cold outside and the fucking wind takes a hike."

"Powerful bad omen, Marsh." Stryker pronounced his diagnosis somberly, both hands cupped against the sky now as he brought a sight-picture up against the distant star around which the insignificant military policemen, patroling their lonely planet, revolved.

"Damned powerful." Marsh joined in on the dramatics, not quite sure yet if Stryker was serious. "Almost fucking ominous, in fact."

"Damned straight . . ." Stryker muttered back.

High above them, the sun was a blinding orb against the blue sky. There were clouds along the horizon, but none near the sun. Extending out from the bright orb, a ring of hazy radiance hung against the sky like a misplaced halo, yet it wasn't something an earthling would even notice unless he was watching the sun, searching for it.

"Perhaps it's caused by—" Marsh started to speculate.

145

"Watch out!" Stryker warned suddenly, grabbing the steering wheel and jerking it to the right as a Honda with two women on it cut in front of them.

"Goddamn chicks!" Marsh started to wave his fist at them as beads of relieved sweat began rolling down across his brows, but Stryker, recognition flashing across his face suddenly, was standing up in the jeep, holding on to the windshield with one hand. He motioned Marsh to give chase. "Beat feet after them whores!" he directed.

His pistol was out of its holster now.

Marsh reached down and activated the overhead lights with the flick of a switch. Feeling suddenly alive, and quite at home, he pressed against a dashboard toggle with the side of his knee, and the sirens on the hood began their powerful electronic wail. As if he had been driving Code-3 all his life, Marsh smoothly swerved out of the heavy traffic onto the sidewalk and expertly scattered the pedestrians as he gained on the Honda rapidly.

"What is it? Who are they?" he yelled against the blaring sirens. He couldn't believe a seasoned veteran like Stryker would get so excited over a simple failure-to-yield violation, though he had often enough seen state troopers back home practically sweep motorists off the roadway with their tail wind while in pursuit of a car with a defective headlight.

"The same cunts who stabbed my partner Carmosino!" Styker yelled as an old *mama-san* sent a torrent of profane Vietnamese after them when Marsh crashed through her poultry stand. For several blocks, a terrified chicken rushed back and forth across the floorboard, knocking loose feathers each time it bounced off the gearshift, until Stryker finally booted it out.

All right! Marsh was thinking as he shifted the protesting gears into second and stomped down on the accelerator. Those chicks tried to kill a cop! Such luck my first day on the street! I'm gonna learn how to smoke pussy right off the bat! But Murphy's Law was already falling in place around every

146

corner: A sidewalk vendor, ignoring the sirens, wheeled a vegetable cart right in front of the MPs. Splinters of wood and multicolored produce exploded everywhere.

The MP jeep continued the chase, undaunted.

"Waco, this is Car Niner!" Stryker now had the microphone off its dashboard hook and up to his dry lips. "This unit has a chase . . . Code One, do you copy, Waco? Gimme the net. . . . We are proceeding southeast on Le Van Duyet. . . . Request units to set up and intercept at Nguyen Du and Gia Long . . . just passing Hong Thap Tu at this time . . . suspect vehicle a beige Honda-five-zero . . . two Victor November Foxtrots aboard . . . unable to read license at this time, over. . . ."

A three-pronged attention-getting emergency tone scrambled both channels of the MP net, but even before the dispatcher could repeat Car Niner's transmission, other units were crowding the radio band in response.

"Thirty-six Charlie on-scene Le Van Duyet and Nguyen Du." A teen-aged voice came across sounding confident and years older than its owner actually was. "Thirty-five and Twelve Alpha are at U-Said One!"

U-Said was short for U.S.A.I.D. or the United States Agency for International Development, which was located a few blocks up from 36-Charlie's roadblock, but across the street on the west side. Stryker smiled as he flicked the safety off on his .45: they'd get them now no matter which way they went.

"Sierra-Five en route from the Majestic," another NCO was breaking squelch. The excitement of the chase infected everyone, regardless of rank.

"Twenty-two Echo is seventy-six . . . from the Capitol. . . ." The private sounded unemotional, even bored, but Stryker could imagine the ear-to-ear grin on Uhernik's face as he grinded gears into overdrive. Nobody wanted to miss out on the action. Besides the gunplay, and perhaps stalking armed men across moonlit rooftops, the street chases were what the men of the 716th lived for. They were what made the low pay and the long hours more than worth it. In a chase—sirens blaring, traffic swerving aside, adrenaline flowing, hearts thumping—cops were flying on a legal high. Something they didn't want to come down from . . . something they often *couldn't* come down from until hours or even days later. It was a world the layman would never experience. Unless, of course, he was the dirtball being chased.

Greg Marsh swallowed hard: *There she goes again!* Waiting until the last moment, then swerving down a narrow side alley through throngs of people, only to reemerge on Le Van Duyet blocks later. And the gall! Flipping them the finger like that on every straightaway . . . it made the private strive to keep up with the two Honda Honeys all the harder.

He decided they were in their early twenties at the most. Slender, the usual long black hair, tight shorts . . . tight *every*thing. And he'd be damned if they weren't even gorgeous on top of everything else, all professional prejudices aside. Half the time, as the chase proceeded down into the densest part of Saigon, he saw them together sometime in the future, under more pleasant circumstances, tangled up in the bedsheets of some Le Loi hotel, getting to know each other. And the other half, as gears grinded beneath him and the deafening sounds of the chase assaulted his senses, he saw their motorscooter slide into a parked tank—saw the squad of hyped-up MPs racing up to be first to break a nightstick over their beautiful faces.

The chase did *that* to you, too, according to what the DIs back at Gordon had told him. On weekends, when the recruits were allowed a few hours at the EM club, the drill sergeants abandoned their prized campaign hats, and privates and NCOs alike were all just cops, dissecting the makeup of the street over an icy-cold beer in some dive in Augusta, Georgia.

Stryker's right arm locked straight out, and for a second

Marsh thought he'd let loose with a couple rounds, but both men knew there were too many bystanders in the distance, and a .45 slug was apt to slam through your primary target and deck whoever was unlucky enough to be standing behind it. Stryker lowered the weapon and grabbed the mike. "Waco . . . this is Niner," he said calmly, even though his throat urged him to scream over the radio waves. "See if you can raise Egor at Tan Son Nhut . . . If they're not busy, we could sure use a chopper to assist . . . these suspects are just toying with us . . . they're going to disappear down territory the jeeps won't be able to follow anytime now," he said, well aware any officers who were listening were probably grinding their teeth at his failure to use military police codes over the air.

"Car Niner, this is Waco." The dispatcher was speaking rapidly, so he could talk by the book yet still save time over the air. "Copy your last . . . will contact Dean for authorization. . . ."

"Waco, this is Lima-six." A line lieutenant's dry voice broke static for the first time. "Believe I heard Novosel over the Dragon net earlier . . . their Dust-Off is Ten seventy-six a firefight north of Gia Dinh, how copy? I doubt they're available; over. . . ."

The air was alive with sirens now. The tenements all around were rising five and six stories high, and the yelps and hi-los were bouncing back and forth off the concrete until it was difficult to tell where the individual sirens were coming from. Stryker tensed up at the slight shudder of danger that shot through his gut and up the hairs on his back, and that was when it happened. The girl on the back of the Honda turned to match eyes with Stryker, she raised her extended finger out at him again, and then the motorscooter shot forward in a burst of power at the next intersection— just as two jeeps loaded down with MPs charged in from opposite directions.

The unit coming in from the east turned left, tires

squealing, and the jeep appearing out of the west turned right to follow the women. They slammed into each other's sides halfway through the skids. That was all that saved them.

Stryker winced as metal tore at metal and the MPs on the inside scrambled away from the impact. Both jeeps remained on their wheels and, sides locked together briefly, roared off in pursuit of the Honda. The motorscooter braked hard suddenly, and, at the last possible moment, swerved down another narrow alleyway. It was one that the jeeps, locked together miserably, would be unable to plunge down into.

Marsh, taking his cue as several MPs waved him past the now clogged alley entrance, shifted into third and continued down Le Van Duyet until his eyes focused on the street sign hanging by one strand of wire from a utility pole: Nguyen Du. He pulled hard on the steering wheel, sliding to the left, and screamed past a squad of *canh-sat*s who had just exited an open-air cafe on foot. The rush of air chasing their MP jeep blew one of the Vietnamese policemen's white hats off and he angrily drew his American-made revolver and took a bead on Stryker's back. Before he could fire, however, one of his associates knocked his arm high, and neither Stryker or Marsh even heard the discharge that sent a steel-jacketed .38 rocketing toward the clouds.

"We got the plate, don't we!?" Marsh was yelling above the whining engine as he swerved in and out of taxi cabs and cyclos, racing toward where the alley should come out on the next street over. "Why don't we just run 'em down that way later?"

He decided, the moment he suggested it, that the MP sergeant would tell him how you never gave up the chase when it involved fleeing felons, but Stryker's explanation was different than he had expected. "We tried that the last time!" he yelled back above a chorus of protesting horns. Marsh took them up onto the sidewalk for a half block when they came upon a snarl of stalled buses, their motors vapor-locked. "But the scooter turned up to be a steal. . . ."

"Stolen?" Marsh added his own horn to the dual singing sirens when an old woman stumbled out of a pharmacy into his path. He swerved back into the street abruptly, taking out a roof overhang beam in the process.

"Yah!" Stryker said. Both MPs glanced back to see if the collapsing roof would fall across the *mama-san*, but she escaped unscathed. "Snatched it right out from under a *canh-sat* on his goddamned coffee break! I'd wager this one's hot too!"

As predicted, the motorscooter emerged nearly in front of the MP jeep, and Stryker could almost reach out and grab the woman straddled across the back of the seat. She responded with a vicious swinging motion of her right arm that caught Stryker in the forehead. The switchblade her slender fingers were wrapped around ripped a horizontal gash above both eyebrows that sent blood spurting onto the windshield.

"Son-of-a-bitch!" Stryker snarled as he ran his left fist across his eyes, swabbing the crimson tide aside. He leaned out across the windshield and jerked off five rounds rapidly, one after the other.

The first bullet missed entirely, ricocheting off the blacktop with a dull zing as it arced out above the rooftops. The next two slammed through the scooter's rear fender, and the back tire exploded with a shower of disintegrating rubber. And the last two slugs pounded into the closest woman's back, catapulting her forward into the driver, and sending a shower of blood back at both MPs as the hollow-points tore a neat crevice down along the backbone between her shoulder blades.

"Holy shit!" Marsh yelled as he watched the driver struggle with the handlebars as her passenger somersaulted over her. The front wheel jerked from side to side, nearly flipping the Honda end over end, but after the wounded girl tumbled to the ground, the driver regained control and sent more gas rushing to the motor with a flick of her wrist. The scooter nearly popped a wheelie as the front end left the pavement, despite the rear blowout, and as the MP jeep raced by the woman sprawled across the ground, Stryker leaned over and pumped another round into her, mumbling, "Insufferable cunt!"

"You all right!?" Marsh fought with the steering wheel as he glanced over at the blood spraying from the sergeant's head wound. Greg wished more than anything just then that he had a firearm.

"I'll be all right!" Stryker was incensed. He reached down and grabbed the mike again, telling Marsh, "Just concentrate on catching our suspect up there!" Already the woman had put a half block between them. "We are now southeast bound on Cong Ly!" Stryker was squeezing down on the microphone button now as if he were trying to squish a slithering rattlesnake. "I want units at Le Loi and spread out along the Central Market!" He was not sure he had gotten through. The radio band was a garbled collage of MP privates fighting to air their locations.

The dispatcher sent the emergency scrambler tone across the net again, demanding silence from the military policemen crisscrossing Precinct One. "Attention ALL UNITS!" his voice carried an urgent and angry tone for the first time that afternoon. "Gimme a Code One at this time!" Static reclaimed the airwaves. "Okay, Car Niner . . . it's all yours, Stryker . . . Talk it up!"

But Sgt. Mark Stryker was busy holding on to the dashboard with both hands as Marsh swerved in and out of traffic, trying to keep up with the Honda Honey. *At least she's lost her fucking smile!* he laughed inwardly as they slowly gained on the motorscooter. *Now she's tits to the wind, sprinting for her life!* Stryker felt like a tiger, toying with a gazelle . . . easily pacing it, lashing out now and then to slap at its haunches with sharp claws—just to let her know he was right behind her. He could almost hear her breathing, panting with the exertion, though he was also aware her legs weren't even moving, except to play with the pedals as she downshifted, trying to catch him off guard or entice him into stacking it up as she veered down another narrow side street.

Stryker wasn't sure how much longer she could keep this up. They had doubled back again, and were now barreling southwest down Tran Hung Dao in excess of fifty miles per hour. He had never seen a motorscooter, with its rear tire demolished, able to last so long on just the rim. With each swerve through traffic, the chrome-edged wheel was throwing sparks back at the MPs like a Fourth-of-July fireworks fountain tipped onto its side. Up ahead, the fortified walls surrounding the International Hotel compound loomed menacingly down the street.

"Hold her steady . . . hold her steady. . . ." Stryker had his .45 extended again, and was bringing a sight-picture down across the female driver's narrow back. He knew he had two rounds left, and he no longer cared if they went astray.

Or did he. The big MP sergeant hesitated just a moment too long. In the distance, pedestrians were scattering out of the way. The woman was all over the road again, dodging the platoon of MPs who had trotted out from the International with the crazy intention of tackling her, Honda and all!

But she made it through the maze, and the bobbing black helmets, like aquarium fish rushing away in unison when you tap against the glass, sprang back to allow the racing jeep by.

Up ahead, two more MP units appeared suddenly across the intersection of Pham Kim, and the woman jerked the handlebars hard to the left. But there was no side alley this time—she would have to double back!

And Marsh was ready for her. Or at least he thought he was. He pulled hard to the left also, and the vehicle responded with a deafening *pop*! as the right front tire exploded under the shifting weight and miles of high-speed stress.

"*Sayonara!*" Stryker managed to say as the jeep flipped

over onto its right side, throwing both MPs through the air. The vehicle, engine still roaring above spinning wheels, and sirens barking as the power went out, rolled several times across the street until it crashed through the southwest wall of the Military Police headquarters.

Stryker landed, like the classic cannonball, on his back in the hotel's courtyard swimming pool, splashing the odd assortment of off-duty MPs who had gathered under the sun umbrellas to read newspapers or write letters home. Marsh, on the other hand, managed to smash into one of the colorful umbrellas *beside* the pool. Their MP jeep's radio clattered across the courtyard, coming to rest precariously on the edge of the diving board, inches from the water. Stryker rushed over and braced a bruised and battered hand beneath it as Marsh rolled down off the umbrella and landed unceremoniously across the cement and one of the dozing housegirls, breaking his leg. He began howling in pain.

Swishing his feet back and forth to keep him afloat in the deep end, Stryker forced a grin up at the groaning Greg Marsh. Still holding the radio up with his free hand, he waved the other arm out to encompass the group of shocked MPs standing on the edge of the pool. "Welcome to the Seven-sixteenth!" he said, the blood from his head wound still oozing down across his face. It began dripping into the warm pool water, with small rivulets spiraling down toward the bottom like fluid crimson screws. Marsh just closed his eyes, exhausted.

In the distance, the sound of a sputtering motorscooter could be heard quickly fading with dusk from the sunset. Marsh clutched at his leg, but even more painful was his inability to do anything when he heard the woman laughing . . . calling back to them, "One, two, three . . . motherfuck MP!"

7. LUCKY CHARMS AT CHECK-POINT 6-ALPHA

"Want a warm-up?" the marine embassy sergeant asked Stryker. Without answering, the MP pushed his mug across the consular desk for a refill.

"I'll tell you, Simm . . . never seen anything like it—there we both went flying balls to the wind right into the hotel courtyard, and that goofy Marsh only got a hairline fracture to his thigh to show for it all. . . ."

"And Captain Harlow?" the marine brought his own cup nearly to overflowing before adding a bit of cream and sugar. Stryker smiled but didn't comment on the sugar. He was thinking that he'd always been under the impression marines weren't allowed cream and sugar!

"Yah, you guessed it . . . such luck. The ol' buzzard was standing right beside the diving board when we made our dramatic entrance."

"Tough break." The tall marine brushed at his thick mustache for a second then swept back his wavy locks—almost unheard of among leathernecks.

"But you wanna know the strangest thing about it all? Standing in the rubble of the wall was this little old *mama-san*. The same woman we had nearly run down minutes before . . . during the chase, when we knocked the roof off a storefront back on Nguyen Du. And I could swear I saw her face among the crowd earlier, when we were parked alongside a bonze bonfire. . . ."

"Damned Orientals all look alike to me," the marine muttered, "once they get past the age of fifty or so."

"Well, I guess it's no big thing. Just kinda nerve-rattling . . . on top of everything else, you know?" Stryker gulped down half the cup, searching for the caffeine lift.

Two young lance corporals appeared in the dim doorway several yards behind the NCOs, and Sergeant Wabbitt motioned them forward.

"Perimeter secure, sergeant," one of them reported.

"Fine, fine," the big marine waved them back out into the night. "Go take in a movie or something . . . just keep your pager on standby."

"Any clandestine activity under the tamarind trees?" Stryker asked before the enlisted men had a chance to proceed very far. Gleaming smiles broke their previously grim features, but they didn't respond to the bait immediately. Instead, Wabbitt waved them off again, smiling himself as he shook his head from side to side, and the marines vanished.

"I'm tellin' you it ain't *my* men ballin' the dinks out there behind the treeline," the marine sergeant insisted, but Stryker only cleared his throat sarcastically. Wabbitt changed the subject like the pro he was. "So what did Harlow say to you anyway. I mean, three strikes and you *are* out, aren't you?" A get-even giggle escaped him.

"Aw, same old shit," Stryker tugged at the bullet-hole scar across his earlobe. "Threatened to bust me a couple stripes if I continued abusing government property in the form of GIs. . . ."

Wabbitt laughed loudly at that one. "So who's scheduled to ride with you tomorrow?" The marine sergeant was never quite sure what Stryker's shifts were. He seemed to be out on the street, in uniform, a patrol jeep close by, at all hours of the day and night.

"Currently . . ." Stryker swallowed uneasily, "I'm a solo unit. . . ." The lanky marine laughed again. "Even The Brick wouldn't drive me around tonight!"

"Another cup?" The sergeant in dress-blues was lifting the coffee pot again. He tried to avoid staring at the two butterfly bandages that held Stryker's split forehead together—the sight required repeated chuckles.

"No, no thanks, Simm," Stryker glanced across at the big man's name tag and wondered, briefly, if he got razzed often about his last name. Stryker started to relay the latest Bugs Bunny joke he had heard, then thought better of it: Simm had nearly handed that goofy Reilly his head when, out of habit, he showed the marine his Bugs Bunny imitation at midnight chow over at the USO one evening. Rumor had it the whole incident had just been a study in comedy, but half the graveyard shift *had* been dispatched to break up the ensuing melee. Stryker glanced down at the bottom of his empty coffee cup and grinned at the decal of a topless waitress staring back up at him. *Crazy jarheads*, he decided. *Anything for a laugh.*

"Sure now?" Wabbit still had the pot suspended in the air. The fumes smelled good, but Stryker could feel his limbs being rejuvenated already.

"Naw, I think I got enough brew racing through my veins now, pal. Appreciate the company, too."

"Maybe that kid, Greg what's-his-name, would be willing to stick it out with you. Ridin' patrol alone in this town could be hazardous to your health."

"Marsh is a good sport, but the Docs say he'll have to remain on light duty for the next few weeks, to make sure his break heals properly. I just visited him before I stopped by here. They're releasing him tomorrow to make more room for all those casualties coming down from Gia Dinh."

"Yah, I heard there's quite a battle raging up there," the marine brushed at the edge of his mustache with his knuckles

157

again. "But you know what else I heard? Talk about the scrap up north not being just another engagement with the bad bad Victor Charlie. Some cats in the know are claiming all the flying lead is actually a private little war over dope-running ops that—"

"I heard that same crap too," Stryker cut in. "I would not lend much credit to the talk. If there was any half truth about it, the papers would have picked up on it long ago and blown it across the front page. What with CIA leaks being rampant like they are these days . . ."

"So did you see Cob and Nilmes while you were at the hospital?" Wabbitt checked his watch. He was stalling for more company. The marine didn't look forward to the next eleven hours alone, guarding the U.S. embassy on Thong Nhut street, watching flares and the world pass him by. Despite the curfew.

"Carmosino should be back on the street in a couple weeks," Stryker smiled, trying to ignore the flashbacks slapping at him: their chase after the Honda Honeys . . . the switchblade being plunged into his fellow sergeant's thigh like a butcher snatching a cold block of meat with an icepick. "And even better news on Carl. He'll be line-ready tomorrow. They patched up his scalp wound pretty good."

"I'm sure he'll be anxious to pay the Saigon Zoo a visit so he can check on his pet ape out there."

Stryker thought back to the night Nilmes was tossing matches at the big monkey, only to get caught off-guard and repeatedly slammed against the animal's cage after it grabbed hold of him. "Yah, I'm sure ole Carl will be back to true form the instant he zips up his jungle boots and dusts off the helmet liner. . . ."

"And the rest of the troopers?" Wabbitt glanced past Stryker, out toward a flare that had broken free of its chute and was plummeting to earth like an angry, falling star. "How's the gang all doing?"

"For the most part, fine. They'll always have their gripes,

and I've been invited to another bitch session after end-of-watch in the morning." Stryker found himself reaching across the table and pouring himself another cup of coffee, however much it pained him to drown the topless blonde at the bottom of the mug.

"What's the topic this week?" He sounded like he too was used to the complaints.

"Oh, now it's the M16s again. They're complaining the damn things jam too much, especially after that sniper attack a few days ago."

"Just gotta keep 'em clean, that's all," and Wabbitt glanced down at the arsenal of weapons stacked strategically under his desk.

"I agree with you—it's not like we were out patroling the boonies, though. One of those clowns on the Decoy Squad even went so far as to suggest that the Saigon smog was the culprit—"

"Naw . . . no way."

"But one of my rooks—the guys are calling him Nasty Nick now, after the way he took out that sniper on Le Van Duyet—claims it's the ammo that's causin' all the jamming. He showed me the problem, and even had documentation in his little notebook he keeps. . . ."

"Good man." Wabbitt poured himself his fifth cup of brew.

"His notes seemed to jibe, so I wrote it up and sent it, through channels, to PMO—just to see how they toss it back at me."

"I hear ya, brother . . . I hear ya."

"Then there's the rash of VC booby traps the guys out at Fort Hustler have had to contend with the last week or so. Seems the Cong have been turning the claymores around so that they face inward instead of out across the perimeter."

"That could ruin your whole morning." The marine lashed out at a huge wasp with a graceful karate kick that sent the insect buzzing out a window.

"And yesterday the armorer, during a routine check of our Alert gear, found that someone had gone and rigged all the grenades with shorter smoke-bomb fuses, so that they'd detonate the second you pulled the pin and let the lever fly loose."

"Damn Charlies . . . you'd think they were trying to win this war or something."

"Then there's this Spec Four in Third platoon. Mailed a goddamned VC finger home as a souvenir and can't understand why his wife has filed for divorce. . . ." Wabbitt laughed at that one, despite its hidden implications. "And of course there's scheduling problems—"

"Naturally."

"Broox caught a sniper's round last month, you know. And the slug lodged dead center in the Gideon Bible he was carrying in his shirt pocket—you know, those little jobbers they hand out when you join the army?"

Wabbitt produced a slight smile just before pulling his own pocket bible from his chest pocket. "I think I know what you're talkin' about."

"So now Broox is the company charm, and everyone—especially the single-digit midgets—wanna ride patrol with him, and *only* him."

"Sounds like you got a whole bucketful of worms to contend with."

"And that's not all," Stryker checked the squelch on his belt radio to make sure the volume was up—it seemed unnaturally quiet for a Thursday. Only a few bar fights so far tonight. Curfew in thirty minutes would get the citizens off the streets, and then there'd be only the VC and the snipers—some of whom were also VC. And some of whom weren't.

"I got this one private on day watch," the MP sergeant continued, "who recently broke up with a Saigon bar girl—"

"Shame, shame," Wabbitt flashed a set of teeth at Stryker.

"And she had a note delivered to him warning the poor guy she had spent the last three days praying in one of them

160

Buddhist temples downtown..." Stryker paused for dramatic effect, "and had put a curse on him that would last the rest of his life!"

"I heard about them temple joss-stick curses, but I never put much stock in them."

"Neither did my man Malboys. But he's had a sniper knock out his windshield the last four nights in a row, and I heard this morning his hootch down in Cholon burned to the ground day before yesterday."

"Total bummer." The marine sergeant's eyes darted around the dark room dramatically.

"Yah, I been trying to look up his old lady to talk to her, but she's more or less vanished. Probably took a hike to Mui Dinh, where she's from, to let things cool down—"

"Or her cauldron simmer," the man across from Stryker added somberly.

"Other than that, it's just your normal Tour-Three-sixty-five in good ole Saigontown, pardner." Stryker poured himself another cup, feeling suddenly in the mood to clean up a bar fight somewhere.

"Any leads on that Honda Honey you guys been chasing?"

Stryker produced one of his better frowns. "You leathernecks really like picking at the scab, don't you?"

"Hey, big guy: The story's all over Saigon. *Honda Honey manages to elude legendary Super-Stryk after blazing high-speed chase.* Don't blame me."

"Nobody mentions that we smoked her passenger, right?" Stryker was grinning now, even though he was growing queasy and feeling light-headed, thinking about how the woman had lashed out at him with the switchblade. He ran his fingers along the butterfly bandages above his eyebrows. If he wasn't such a big man, they'd look almost comical. "Nobody mentions that I dusted her commie ass even though I was blinded by my own blood, right?"

"Do they ever?" the marine was noncommittal. He reached out suddenly and swatted a mosquito in midflight with an open palm. The insect was so big both men could hear it smack against the far wall, drop to the floor, snort a couple times (like a lawn mower that was refusing to start), then buzz its wings angrily as it tried unsuccessfully to get off the ground again. "So did CID ever ID the chick?"

"Nothing," the MP sounded both disappointed and drained. "Nothing in the mugbooks, no prints on file . . . an absolute zero. She didn't even have an ID card on her. . . ."

"Did you expect her to?"

"Not really, I suppose."

"All the time you've spent patroling this town, I'm surprised you didn't recognize her yourself . . . everyone knows about your photographic memory when it comes to Saigon's ladies of questionable virtue. . . ."

"Wasn't much left of her face, *amigo*. After I canceled her—"

"Yah . . . stamped a real visa across her ugly puss, eh?"

"I'll tell ya, Simm . . . that cunt that got away—I'm positive I've seen her somewhere before. Maybe just some boom boom girl hookin' in a Tu Do Street bar, but I'm gonna locate her if it's the last thing I do. It's only a matter of time. Sooner or later, she's gonna find an MP jeep bumper rammed up her tight little ass."

"I love that kinda talk!" the marine feigned enthusiasm.

"I've poured over a dozen mugbooks down at the Vietnamese police station on Vo Thanh" (he didn't bother to tell Wabbitt about the cute policewoman whose coffee was a shade better than the husky marine's) "without luck. Several hours logged dumping watered-down drinks in the bars downtown, searching for leads of course, have also proved futile."

"I'm sure you'll get your man . . . I mean—"

Stryker held his hand up for silence as a garbled transmission from his pak-set broke the silence in the room. He quickly turned up the volume. ". . . at Checkpoint-Six-Alpha!" An excited voice, miles away, filled the quiet room, adding electricity to the already tense air. "Signal three hundred at this fourteen . . . Gimme backup, ASAP!" Shots were ringing out in the background, and suddenly a magazine of twenty M16 rounds were sprayed off on full automatic only a few feet away from the man calling for assistance. Stryker envisioned either of the SPs at the joint army-air force outpost returning fire at hostile forces. "Repeating . . . Code Zero: Shots fired! MP needs help at checkpoint-Six-Alpha!"

Stryker was sprinting from the room, disregarding formalities. A brother cop was in trouble.

"Watch your ass, Mark!" the marine sergeant called out. He poured himself another cup of coffee, then walked casually over to the short-timers' calendar tacked to the bulletin board and Xed out another date.

Sgt. Mark Stryker would have been surprised to find Greg Marsh manning the kiosk at Checkpoint 6-Alpha only a few hours after he had visited the private at the army hospital on Tran Hung Dao. And Stryker would have been mildly upset if Marsh had called him up on the field phone to complain that some crazy lieutenant at the International, spotting him getting off the 17th Field shuttle bus, had hustled him right onto an outgoing jeep after throwing a spare helmet and flak jacket at him. "Short on manpower tonight, troop! Need you out on the static posts! Sign for the weapon of the MP you relieve." But Marsh had not protested. From all the small talk at the hospital, he already knew Checkpoint 6-Alpha was a four-man post where you monitored vehicular traffic funneling out from busy Saigon up north into the military complexes along the edge of the airport. Very little strenuous activity, but the place was a no-man's-land, famous for its disproportionately high number of sniper incidents. Marsh's leg was not even in a cast—just a tight fiberglass brace that was fairly comfortable, and he decided to comply with the abrasive, no-nonsense lieutenant without argument rather than be forced to recount for the umpteenth time the bizarre circumstances surrounding his landing in the Republic of Vietnam.

And it felt good to get back outside for a change.

Until the first rounds zinged in along the edge of Checkpoint 6-Alpha. A burst of AK fire from a distant rooftop exploded across the windshield of a brightly decorated passenger truck, and, amid the screams of scattering commuters, Marsh found himself diving for cover and trying to keep his rifle out of the dust while he frantically scanned the charred skyline for muzzle flashes.

Directly in front of him: the ridged boot bottoms of the three Americans who had been manning the post with him. They too had immediately taken cover and were desperately searching for someone at which to return fire. Behind him: a huddle of terrified Vietnamese who had stampeded off the passenger truck to take refuge beside the heavily armed MPs. Sirens from all sides of the city were converging on their location, and the portable radio inside the kiosk was nonstop chatter as Dispatch and approaching units tried to raise them on the air. Pinned down as they were, none of the Americans cared to venture across to the radio just yet, solely to answer a transmission. PMO was probably fearing the worst: total wipeout. Hopefully, they'd be pleasantly surprised.

There came a sudden tugging on Marsh's thigh pocket from the mass of bodies beside him, and then the words, "Gregory! Gregory Peck!"

The sweat rolling down into his eyes, Marsh turned to find Judy, the Vietnamese woman who had tried to hustle him back at Tan Son Nhut. His eyes fell to the swell of flesh being pressed tight against the plunging neckline as she too hugged pavement.

"Well, hi!" He couldn't believe they were actually exchanging greetings while under fire. Another shower of lead swept across the snarled intersection, but cars continued to squeeze through, and some irate motorists, their windows rolled up and air-conditioners cranked to full blast, lay on their horns as they protested the unexpected traffic jam. 'I haven't been by to see you because I just got out of the—"

The other MPs were turning to look back at them. He found it just as incredible that they found time for small talk as the rounds zinged in all around. Marsh felt himself going red: It was happening again. . . . But he didn't know if he was growing hard from the fire fight, or the "lucky charms" beckoning him from beyond the edge of silky fabric.

The first patrols were skidding up to the scene now, and as soon as two flapping gunships descended from a ring of flares, the sniper melted into the mobs of reporters crowding the rooftops to see what all the commotion was about. And vanished with the gunsmoke.

"Marsh!" It was Stryker. Still in the air, hopping from his jeep, his eyes were locked on the M16 in the private's hands as the newbie rose from the ground. "What you doing working the street, son?" His eyes narrowed as he spotted the slender girl clinging to his arm. "Christ," he muttered at the sight of her disheveled halter-top. "Something tells me I don't want to know. . . ."

But then the other men at the checkpoint were explaining to Stryker about the overzealous lieutenant, and a deep frown creased the ex-Green Beret's features. He looked like he wanted to break a fencepost with somebody's head. "Wasn't Slipka, was it?"

"'Course not, Mark," the PFC in charge of the post grinned. "From the description Greg here gave me, it sounds like none other than that goofy-fuck, Calloway."

"Cowboy-boot-Calloway!?" Stryker was fuming. It wasn't bad enough the butter-bar had dropped in on the Saigon Commandos without warning, fresh from the attitude adjustment academy at Disneyland East, intent on making waves in the Big V. The men could cope with that. They had in the past . . . they would in the future. But it was hard for anyone to keep a straight face when the lieutenant showed up on the graveyard shift, sporting black cowboy boots that were an embarrassing eyesore beneath the bloused khakis. Stryker had set him straight quick over that escapade, and the men all wished he had lost his commission over the incident. The lieutenant was a royal pain in the buttocks. "Ole Bobby-A gonna lose a piece of his ass before I get through with him," the MP sergeant grumbled, turning back to face Marsh.

"How's your leg, Greg?" he asked, but it was the girl's legs his eyes were inspecting.

"Oh, I'll be fine, sarge. Slammed it against that cinder-block back there diving for cover, but I'll make it through the night."

"Bullshit," Stryker muttered under his breath. Then, turning to face the senior man present, he said, "Think you can handle the army half of this post by yourself the rest of the shift? Marsh here just got discharged from the hospital, for Christsake. Broken leg."

"Hey, no sweat, sarge!" The man was all smiles. "You know that." He spoke to Marsh next. "You gotta forgive numbnuts," he referred to Calloway. "Most of the officers in the Seven-sixteenth are first class, let me tell ya. Us guys on the line really respect them. But now and then you get a jerk like Bobby-A passing through, trying to make his reputation at our expense."

"Those are the key words," Stryker cut in. "*Just passing through*. Now gimme your rifle, my friend. And take a hike. You're off for the next forty-eight hours. Report to me Saturday evening at twenty-three hundred hours. Think you can put your time to good use?"

Both Stryker and the other three soldiers present were staring at the woman standing silent in the shadows, but Marsh felt uneasy. *They* assumed he was already deep into her pants, but *he* knew different. Of course, there was the reputation of the MP Corps to uphold. Couldn't let a tiny five-foot-tall tigress make you look ball-less. "Sure sarge," he said, deciding to use the favorite expression in Saigon next. "*No sweat.* I'm sure Judy here will take good care of me. . . ."

"Good evening, Judy!" All four men bowed in unison after finally learning the woman's name. She smiled shyly, placing her hand across her mouth, relieved this huge man with stripes on his arm like a jungle cat had lost some of the hostility he had shown her the previous day outside Tan Son Nhut.

"So beat it." Stryker motioned him off the concrete island in the middle of eight lanes of traffic, and, as if on cue, Judy tugged on his arm and led him over toward a cyclo that was slowly making its way in and out of the snarled automobiles. Marsh tried to listen to what they said as he was leaving— something about how a follow-up search for the sniper would probably prove fruitless—and then he was climbing up into the three-wheeled contraption, and they were sputtering toward Cach Mang Boulevarde.

Three days later, Pvt. Greg Marsh sat beside The Brick as they cruised west Cholon. He was being given the royal tour of the city, but Sergeant Ron, as the men lovingly referred to the huge NCO, seemed unusually quiet. Marsh believed it had something to do with the menstrual period cops suffer from. After they lose too much blood on the street. Go up against one too many bar fights or domestic disturbances. They become irritated, cranky. Threaten to ram the damn badge up their supervisor's rectal cavity if they don't slack off on all the petty busy-work assignments. (They had already been to five family fights tonight, and when an off-duty gunny sergeant uttered the classic I'll-have-your-badge threat, The Brick had stuffed him into a trash can and replied, "Son, you wouldn't *want* this job!"). Yes, Sergeant Brickmann was fighting burn-out, Marsh decided. Something the private had yet to experience personally, but a phase he was sure the legendary Saigon Commando beside him would quickly pass through.

As martial law curfew fell across the metropolis, they too fell silent, and through miles of alley mazes and confusing side streets, Marsh found himself thinking more and more about the girl he had spent the last two days with.

After the sniper attack on Checkpoint-6-Alpha, she had taken him to a tiny buffet overlooking the railyards behind Minh Chieu. Had prepared a sumptuous feast of steamed rice, shrimp, and twice-cooked pork for him. Had massaged his aching muscles late into the night. Had played the soothing Vietnamese music tapes for him as flares floated like wandering stars past their windowsill outside.

And he, notorious newbie that he was, had gone and fallen asleep on her.

But the next morning Greg took her out to an open-air cafe down on Truong Tan Buu, and after spending nearly three dollars on her and the five-course seafood meal, he handed her another fifteen to pay the month's rent. "Then you move in with me, Gregory?" she had asked, excitement in her eyes.

"Yes . . . yes, of coure," came the uneasy reply, and she had spent the entire day escorting him to all the addresses in his carefully researched notebook. Addresses his brother Nathan had written about in his lengthy letters from the jungles of the 'Nam. Addresses where Marsh showed the tenants pictures of his missing brother, but where nobody claimed to know the infantry sergeant. Doors were repeatedly slammed in his face.

And that evening the fruitless search had left him exhausted. He had collapsed across the fancy bed with the satin sheets, beside the stereo speakers that continued to hum singsong melodies into his dreams of jungle fire fights and checkpoint snipers.

Not that any of it made Judy angry. She had finally found a gentle GI. And hadn't he showered her with little gifts and paid the rent in advance? What did it matter to her if he preferred to snore into his pillow all night instead of pounding her pelvis against the mattress springs like the others?

Marsh had mixed feelings about moving downtown so soon—before he had even had time to mingle with the MPs at the International. He had come across Stryker downtown the day before—they were purchasing baggies of steaming sugar cubes from the same old *mama-san*—and the sergeant had spent the mandatory half minute lecturing the private about the evils of Sin City. But deep inside, Marsh knew it would end up being just like the way it had been back at Ford Gordon. He would remain isolated from the other men, for the most part. Oh sure, he'd work beside them here in the streets, same as he had drilled with them back at The School. But after his twelve or eighteen hours were put in—after he earned his paycheck—the kid was off on his own. Secreted into some cubbyhole, studying the evidence his brother had left him: the pile of letters. The clues were there. Somewhere. And there was no way he could crack the mystery if he spent his free time bar hopping with his buddies. So he didn't make many friends. Not back at the academy. And not yet in Saigon. A man had to have his priorities. And Marsh believed he knew what his were.

After his brother was back safely among free people, he could enjoy life. Until then, Greg would press for the truth, no matter where it eventually led him. *Just the facts, ma'am* . . . Jack Webb's grim face laughed at his predicament.

Judy would provide him with a warm bed, two hot meals a day. Someone to yell at when the dead ends became too much to handle. Someone to hold at night when darkness settled in and the loneliness screamed back silently at him.

169

"We got trouble." Brickmann spoke the first words in three hours. He motioned toward a woman lying in the street ahead, totally nude, breasts not quite flattened out across her rib cage. Marsh shook himself out of his trance and popped his holster flap open.

"Yah, I'll check on her," he whispered, stepping out of the unit.

"Watch your ass," Brickmann muttered, sounding annoyed. He reached for the mike to call it in.

In ten cautious steps, Marsh was upon her. Pistol out, he scanned the shadows to his left and right—no activity. No movement. Then he stared down at her.

Early twenties. Long black hair fanning across the pavement under her neck. One slender leg crossed over the other. Entire body lined with sweat, glistening under the starlight. Chest still—no breathing. And no sign of blood.

Marsh went down on one knee and gently felt her throat for a pulse. At the same time there came a scurrying of feet from the alleyway up the block and he could hear his partner yelling, "Aw, fuck!" as he drew his automatic and hastily jerked off a poorly aimed round.

Pvt. Greg Marsh looked up just in time to see a shadowy figure, caped in a long rain poncho, rush up to Brickmann and hurl a glowing Molotov cocktail at the MP sergeant.

"Stop!" Marsh was shaking as he raised his .45 and pointed it at the phantom in green, but before he could fire, the woman at his feet had reached up and clamped her own sharp fingernails around his throat. She tightened her death-hold, like a hawk squeezing its talons into a frightened rabbit, and the last thing the army private felt before blacking out was someone slamming a board into his helmet liner from behind.

8. HOLLOW-POINT HELL

Two miles away . . .

"Stryker's gonna have a case of the ass if he finds out we're away from our unit again," Anthony Thomas mumbled his reservations as Bryant doused their jeep's headlights, cut the engine, and coasted down into the dark maze of alleys behind his Dau Street bungalow.

"Never fear, Motorola's here," the Spec4 slapped the portable radio clipped to his web belt. "We'll know where the Stryk's at at all times . . . but he's cool, compared to Grumpy Gary—yah, it's Richards *I'm* worried about. . . ." Tim brought the vehicle to a stop a few inches beside a run-down Bluebird sedan, and both MPs silently dismounted and started along the narrow, swaying footbridges that crisscrossed this poorly lit neighborhood. Suspended a mere foot above the stagnant canal channels that branched out behind Tu Do's raunchy nightclub district, the loose and splintered collage of planks had been here since before the French, and they served to connect the odd assortment of converted tenements, tucked down beyond the mangroves and tamarinds, with the tangle of side streets west of the river.

"I still can't believe you sacrificed a hundred bucks of your own paycheck to buy that PR," Thomas motioned toward the portable radio, but the movement was lost in the darkness.

"Stryker's got one, don't he?" Bryant responded, as if that were reason enough. "You can get *any*thing put together downtown . . . plus, I can listen to the calls when I'm off duty."

"Why the hell would you want to do that?" Thomas was shaking his head back and forth now. His bewildered expression was also masked by the black night. The usual ring of flares drifting along the edge of Saigon was even gone—perhaps the gunships and C-130s were off refueling at Tan Son Nhut.

"So okay . . . okay. Knock off the chatter," Bryant pleaded, aware they could and probably would argue the rest of the shift about this or that—it was why they got along so good. "I don't wanna piss off the neighbors. . . ."

They were out of their district again. Stopping by to check on Hue Chean, Tim's wife. The dwellings on either side of their bungalow had been burglarized in the last couple weeks, and Bryant wasn't taking any chances. The suspects were Americans—probably deserters scavenging for their dope money—and in the latest incident they had attempted to rape a young woman sleeping alone before they were scared off by Chean herself, ever alert to suspicious noises in the night.

Bryant wasn't really worried about her. The bungalow was practically an arsenal: an AK under the bed, revolvers under the pillow and tucked behind the rattan lounge chair cushions.

When they were a few feet from the rear door of his hooch and it was magically pulled back by the woman herself, as if she had been expecting them, Thomas glanced down at the "reason" Bryant was so worried.

Even at this late hour, Chean was radiant as ever—hair clipped atop her head with jade bobby pins, and face scrubbed clean as ivory . . . looking youthful, healthy. She

172

was wearing a light, flowered nightgown that almost hid the slight swell below her breasts.

They were expecting the baby in about three months.

She had the wok sizzling as they entered, and Thomas was amazed, again, at how his cheeks drew back in an automatic smile as the rich and spicy fragrances rushed up to slap at his senses.

She was motioning for him to sit in front of the small black and white TV set, beside the carved teakwood game table, upon which a *Go* board was set up ready to be played. There was nothing on the battery-operated television this late at night, but its silver screen provided a glowing light by which they would eat. Power in the neighborhood was out again, and *mama-sans* in the market had raised the price on wax, making candles cost-prohibitive.

"Why, thank you, Chean." Thomas nodded his appreciation as she set a plate of steaming seafood in front of him. The three of them ignored the rattan chairs for the most part, choosing to sit on a plush Indian floor mat instead. He couldn't help but notice Tim's wife was all smiles herself this evening, and he wondered if the spark of life growing in her belly had sapped her of some of her wild impatience for everything American . . . had put out some of her fire. After all, her baby *would* be Amerasian.

On the walls were tapestry enlargements of their honeymoon in Hong Kong: photos of them posing on Victoria Peak, the magnificent harbor skyline spreading out below them. Of the two of them in Aberdeen, trying comically to both keep their balance atop a floating junk and push the other overboard at the same time. Riding the two-cent ferry between Kowloon and Wanchai, the notorious Suzie Wong district. Tim had even bragged that they had stayed at the original Luk Kwok Hotel.

The volume on the TV set was turned down all the way, so they were not bothered with static. Instead, Chean had inserted one of her Vietnamese cassettes into the wall recorder Tim had brought back from Taipei, and the room was soon filled with the long, sad love songs of Thai Hien. In the background, their tiny blue-green parakeet, Tu Do-san, sat perched in his bamboo cage, suspended from the ceiling beside the east window, head turned around so that its beak rested in the ruffled feathers between its shoulder blades. Thomas noticed that the silent bird, balanced on one leg, was watching him. When he returned its intent gaze, the parakeet fluttered its tail feathers briefly, as if in a shiver, then began a quiet, muffled series of chirps and half whistles that mingled with the melody coming from the stereo speakers.

"That goofy parrot of yours is humming along with the tune," Thomas finally decided, after watching Tu Do-san for several seconds. "Does he talk?"

"It's not a parrot," Hue Chean corrected him matter-of-factly. "Tu Do-san is para*keet*!" and she playfully slapped him against the ear. Anthony made as if to chase her, but, despite the added weight she had picked up in recent months, Chean floated out of his reach. "He knows how to say 'Ants in my pants' and 'Thomas is a boom-boom novice,'" she laughed.

"Ants" Thomas turned to Bryant and grinned, "Your wife there is nothing but a goddamned cocktease."

Tim smiled back. They were close enough partners for him to talk that way and get away with it. "Yah, that goofy bird," he motioned up to the parakeet, still chirping quietly in harmony with the singsong notes but with its eyes closed now, "is a regular Beatles groupie, too. You oughta see him when she puts on "All You Need Is Love." But enough about Tu Do-san. Gary said you got woman problems. Spill it, my man."

"Oh, it's no big thing . . . you know I never let women blow my mind . . . just my—"

"Yah . . . so anyways . . ." Bryant had folded up one of his MP reports into a paper airplane and tossed it up at his feathered pet. Tu Do-san screeched down at him briefly, flapping his wings, then turned around on its perch so that his chest was facing proudly down at the humans. Then he casually twisted his head around again to rest it on his back so he wouldn't have to look at or put up with the two Americans.

"So anyways, my old lady keeps this eight-by-ten picture of me on her nightstand, right? Well, when she was in the shower couple nights ago, I picked it up out of boredom . . . you know, just to brush it off—"

"And admire yourself," Chean cut in loudly.

"And what do I find under my picture?"

"I'm breathless," Bryant said sarcastically.

"Another fucking photo! Can you believe that?"

"You mean of some other guy?" Tim sat up straight, laughing now.

"Not just some other guy! She had that goofy Jeff Reilly's picture under mine!"

"Jeff the kangaroo-killer?" Chean was laughing now too. She had heard of the handsome Australian and some of his antics from her husband.

"And not only that!" Thomas himself was smiling now, though, at the time, he had seriously considered killing his girlfriend over the matter . . . just to see if he could get away with it. "Under jolly-Jeff's picture were eight-by-tens of Mikey and Nasty Nick!"

"Nasty Nick?" Tim said incredulously. "I don't believe it. Angi never lets him out of her sight."

"Hey, it was Nick's ugly mug, all right. He was wearing that stupid boonie hat and everything—the one with the 'Peace hell—nuke Hanoi' patch on it."

"So what did you do about it, mighty man?" Bryant was still chuckling over the whole thing, but Chean had lost her smile: If Mike Broox's picture could be there, perhaps Tim had a mistress stashed away somewhere, too. She glanced down at her ballooning stomach. Everyday it grew just a bit larger. More unattractive. Would she ever regain her figure?

175

Would Tim ever again find her attractive? Did he find her attractive *now*?

"Nothing. Yet," Anthony answered. "You think I should ask Nick or Mikey about it, or just confront her with—"

There came a sudden pitter patter overhead, across the roof. The muffled noise made Bryant think of the saying: *When you hear the pitter patter of little feet, it's the Arvin Army in full retreat.* It made Thomas think of the play "Cat On A Hot Tin Roof." Hue Chean didn't waste time thinking. She reached for the nearest revolver and cocked the hammer back: Bryant had often bragged in the past that she could outshoot the entire Decoy Squad on the firing range.

Another set of feet raced past on the other side of the ceiling.

"What the hell was that?" Thomas's hand automatically went to his gun butt.

"Cat burglars," Bryant whispered, his finger up to his lips now for silence. Chean reached over and turned off the TV, but she left the music on.

"You gotta be shittin' me," Thomas now had his .45 out of its holster.

Bryant was now on his feet. "You take the front door," he told his fellow MP. "I'll go out the back. Chean can hold down the fort in here." He was rushing toward the door already. "They're probably long gone, but let's see if we can scalp us some cowboys!"

He wasn't out the back door two seconds when he bumped straight into a stocky form that towered over him by nearly a foot. His instincts told him to fire off the entire seven-round clip into the man, but his fingers held back. "Sergeant Stryker . . ." his eyes were starting to adjust to the dark. "We were just—"

"Save the explanations," the ex-Green Beret whispered back, brushing the .45 aside. "Looks like you got roof rats," and he pointed to shadows racing to the other side of the building.

As the thieves disappeared from view and began jumping to the ground, the Americans could hear Thomas yelling his warning in both Vietnamese and English, "*Dung Lai!* MPs! Hold it right there, suckers!"

But the suckers didn't hold it right there.

Taking their chances, they bolted to the left, and began a spring toward the rear of the line of bungalows. "Coming your way!" Thomas yelled back to Bryant as he took up the foot chase.

Stryker and the Spec4 were waiting for them.

As the two cat burglars rushed around toward the footbridges, a long board swung into their path, and both belly-flopped into the nearest canal.

Itching for action—anything to liven up the night— Stryker jumped in after them and started throwing his fists about.

That was when he made a startling discovery. "They're round-eyes!" he called out to Thomas and Bryant. "GIs!"

Bryant handed Thomas his pocket camera and gunbelt and jumped in to assist Stryker with the suddenly looming Occidentals. Thomas caught the sparkle of cold steel slicing through the air and he brought up his gun hand, but there was no way he could fire without risk of hitting his friends.

Stryker knocked the man's hand away before the blade could be slammed home, and they both disappeared beneath the polluted pool again. Thomas was moving around the edges of the canal in a circular pattern, hoping for a clean shot, but the two sets of combatants were flopping about in the muck so fiercely he was rapidly losing track of who the "good guys" were.

"Consider yourself under apprehension, asshole!" Stryker had come up with a choke hold on his suspect. He quickly had the man's right arm twisted back, and Thomas threw the MP sergeant a set of handcuffs.

Thomas felt himself wince as the man fighting Bryant slammed a fist into the MP's groin, then batted him in the back of the neck with both forearms. As Tim was forced face-first back down into the stagnant canal, his assailant produced a long, gleaming stiletto and brought it high over his head with both hands in preparation for plunging it down into the MP's back.

Thomas gulped in a lungful of the hot, sticky air, then held his breath, brought the focus of his eyes down across the man's torso, and hoped his reflexes would bring his automatic up to just the right angle. Then, without taking in a sight-picture, he gently squeezed off two rounds, one after the other.

The .45 caliber hollow-points both hammered the man off his feet when they smashed into his chest. Before the impact catapulted him out of the muck, the slugs exploded from his back, misshapen and expanding, and slammed into the bungalow walls in the distance with a dull thud that echoed against the black thick of night.

A choking, gasping Tim Bryant struggled back to the surface as the crack of the discharges was still heavy in the air. The first thing he saw were the soles of the boots of the dead man floating a few feet away from him.

"Hey, thanks brother!" Bryant yelled over to his partner as candlelight began flickering in several nearby dwellings, "I owe you one!"

Thomas just smiled nonchalantly and brought the barrel of his pistol up to his lips as if to blow the smoke away, then he slowly, dramatically, holstered it, gunfighter-style.

"You've some underserved rights I gotta explain to you, scumball." Stryker was trying to drop-kick his prisoner out of the canal, but the four feet of oily water made it difficult. "You've the right to keep your mouth shut," and Stryker punched him in the mouth after he was unable to boot him to dry land.

"Fucking deserters," Bryant muttered as he pulled himself up out of the canal.

"You've the right to one of your long-haired punk

attorneys." Thomas was at Stryker's side of the canal now, helping drag the prisoner up out of the water. "You've the right to—"

"I know my rights, motherfucker!" And the guy kicked out at Thomas. The MP drew his nightstick and made as if to ram it down the prisoner's throat, but when the man ducked, he held back at the last moment.

"Want me to call for a prisoner-relay?" Bryant was holding his portable radio upside down, frowning as the water trickled from its insides. He had forgotten to take it off before jumping into the canal.

Stryker was up out of the water now, and he took some flexi-cuffs from his belt to further restrain the prisoner. "Naw, I think we can handle—"

A muffled cry, weak and laced with pain, managed to slice through the noisy atmosphere at the edge of the canal, and the big MP sergeant fell silent. "Did you hear that?" Visions of a stray round hitting an innocent bystander flashed through Stryker's mind.

Bryant's concern for his waterlogged radio vanished as his head whirled around in the direction of his bungalow. His wife should have been standing in the back doorway. But the windows were deserted, and his eyes fell, attracted like magnets, to the two craterous bullet holes in the kitchen wall.

"Hue Chean!" he yelled, dropping the radio as he rushed over to the bungalow. Thomas, feeling suddenly faint—like he already knew what had happened, and he was going to throw up—raced to catch up to his partner.

In seconds, Tim was through the rear door and at Chean's side, holding her head up out of the rapidly spreading pool of blood.

Thomas came to an abrupt stop in the doorway as the horrifying scene splashed back at him: One of his hollow-points had not only killed the cat burglar outside and passed through the bungalow wall, but had come to rest in the belly of his partner's pregnant wife.

Hue Chean was on her side, curled up in the fetal position, arms wrapped across her wound, face contorted in unconscious agony. Bryant, his own face a mask of shock and helplessness, looked up at Thomas briefly. Their eyes met, and as the emotions of anger, rage, sorrow, and forgiveness were exchanged in the searing flash of the moment, Timothy Bryant exhaled a deep sigh and slowly closed his eyes, bringing his wife closer to him in a protective embrace.

Thomas swallowed hard, wanting to die right there, on that very spot. How could he ever hope to atone for this terrible accident. When she fell, Hue Chean had knocked over the TV, and shards of glass lay everywhere. The wok was still on, and the seafood was smoking, filling the room with a surrealistic haze.

PFC Thomas's eyes were drawn toward the far ceiling just then. To where blue and green feathers were still fluttering from the mangled bamboo birdcage.

The MP's other hollow-point had decapitated Hue Chean's parakeet, Tu Do-san.

9. FIRE ALLEY'S FLEEING PHANTOMS

Saigon Police Sgt. Jon Toi jerked bolt upright in his bed, drenched in sweat. He glanced about the room frantically, trying to shake the nightmare visions of *the woman* out of his head. He realized he was holding a chestful of air in, and he slowly let it out. The room was still bolted tight against the outside world, the shades were drawn, the ceiling fan above was slowly twirling, his wife was under the sheets beside him . . . far away in her own dreamland somewhere. He carefully lay back down, hoping he wouldn't disturb her.

The nightmares were returning to haunt him more often now. And they were always about the woman in the crimson dress who had held a knife to his throat. But the MPs had blown her out of her high heels, and now she came back to visit Toi every night.

Toi rolled over onto his side and buried his nose between the filmy negligee-covered breasts, smugly aware they would offer him more security than arousal. Uncaring. He needed desperately to get back to sleep. Tomorrow would be a hectic day. He would have to—

There it was again.

Something going on down in the alley outside. Toi quietly rose from the bed and slipped on his pants. Was that what had awakened him? Not the nightmare of cold steel against his throat but someone down in the street below. Out of habit, he grabbed his revolver from the top drawer of the nightstand, then tiptoed over to the window and slowly moved the drapes aside.

Toi's eyes went wide at the sight below, and he wondered if he might still be dreaming: A young woman was unzipping her miniskirt . . . letting it fall to the ground as she stood with two other women in the shadows. He watched her quickly unhinge the bra by swinging her arm around behind her, and then her breasts sprang forth, bouncing slightly as she stooped to slide off the panties. Somewhere down the street there came the rumbling of a muffled yet powerful motor, and then Toi could see yellow-coated headlights.

American MPs.

He watched the woman walk out into the middle of the alley and . . . *Christ!* he thought. *She's lying right down in the middle of the road!* He watched her lay her head to the side, making herself comfortable, then she bent one long, slender leg sensuously across the other. If she was trying to make herself look like a traffic accident victim, it wouldn't work. Toi smiled to himself, both bewildered and intrigued. She looked more like a free piece of ass, with a thing for round-eyed cops. A chippie . . .

Thinking he'd better get down there to see what was going on, Toi left the window and took his police shirt from the closet, but the MPs were already rolling up to the scene, and he didn't want to miss *anything*. He stepped back to the window.

Toi recognized Sergeant Brickmann, but the young private must be a new man. The *canh-sat* frowned. He felt sorry for these American youngsters torn away from their colleges and life of plenty back in The World (as the MPs jokingly called the United States) to patrol the streets of South Vietnam, fighting snipers, sappers, and often bar girls, before some of them had even lost their virginity, but what could he—a mere VNP sergeant—do about it? So Toi just sat back against the windowsill and watched, confident that crazy giant they called The Brick would live up to his notorious reputation as a lady's man. Toi wondered how far the huge NCO would actually go in public. If he thought nobody was watching so late at night. The Vietnamese policeman could not believe all this was happening in the maze of alleys that plunged, like an eyesore, down into the rows of tenements directly behind the *canh-sats'* family housing project.

What followed was even harder to comprehend: Someone in a rain poncho was rushing up to Sergeant Brickmann from the side, while his rookie partner was down on one knee, checking the nude girl sprawled across the pavement.

Toi's eyes flashed wide with surprise when he saw that the caped figure held a glowing object. The woman lying on her back was reaching up to lock onto the rookie's throat with a stranglehold! Brickmann was yelling something, and then the night silence was shattered by gunfire—the MP was shooting at the figure rushing toward him!

The third person! Where was the third person? Toi was leaning halfway out the window now, scanning the shadows. But then even the shadows were destroyed when the caped figure threw the Molotov cocktail at Brickmann.

The sergeant shielded his face with a thick forearm, and the wine bottle, filled with gasoline and chips of soap, bounced off it and exploded across the brick wall behind the MP jeep. As the ball of hungry, spinning flame billowed up past Toi's window, destroying his night vision, the *canh-sat* fired two rounds down at the subject in the rain poncho, but the bullets only kicked up sparks across the few feet of blacktop separating The Brick from his attacker.

Gasoline, like some liquid sheet of napalm, splashed back off the wall, down onto the soldier in the jeep, but he continued firing until his clip was exhausted, and then the caped phantom was gone and Brickmann was running toward some woman who was slamming a two-by-four across his partner's helmet.

More shots were ringing out—from above and behind him—but somehow Sgt. Ron Brickmann sensed it was friendly fire and he didn't turn to shoot back. He knew the VNP barracks were in the vicinity, and soon the whole neighborhood would be crawling with the beautiful white shirts.

Brickmann lunged at the woman swinging the board— caught the object while it was still in the air, and flipped her onto her rear.

And damned if she hadn't produced a pistol of her own and was shooting at him now, point blank.

The small 32-caliber slugs punched at Brickmann's flak jacket like a string of firecrackers that go off when you're standing on them, and though he was on his own back now, the wind knocked out of him, he wasn't losing any blood. The vest must have stopped all the lead!

He rolled over, groaning loud, stalling for time as he moved away from her—hoping she'd think he was already mortally wounded. Hoping she wouldn't rush up to finish him off with a slug or two to the back of the head. Time to slip in a fresh clip as he rolled hard across the gravel on the blacktop. He could see Greg Marsh a few feet away, out cold, and in the distance, a set of firm, bouncing haunches trotting off into the night. When Brickmann, his pistol's supply of ammo replenished now, turned to confront the woman with the .32 automatic, she was gone.

He glanced to his right. The Torch had also vanished.

Behind him, melting glass from the firebomb was starting to crackle amid the dancing flames and swaying shadows. A door slammed open and an iron grating was slid back.

Moments later, Jon Toi was beside him, huge American-made revolver still smoking. "You all right, sergeant?" he was asking.

Brickmann slapped at the few spots on his shoulders where the mixture of clinging soap and flammable liquid had burned through his fatigue shirt. He could already tell his entire back would be sore for weeks to come.

Without answering, Brickmann got up, patted the tiny *canh-sat* on the arm, then started over to check on Marsh. "This is really beginning to suck," he muttered. "They never gave me any fire fighter training back at Fort Gordon."

Sgt. Mark Stryker was still sitting up in bed as the wall clock in his third floor room at the Miramar Hotel showed four A.M. Though it was the evening following his fellow NCO Ron Brickmann's brush with death, and though Stryker himself hadn't had any sleep in three days, the ex-Green Beret was finding it difficult to clear his mind enough to close his eyes, let alone stop the rush of adrenaline still coursing through his veins. Mark glanced up at the wall across from the bed. The wall portrait of Lai, done in bright oils on black felt, was missing. He could still see it there—could still visualize the beautiful Montagnarde girl with the rim of her straw conical hat just above the haunting, almond eyes. But the portrait had been taken off the wall.

Kim lay across his heart now, left arm wrapped securely around his shoulder, one leg tangled loosely between his. Stryker knew *she* had hidden the portrait. Might even have destroyed it.

After the incident with Miss Nguyen, the policewoman.

Stryker smiled now as he thought about the whole affair. It had started out innocently enough. Sure, he had been spending more and more time down at the Vo Thanh stationhouse, trying to identify the second Honda Honey—the one that had gotten away. And yes, he had become quite friendly with Miss Nguyen. It was hard not to—the girl was always fluttering somewhere nearby, waiting to refill his coffee cup.

And she had even asked *him* out for a date. Highly unusual, especially in Asian culture. That's when Kim must have seen them together. At the restaurant where Miss Nguyen treated him to a ten-course meal of wonderful Vietnamese cuisine. It had all been totally innocent enough. But try and explain that to Kim.

She had not even challenged him about it.

The next day she had bravely stalked into the station-house, and, in front of a dozen uniformed police-persons, roughly delivered two black eyes to the dainty Miss Nguyen.

The *canh-sat*s had promptly subdued her, but Miss Nguyen refused to have her arrested after it was learned that Stryker had been sharing a hotel room with Kim for several months now. He now winced as he thought about the looks he received from the department employees as he arrived to pick Kim up. And the way Miss Nguyen's eyes had swollen nearly shut! *Christ* . . .

He had rather expected Kim to greet him too with a few wild swings of her fists, but neither that nor the torrent of accusations in rapid Vietnamese he was waiting for ever materialized. She just seemed relieved that, passions spent, she wasn't going to have to pay the consequences of her actions. She hugged Stryker like they hadn't seen each other in years, and stared straight ahead, shivering when they passed the bleak-looking holding cells, as he escorted her from the stationhouse.

Stryker had sent Miss Nguyen some flowers, more out of friendship than any misguided loyalty, and he had seriously considered booting Kim out into the street because of the embarrassing incident. But he'd be damned if she hadn't made his day by treating him to a surprise tarot card session—*that revealed his bad luck cycle was coming to an end!*

Stryker wasn't a fool. He was aware the woman could manipulate the cards to read whatever she wanted them to. But the MP sergeant had never mentioned to her he was feeling depressed about his recent bad run of luck. She had come up with the phrase herself, read straight from the cards of course. And he had given her the benefit of the doubt.

Outside, two Phantom jet-fighters swooped low over the city, just under the speed of sound, and through the open window he watched them waving their wings at some sentries on the round, red afterburners glowing against the shifting black shades that marked the horizon in the distance. He dropped his eyes to the bureau dresser.

To the stack of letters. And the one on top, its red and blue airmail stripes making the edges stand out, from his sister. He had read it a dozen times. Practically had the damned thing memorized. He could not believe they were blood relatives. After all these years, her unannounced attacks of sheer stupidity still caught him off guard, amazing him each time. *She's gotta be adopted!* he'd laugh to himself every time, but he loved her just the same. She was the only one in the family who still wrote to him.

I can't believe I didn't send you Lai's letter, she wrote. *How stupid of me! And yet, when I checked my desk drawer . . . there it was, sure enough! Can you ever forgive me for keeping you in such suspense? Anyway, I can't really believe my brother Mark, the notorious lady's man, would ever lose any sleep over a woman. Even one of those dark, mysterious Orientals they have in Vietnam, husband-hunting, constantly on the prowl for that precious ticket to the Land of the Big PX stateside. . . .* There she went subtly running hints of disapproval past him again. One of these days he was going to mail her home a belligerent shoeshine boy, fresh off a gutter curb, for Christmas!

Anyway, the letter continued, *I'm enclosing some snap-shots of the family, taken at Scott's graduation last spring—hope you like them.* (Last spring!) *Can you believe the way time flies, Mark? It seems like you just left for Vietnam last year, but you've been over there ages now, haven't you? Aren't you ever coming home, dear? Please take care, Mark. And stay out of the whorehouses, even if you are a big boy! Love, your sister.*

And once again she had forgotten to enclose the letter from Lai.

Stryker shook his head again as he recalled ripping the envelope apart. But no: absolutely no address for Lai anywhere inside. Goofy space cadet. Was she trying to tell him something?

Kim rolled away from him just then, mumbling in her sleep about something, and Stryker wondered, briefly, what ex-hookers dreamed about. Somewhere, beyond their window, in the distant dark, an exchange of intense gunfire was taking place, but it ended just as abruptly as it had begun, and the MP sergeant, free to shift about in the bed himself now, wondered how many people had died within the last minute, and how many of them had been Americans.

He slowly eased himself up off the bed, careful not to disturb the woman beside him, and walked toward the bathroom, clad only in his o.d. green GI shorts. They were a size too small, so they fit Stryker rather tight, as opposed to being baggy on all the Vietnamese men who coud be seen wearing them on the street more and more these days. Sometimes Mark would wear them to take a morning dip in the pool at the International—it was funny to gauge the expression on the housegirls' faces when he climbed out, soaking wet, the thin fabric clinging to his lower torso. The housegirls always went wild, giggling at first, in his presence, then breaking into excited chatter after he commandeered his towel from the nearest private and disappeared into the hotel lobby to see if he could make the cute receptionists blush.

Stryker slowly closed the bathroom door and surveyed his forehead after turning on the dim, twenty-five-watt bulb. The butterfly bandages had come off yesterday, and he gently tried to pry the wound apart, but it had already scabbed and was holding firm. The medics had told him it probably wouldn't scar—which was the least of his worries—especially since it ran horizontally along one of the slight wrinkles above his eyebrows. Stryker's mind flashed back to the exact moment the Honda Honey had whirled around and lashed out at him with the switchblade. Two inches lower, and she would have sliced through both eyeballs. Maybe he wasn't having such a run of bad luck after all.

He walked back out into the bedroom, careful to extinguish the light before opening the bathroom door, and walked up to the open window overlooking Tu Do Street. It was hours after curfew had begun, so the streets were, for the most part, deserted. At the corner with Le Loi he could see a militia checkpoint, and several blocks away two dim yellow headlights were slowly approaching. An MP patrol, prowling for prowlers. Gunning for gunmen. Hunting the beasts of the concrete jungle.

Something twitched at his gut, and he thought about Hue Chean. And Tim and Anthony. She had lost the baby. And Stryker was worried he might lose one or both of the MPs from his platoon. How could they ever be expected to work together smoothly after experiencing something like that?

Chean was in 3rd Field Army Hospital. Getting the best medical help available. They were still not sure she would make it. The men were volunteering their time to stand guard shifts outside her door.

You never knew about Saigon. Word quickly got out a cop's wife was on the ward, and with a gunshot wound. It could easily set the clandestine VC machinery rolling. The communists loved capitalizing on tragedy. They would expand the hurt tenfold, given the opportunity.

Stryker watched two militiamen starting a trash can fire on a hilltop beyond the now quiet nightclub district, trying to stay warm. Two thoughts immediately struck him. *Staying warm* . . . he was constantly amazed at how Vietnamese soldiers got cold in *this* climate. Even after dark, the humidity and the heat followed Stryker everywhere he went. But he had long ago come to terms with the tropics. He liked it hot: his job, the street, his woman. Nothing else mattered. If the Cong 'ever got him, he wanted to be cremated, and his ashes spread across the Saigon River by a gunship. He had made Gary promise. Richards had grinned, shaken his head, and muttered something about the ex-Green Beret going goofy on him again, but Mark had not let go of the Decoy Squad sergeant's twisted wrist until he had promised. *The hill* . . . Stryker stared out at the hill, glowing in firelight now from the burning trash can. The teen-aged militiamen were rubbing their hands over the flickering flames now, even though they wore GI fatigue jackets. *Over the hill*—he felt the shiver go through him again. *In my early thirties now, and still a buck sergeant. Fuck the promotions . . . I'm happy as hell working the street with my men. . . .* But his fingers went up automatically to the wound on his forehead. What if that crazy whore *had* cut out his eyes with one lucky swipe of the blade? *Had* ended his career with a backhanded slap of cold, razor-sharp steel? Visions of a steak knife breaking the yoke on a plate of eggs, prepared sunnyside up, shot through his mind and he tried to imagine how painful such a wound would be. *Harlow would love that*, he decided, biting his lower lip now. *He'd retire me medically . . . what other choice would he have? And then what would come of Sgt. Mark Stryker?* Where would he go? What would he do? What *could* he do . . . on two hundred lousy bucks a month disability pension?

Stryker shivered and turned away from the window and his ghosts in the night. His fears.

He stared down at Kim, but instead he saw the pizza girl. The woman who worked in the bowling alley, back at the post. The girlfriend of the MP who had died in his arms aboard the colonel's gunship as it tried desperately to race him to the hospital. The MP who had been gut-shot by a sniper. The man who was more worried about whether his woman would wait for him than about his wound.

He had sat at a table for nearly an hour, watching the off-duty MPs drinking beer and laughing while they bowled and stumbled around. But he was watching the pizza girl, too. Trying to decide how to tell her that her man was dead. Murdered. By one of her own countrymen.

And then, just as he was about to walk over to her, two of her girlfriends rushed up to the pizza counter. Jabbered nonstop in rapid Vietnamese for several minutes . . . and he watched her smiling, youthful face slowly turn into a desperate, tear-streaked mirror of every cop's wife who ever spent the night shift alone, dreading the possiblity that the phone might ring or that knock at the door would finally come.

One of the girls was still jabbering—long after the MP's girlfriend had dropped her pizza pan and fallen to her knees, faint, unable to breathe. And the woman beside her was almost smiling . . . *almost smiling!* And repeating something about *GI Insurance*, over and over. But the loyal girlfriend was screaming them out of her face now, and she ran off. Abandoning her job, abandoning her friends. Never to return.

At the morgue they wouldn't even let her see him . . . touch him . . . say goodbye. . . . "He's already gone, ma'am," they told her. The Officers of The Dead. "Already on his freedom flight back to The World." No, there was nothing they could do to help her out . . . nothing more anybody could do. After all, she wasn't really his wife now . . . was she?

And now the major in charge of clubs and services had gone and hired some old *mama-san* with black teeth to make the pizzas. Yes, he had learned his lesson . . . wasn't no young oversexed boom-boom girl gonna leave *him* high and dry again! So there'd be no job for her to come back to, if she chose to return to the post. After her period of mourning. After she had controlled her grief.

Stryker could still see the old *mama-san*'s face as he

thought back to that day. He'd be damned if they hadn't gone out and hired that same street-corner vendor woman who sold steamed sugar cane cubes on Tu Do, and almost got zapped by a speeding MP jeep on Nguyen Du, and seemed to be turning up just about everywhere these days.

But then again, maybe that marine sergeant back at the embassy was right. After fifty, they all started looking alike. . . . Stryker rubbed the fatigue from his eyes—was the urge to sleep finally sneaking up on him, unannounced?—and focused on Kim. She was wearing a nightgown for a change. A filmy, scarlet affair that didn't do her curves justice. And she was under the sheet now, too.

He slipped off his shorts and slowly, silently climbed up onto the edge of the mattress, then let out a boisterous war cry and leaped onto the now wide-eyed woman, wondering how long it would take for him to rip the nightgown off.

Greg Marsh stepped out of the blue and yellow taxi, slipped the driver several brand new Dong coins, and stared up at the building before him as the vehicle swerved away from the curb and rejoined the traffic rushing past on busy Lam Son Boulevarde. He glanced down at the piece of paper in his hand. The addresses matched. He swallowed hard, wondering why he was doing this, then nodded to the porter struggling to get the huge glass doors open for him and entered the cool, brightly decorated lobby.

The Caravelle Hotel.

New, modern. Contrasting sharply with the crumbling Continental that sat catty-corner from it, across the street, on Tu Do.

He took the elevator to the third floor, and before he knew it he was standing before room 313.

Greg stared down at the napkin with Sharon's name on it. His eyes focused on the red smear of lipstick, and again considered the manner in which it had been applied to the invitation she had slipped him.

He wondered, briefly again, what Judy would do if she found out he was here, but there wasn't much time to ponder the situation. The door was swinging open. Even before he had knocked.

"Well, hi there, solllldier-boy." She was wearing only a long man's shirt that came down to the tops of her thighs, and she slurred the word *soldier* until it sounded dirty. He glanced over her shoulder, wondering who was with her . . . if he had disturbed them. Why was she so scantily dressed? He wanted to glance at his watch, but he already knew it was late afternoon.

"I didn't mean to—" he started to apologize for coming over without calling first, but she was moving closer, running two fingers across his lips to silence him. And then her lips were against his, and she was slowly prying them apart with her tongue, running it along the edge of his teeth.

Her hands were expertly loosening his belt, slipping the top button free, tugging on the fabric so that the zipper came apart by itself.

Greg wanted to check the hallway, look over his shoulder—surely there were porters, housegirls, maids . . . was that squeaking noise a load of suitcases being wheeled toward them?—but now she was raising one hand, brushing his chin with it, forcing him to ignore the hallway.

Sharon kissed him harder, her eyes staring into his now as she worked on making his lips sore, and then she was unbuttoning his shirt, pulling it apart. Kissing his chin, then his throat. Sliding her tongue down his chest.

She fell to her knees and engulfed him, wrapping her arms around him until her fingers were buried in his back pockets and she was pulled him closer, hard into her face.

Someone rushed past behind them, silent as a breeze yet obvious as thunder, and he wanted to pull away, turn his head, explain . . . But instead he found himself tangling his fingers in her reddish-blond hair, grasping the back of her skull, working it up and down in the manner that pleased him most, his own head bent back in the rapture of it, the skin of his throat taut, eyes tightly shut.

When it was over, she fell back playfully on the rug, totally collapsing with bliss, yet managing to drag him down on top of her. Like magic, her shirt fell away and she was guiding his lips down onto her breasts. He was amazed at how large they were—or was he surprised at how the stewardess outfit could so cleverly restrain . . . conceal them?—the nipples seemed as red as her hair and jutted out full and wide . . . looking almost swollen. Ready to burst with anticipation of what was to come? Of what this young, eager soldier-boy could offer her . . . do to her?

"Bite me . . ." she was whispering to him, but all Greg could think about was kicking the door shut with his foot. Another maid, sheets and pillowcases piled high in her arms, was passing by, oblivious of what was transpiring on the floor a few feet away.

"Bite me!" she yelled this time, just as he got the door closed, but Greg was still kissing her chest . . . lips absorbed with the pleasures of her flesh, while his eyes darted about the room, afraid of what he might find. Onlookers? An audience to perform in front of? A roommate, patiently waiting to join in? But the only eyes staring back at him belonged to the stuffed tiger rug a few feet away, gleaming teeth still intact, the green glass marbles retaining none of the beast's old jungle magic.

"Nice place you got here, Sharon," he whispered slowly as he worked tongue down along the moist valley between her breasts, but she was slapping him against the back of the head now.

"Bite me, goddamnit!" and she grabbed him by the hair and pushed his face firmly against the swell of flesh over her thumping heart. Greg started to protest her rough style of making love, but she had suddenly changed her own mind and was pushing his head down along her belly, toward the point where her thighs came together.

"Now wait a minute!" Marsh braced himself up on one arm, pushing away from her. "What's wrong with slowing it down a little bit . . . showing a little tenderness. . . ."

Sharon reached out and grabbed a handful of hair. "You know you love it, Cory!" She hissed the words at him, grinning. "Now get down there and give the little beaver a big French kiss!" and she pulled him back toward her.

But Greg resisted. "I said *hold on*, lady—"

"You weren't complaining when I was sucking on your cock a second ago!" she lashed out like a striking cobra, and then she slapped him. The lust drained from her like sand from a broken hourglass. "Get out of here!" she screamed, pushing him away and rolling to the side. She grabbed the edges of her shirt and pulled it tight, concealing her breasts, then kicked him in the thigh.

"Okay . . . all right!" Marsh fought to zip up his pants without hurting himself, and he limped over toward the door.

"And don't ever come back!" She slammed the door after him and smashed a cheap vase against it for good measure.

"Christ," he muttered, massaging his leg as he slowly walked past two giggling maids folding sheets at the end of the hall, "goofy American broads . . ."

One of the housegirls reached out and touched his side with a probing finger, trying for a mild tickle. "Round-eye woman bookoo dinky dau," she told him matter-of-factly, like he should have known better from past experience.

"Crazy ain't the word for it, honey," he winked at her and stepped into the elevator, sighing as the doors shut smoothly in front of him.

As the lift made its way down to the lobby, he found himself thinking about some of his old girlfriends. In high school. There had only been three, actually. . . .

He had tumbled around in the back seat with all of them, at the drive-in movies, but had never really gotten very far.

Certainly none of them had ever done to him what Sharon had just done!

Then his thoughts shifted to Judy, waiting patiently for him back on Cach Mang street in her sexy silk nightgown. She had sewn it herself, from a flare parachute some GI had given her. He could see her now, lying in the fishnet hammock that was suspended above the bed, her legs spread ever so slightly for him, beckoning the man behind the boyish face, teasing him. But he had always been too busy . . . too tired to take advantage of her. Until now.

Of course, it wasn't really "taking advantage" of her. After all, he *had* paid the rent. And she *did* come with the apartment. Didn't she?

Marsh smiled as he stepped out of the elevator, wondering if what had just happened up on the third floor was officially his "first time," or if he could still, as Stryker would say, "lose his cherry" between Judy's legs.

"Back so soon?" the doorman grinned as he opened the door for him.

Smart ass, Marsh thought as he walked out into the afternoon heat. He glanced up at her window and had to grin himself. *Cory? Who the hell was Cory!?* Her only answer was to flip him the finger, then the drapes were drawn roughly shut.

He pulled his small pocket notebook out and ran his finger down the list of addresses he had compiled from his brother's letters. There were only a few left. He had already been to several dozen places. And nobody knew anything.

Or so they said. Of course, *he* knew what *they* knew. But weren't telling.

He checked the small change in his pocket and considered going straight back to Judy. He still wasn't sure why he had come all the way down here to the Caravelle in the first place. Probably curiosity more than anything. Trying to prove his manhood. But to whom? Himself?

Stryker was surely nowhere around. And Sergeant

196

Brickmann was probably still sleeping it off in the barracks—the nightmare of having homemade napalm blister your back.

Greg rubbed at the knot on the back of his head. He still couldn't remember much about that patrol, three nights ago, except that he had seen someone trying to light up The Brick's life with a lousy Molotov cocktail. Then someone high above them, leaning out a window, was blasting away, and the nude woman lying in front of him was trying to choke him out. Before he could cancel her ticket in a fashion that'd make Brickmann proud, someone was bashing a board against the back of his head.

When he finally came to, in the ambulance, Sergeant Ron was sitting across from his stretcher, wincing as the medics applied disinfectant to his back and trying to explain to his rook partner that the naked woman, now apparently braver than ever and even turning to decoying MP patrols down into her target zone, was probably the Honda Honey Greg and Stryker had lost earlier.

Marsh could not be sure—during that chase along Tran Hung Dao he had never seen enough of the driver to make a positive ID.

Only the back of her head.

"You want taxi, Joe?" A Renault had coasted up next to him.

Marsh glanced back at the list of addresses. He decided to take a chance, and showed the notebook to the Vietnamese man. "How far?" he asked, trying to look both bored and worldly. Grim.

The hack driver, in his early forties and wearing only greasy jeans, barely glanced at the page before saying, "Oh, veddy far! Veddy far! I take you, Joe . . . no sweat! Too veddy far for walk!" And he was tugging at the American's arm, leading him over to the Bluebird.

Forty minutes later, Greg found himself a dozen circles and only about five blocks away from where the cabbie had first picked him up.

"Fifteen hundred p!" the driver smiled proudly, pointing to a leaning tenement on the banks of the Song Saigon. The ear-to-ear grin revealed several chipped and broken teeth. The man had been in some real scraps before. Either that, or he had been hit by a bus sometime in his past.

"You gotta be shittin' me!" Marsh refused to take out his wallet.

"Fifteen hundred p!" the man repeated adamantly.

Greg wasn't in the mood to argue over three dollars. And he didn't wish to bring attention to himself in such a dangerous-looking neighborhood along the riverfront. So he just walked away. Without paying.

The cabbie was right on his heels, tapping on his back. "You give me fifteen hundred p! Or me call MP!" The demand actually rhymed.

Marsh whirled around, his customized badge out now. He had only picked it up that morning—at the shop where the guys said he could also buy the fancy MP business cards. *They* were now on order. He was well aware that using his position as an MP in such a manner could get him stockade time faster than he could hope to talk his way out of it, but he was in no mood to accommodate a con artist, either.

The cabbie focused his eyes on the silver shield with the gold crossed pistols in the center, below the American eagle. Then he bit his lip, eyes furrowed in concentration above the deep frown, and slowly backed off. "You numba *ten* cheap Charlie!"

Marsh pointed past the tenement roof. The top floors of the Caravelle were visible only a few blocks away. "And you *nguoi lura phan doi!*" he snapped back, repeating the words Judy had taught him for "cheating con man." The cabbie shook his fist at Marsh, got back into his taxi, and made the rear tires spin.

The American frowned, feeling no sense of accomplishment in the wake of the confrontation, then turned and

198

walked into the filthy housing project looming threateningly behind him.

The woman who opened the door to apartment 7 was young and skinny, with dark circles under her eyes and needle marks on both wrists. Her long black hair still shimmered as she moved, but a dirty white dress, torn along the shoulders, made her look like trash. A doper. *Scum*, his associates back at the 716th would call her. *Human garbage*.

"Nathan Marsh." He wondered how many times now he had repeated his brother's name. "Sgt. Nathan Marsh . . . Nathan . . . Nate."

The woman just stared back at him, not comprehending, or at least showing no sign she understood what his visit was all about, what he was saying. "Do . . . you . . . speak . . . English?" He spoke the words slowly, but the woman just stared out past him, at the street, then made as if to close the door since no one was really there.

Greg held his hand out, stopping the door as he tried to look over her shoulder into the dim room.

And he saw something that made him brush past the woman, excitement suddenly slapping him alive again.

Greg Marsh picked up the small wallet photo of his brother from the desktop in the corner. It was in a small brass frame and showed Nathan in his uniform, holding a carbine in one hand and a cluster of small tropical bananas in the other. Across one top corner was written: "For the star over my jungle . . . Tem. Love, Nathan."

"You are Tem?" Marsh walked back to her, carrying the picture with him. "Tem?"

"Pham Thi Tem," she spoke her name trancelike, as if in a daze.

"Nathan," Greg pointed to the picture. "Nathan Marsh."

The woman slowly brought her finger to the glass and held it against Nathan's chest for several seconds. Was that a glimmer of recognition the young MP was seeing in her eyes? Love rekindled? But the slight smile in her eyes never made her lips move out of its scowl, and with a pitiful expression on her face she finally said, "Nathan *chet.* . . ."

"No, no," he grasped her shoulders firmly. "Nathan is alive! He's alive. . . ." And he pointed down at his brother's smiling, one-dimensional face and resisted the urge to shake her from her drug-induced trance.

"Nathan *chet,*" she calmly repeated the Vietnamese word for dead. *"Khong cu dong.* . . ." And she pulled herself loose from him, glided over to the bed, and collapsed across it.

He spent the next several hours going through the scrapbooks on the desk, but, aside from several recent photos that brought tears to his eyes, Greg found nothing that could guide him closer to his brother. The pictures had all been taken indoors—there were no backgrounds that could provide clues to Nathan's present whereabouts.

There was a shoebox containing some notes his brother had put together, but no dates on them. No shocking revelations. They were months old and looked like a child's scribblings in many places. He scooped some up and stuffed them down a pocket, then turned to the woman.

"You cannot tell me anything about Nathan?" he asked, but she remained silent. Unmoving.

He noticed for the first time that the streets outside the closest window were dark. He checked his watch: only nine o'clock. Three hours until curfew. "Thank you for your time, Tem," Greg was beside her now, brushing the long strands of hair from her face. She felt unnaturally cool to the touch, and a shiver ran through him as he came to realize for the first time that she must be dead. But he did not search for a pulse. He did not even bat an eye.

Greg stood there several more minutes, staring down at her still, silent form, then walked over to the window and looked out.

In the street, armed with clubs and machetes, the insulted cab driver was leaning against his taxi, waiting, a dozen of his hostile-looking friends clustered beside him.

10. PUTTING OUT THE FIRE WITH GASOLINE

The three military policemen routinely shielded their eyes from the sudden flare with a hand motion that looked like a casual salute, then, after the yellow floating "star" disappeared on the breeze, they resumed their unruly, whispered chatter.

"Yah, I got some hookers, sarge," PFC Michael Broox leaned closer to Richards, ". . . waiting right down the block there . . . and they're gonna fuck us over more than Uncle Sam. . . ."

Gary Richards continued fiddling with the small pocket flares his father sent him on a monthly basis, from an army surplus store back in Florida that was better stocked than Saigon's MACV. "Tell me about it, Mikey. . . ."

In the back seat of the black, unmarked jeep, Anthony Thomas sat alone, in deep silence, hoping for another flare to break the tense silence that followed Richards's sarcastic response. Broox's attempts at his old brand of humor were failing miserably. The Decoy Squad was just not the same anymore, without Bryant. The three of them were feeling uneasy, now that they were a man short. And that man was Tim.

The MP Specialist 4th Class had been granted emergency leave, to remain by his wife's side until she was taken out of the ICU ward.

"Got one with coconuts for tits, waitin' just for Ants back there," Broox tried again to make Thomas feel better . . . less guilty. Every man in the squad, including Bryant, knew there was no way blame could honestly be placed on anyone back at that shootout, except, perhaps, the knife-wielding assailant. Who had, of course, been the primary target, and who had died. Hue Chean's child had been, in effect, sacrificed so that her husband could live. It was a no-win situation.

Anthony responded to Broox's offer with a forced smile, but his eyes closed involuntarily, and he sighed just then . . . as if a strong headache had hit him by surprise and a huge weight from the heavens was slowly lowering to rest on his shoulders.

The men were in civilian clothes, but armed to the teeth, in true Decoy Squad tradition, with automatic weapons and the best field radio PMO had to offer. Stryker had been keeping careful track of the "Torch" incidents on his color-coded city street map that broke Saigon down into patrol sector grids and separated different types of crime by color: blue pins for robberies, green for burglaries, white for homicides, silver for sex crimes, and on and on. Red pins were reserved for arsons and terrorist bombings. The "Torch" incidents were plotted with red pins that had a little yellow flame painted on the eighth-inch-diameter pinhead, and Stryker felt he had detected a rough pattern to the unprovoked assaults on Americans by this Molotov maniac. He had talked the provost marshal into assigning what was left of Richards's Decoy Squad to stake out a ten-square-block area where it was predicted the "Torch" would strike next.

"What's that?" Richards grinned, motioning at Broox's crotch. "You carrying a throw-down again?"

Mike shifted around behind the steering wheel, and even in the dark it was clear he was turning red. "Nothing," he

202

maintained. "Nothing that's any of *your* fucking business anyway. *Sergeant*." The tone was not really disrespectful. The retort was made more friend to friend, or man to man. Not private to NCO. Broox grinned now, and looked the other way.

"Mikey ain't as macho as all the little Tu Do streetwalkers think he is." Thomas spoke for the first time since leaving the guardmount four hours earlier.

"Oh yah?" Richards knew it woud be only a matter of time before stake-out talk turned nasty and Anthony's gutter personality got the better of him. The squad sergeant turned back in his seat to face the MP, curious, teeth flashing.

"He carries a big, leather sapp down there," Thomas revealed. "Right at the bottom of his crotch. Thinks it makes him look more . . . 'hung.'"

Richards almost laughed out loud—the Vietnamese girls usually went wide-eyed when American men dropped their pants already—but he remembered the stake-out code of silence, especially in an open jeep. He leaned over again and whispered harshly at the squad's driver. "No shit, sweetheart?"

"I keep it there so it's close at hand," Broox countered seriously. "In case I need it."

"It's close at hand 'cause he's always got his *hand* down there," challenged Thomas.

"Mikey probably uses the damn sapp to beat his—" Richards started to say, but before Broox could argue, the sergeant held his hand up for silence.

"Did you see it too?" Thomas was leaning forward, between his two fellow MPs.

"Something . . . someone moving through the shadows," confirmed Richards, but now there was nothing moving at all. Even the rats had called it a night.

"There . . ." Broox pointed out at a dark side alley where the street lights had all been shot out years earlier. It branched off halfway down the block.

"I saw it again too," confirmed Thomas.

"Get ready to move out." Richards slowly reached forward to grasp the MP40 submachine gun lying across his thighs.

The words had barely left his lips when the Molotov cocktail hit them from behind, taking the Decoy Squad totally by surprise.

Sgt. Mark Stryker reread the sentence on the MP report again—this was the third time—but it still made no sense, and he dropped the set of neatly typed papers across his desk and rubbed at his eyes. He could feel the migraine chasing after him, sneaking "up through the bamboo."

He hated circling the man's errors in red ink, like the PM wanted him too, especially after the guy had gone through so much trouble typing—probably two fingers at a time—the simple burglary report, but what was a lowly buck sergeant to do? He made a notation in pencil and dropped the report in the Return To Line basket, then slid his chair on wheels to the side so he could plop his boots up on the desk. The graveyard shift had been on the street five hours now, but Stryker had been in uniform since noon, and he still wore his khakis and polished jump boots instead of the fatigues and green canvas jungle boots the night troopers had on.

Stryker folded his arms across his chest and sighed as he surveyed his color-coded Saigon district map on the wall. Somebody was shifting pins again . . . moving all the silver sex-crime markers closer to Tu Do so they could justify spending more time cruising the neon-lit nightclub sector.

He nodded his head from side to side in resignation—MPs *would* remain pranksters regardless of morale—and decided it would do no good to correct the map. He picked up the top file on his In basket and glanced at the heading.

MPI FINDINGS, SPEC4 MURRAY

Stryker tossed the report back into the box. Murray was the MP from Charlie Company who had run into some financial problems and decided to sell photo enlargements of colorful Vietnamese scenery to the GIs downtown to supplement his meager income as a soldier. Trying to buy more than one bungalow downtown was what had started his troubles. MPI (Military Police Investigations—one step below CID) had gotten involved when his classified ads in the *Saigon Post* began detailing how his small mail order "company" had gone from selling eight-by-tens of kids frolicking on the backs of mud-caked water buffalo to rather revealing pictures of scantily clad Oriental women. When the investigators raided his studio to check into Murray's extracurricular activities, some of his nude models turned out to be the girlfriends of rather high-ranking warrant officers and senior NCOs in the criminal investigations division.

Stryker didn't want to know what was in the report. He had enough on his mind already.

Like that goofy old *mama-san* that was turning up everywhere lately. Always giving him the evil eye. He had approached her one time, deciding to apologize for the wild jeep ride that had left a storefront roof collapsing all around her. She had tried to scamper off, but Stryker caught her arm and gently stopped the old woman. He noticed then, for the first time, that she had a badly mangled elbow. It was now hidden under several layers of crimson-stained bandages.

"Why *mama-san*," he had said in Vietnamese, "How did you do *that* to yourself?" but her reply was to just glare back at him until one of the blue *ao dai*-clad militiawomen at the compound gate glided over to assist him.

"She say the injury from last week's rocket attack . . . in Cholon," the woman said before returning to her bomb-checking duties.

"Oh, that's too bad." Stryker gave his most sincere smile, but the *mama-san* just jerked her arm away and started off

205

down the road. He had noticed she was wearing some heavy brass jewelry common to the hill people of the Central Highlands—five- and six-inch-diameter circular plates, often a half inch thick, hanging necklace-fashion around her neck and decorated with bits of coral and blue stone—and the items made him think back to Lai, and how she had never worn any jewelry at all.

His sister had finally cabled him the address the Vietnamese woman had printed on her letter to Mark, but when he rushed to the home on Luc Tinn street, he had found that it, along with a half-dozen others on the block, had been destroyed by the same barrage of rockets the old *mama-san* had told him about. Stryker spent the whole day asking questions, but the neighborhood was composed of government housing projects that housed war refugees and even confined some mental patients. Nobody knew anybody else. No one remembered his Lai. Fifteen had died, all males or young children.

All he could do now was wait. Lai would think he was still a private investigator—from that short period in his life when he had left Special Forces during a height in the war atrocities up north. She would have had no way of knowing he had gone back into the service after the Rodgers affair. He couldn't remember telling her about his years as an MP before he had switched the black and white helmet liner for a green beret. But she had seen his photo album, hadn't she? Perhaps Lai would eventually turn up at headquarters. He could only hope. . . .

Stryker started to reach for his coffee mug, mentally exhausted by both the pile of MP reports in front of him and guilty memories of Lai when . . .

"Let me out! Let me out!"

Stryker pushed himself away from the desk, and, out of reflex more than fear, drew his pistol. The voice was coming from the top desk drawer!

"Let me out, goddamnit! Hurry! Let me out!"

The male voice carried an urgency in its tone that started to infect the big MP sergeant.

"Let me out!" it screamed on. "Please hurry!"

Stryker quickly reholstered his automatic and reached for the desk drawer, but it was securely locked.

"Please!" a long, drawn-out, tortured scream punctuated the plea. "Let me out!"

Stryker, jaw practically dragging across the desktop now, fumbled with his keys and struggled to get the drawer unlocked, but his fingers were shaking too much. *This was unreal!*

"Let me out! Let me out!"

But this time the voice lost some of its terrified tone, and a few seconds later a muffled laugh emanated from inside the drawer.

Stryker froze as if he had just been slapped by a girl who caught him sneaking a peek up her dress back in gradeschool. His fingers stopped shaking, and his lips curled up in a wicked grin. "Gary, you goofy fuck . . ." he muttered under his breath, slipping the key into the lock easily now. "You're gonna pay for this, brother . . . you're gonna pay dearly!"

The tumblers flipped aside, and the lock released the drawer. And Stryker pulled the small tape recorder with its hundred-minute tape out of its hiding place.

"Let me out! Let me out!" the recorder was still screaming. He turned the volume down and set the small portable machine on the destktop. He watched the reel slowly run out.

It didn't take long to figure out how the Decoy Squad sergeant had tricked him. Richards had been in the office earlier—was just leaving, in fact, when Stryker walked in. The desk was used by a dozen different NCOs, but Stryker was watch commander the majority of the time, and he was in the room the most. Richards had left the first ninety minutes of the tape blank, so the room would remain quiet as

Stryker went about checking his troopers' reports. But he had recorded the chorus of "let me outs" onto the last five minutes, then rewound the tape to the beginning and switched the battery-operated machine to "play" before locking it into the drawer just as he saw Stryker driving up.

No wonder that sonofabitch had been grinning so much before he hit the bricks that night! Stryker smiled dryly, recalling some practical jokes he had played on the Decoy Squad sergeant in the previous weeks. *Well, payback gonna be a bitch, douche-bag. . . .*

Stryker shifted around in his seat. Were those shots mingling with the sirens outside? Hell, that was the best way to describe Saigon: sirens wailing and shots in the night.

"Waco, this is Delta Sierra Two!" the metallic voice crackled from the MP radio monitor suspended from the ceiling. "MP needs assistance at . . ." Static and fade-out covered his location.

Stryker whirled around in his seat, at first unsure whether or not he was the victim of another practical joke. *But you just didn't joke about a Ten-100!* He recognized Broox's voice immediately.

"We've been ambushed by the "Torch"! Need a Ten-fifty-two this location, copy? A burn unit! Make it ASAP, Waco, you copy? *ASAP*!"

Stryker was on his feet that quick. Running out to his unit.

As he flew through the door, he saw the half-dozen MP jeeps that had been parked outside the Orderly Room, racing Hot, Code-3, to be the first out the compound gate onto the city streets. Ten-100s were becoming more like drag races lately.

Army deserter Julian Ramirez shook his head violently, trying to shake off the drug-induced stupor. It had been nearly twenty-four hours since he had injected the heroin between his toes, and now his dreams of living on clouds

208

were rapidly evaporating, and the room around him was completely dark—no silver linings—and he was beginning to wonder what all the noise was about.

Ramirez lifted his face from the pillow and glanced about. His eyes were already adjusted to the dark, but sparklers and opium poppies were still blooming in them and he was not sure where he was or what he was looking at. After a few moments, he pushed the young girl beside him to the floor, out of the way, and stepped over her crumpled form toward the window. The air seemed alive with garbled radio transmissions—his head was about to explode.

The smut peddler leaned against the windowsill and looked down upon the street below. His fingertips against the rough grain of the bamboo reminded him he was in his own apartment overlooking Tu Xuong Street.

Below, three white men in a black jeep were scrambling to jump clear of the vehicle as a figure caped in a rain poncho charged toward them, hurling a flickering Molotov cocktail. The wine bottle filled with gasoline and soap chips hit the man in the right front seat in the elbow as he flew through the air, trying to shield his face at the same time. The bottle burst upon impact, sending shards of glass and fingers of flame all over the man's left side, and the night exploded with screams. As he tumbled to the ground, slapping frantically at the soap chips melting into his skin through the thin silk shirt, the sheet of flames engulfed the handful of objects Sgt. Gary Richards had been toying with, and the dark street erupted with sizzling light as his "pocketful of miracles"— the tiny flares his father had sent him—ignited and arced out in all directions like a careless match dropped into a bucket of holiday skyrockets. Julian Ramirez instinctively went to his knees behind the windowsill as the man dropped the long black object from under his arm too, and Gary Richards's MP40 submachine gun clattered onto the blacktop, sending a burst of red tracers in a glowing spray toward the stars.

By now curious spectators—families of Vietnamese

awakened by the racket and drawn to their teetering balconies—were watching as Mike Broox stood up in his seat and fired four wild rounds at the caped "Torch" as the suspect whirled around, ready to throw a second firebomb at the two unscathed enlisted men.

One of the bullets caught the suspect in the center of the chest, inches below the throat, and the impact of the .38 slug knocked "the Torch" to the ground.

Both Thomas and Broox, weapons ready, arms outstretched, glanced about, breathing heavily, but there was no sign of the accomplices who had shown up when Sergeant Brickmann had been ambushed earlier. A split second later, Thomas was at Richards's side, smothering the flames out with the sergeant's own jean jacket. He had discarded it earlier, in the back of the jeep, because of the heat choking the city that night.

Broox, intent on handcuffing "the Torch" once and for all, was halfway off the jeep when two bullets, fired from the dark alleyway down the street, slammed into him. One round caught him in the left chest, knocking the breath from him, and the other tore into his arm, spinning him through the air and onto his back in the street.

"My God!" Thomas, for the first time since coming to Vietnam, felt suddenly sick inside . . . all alone, deserted. His friends unable to help him. The enemy closing in on him. *The enemy* . . . he thought as he snatched up the team's riot shotgun. It was an Ithica 12 gauge, loaded with seven rounds of double-00 buckshot. *Just who is the fucking enemy out here tonight? Who* are *these people!?* He blasted away at the distant alleyway, knocking over trash cans and taking out the entire wall of a vendor's shack that was closed up for the night.

With one live round left in the weapon, he rushed over toward Broox, but the MP hadn't even lost his prescription sunglasses in the fall. His right arm was a mess, but Mike's reputation as the company charm would be magnified tenfold after tonight.

"Get back over to 'the Torch!'" he yelled, rolling toward the cover of the jeep. "Get the cuffs on his ass, Ants!"

Michael Broox's heart had been spared the killing force of hot lead again. The Gideon Bible in his breast pocket had stopped another slug.

He frantically wrapped an M16 bandolier around the severe wound to his right arm after dumping its ammo clips onto the pavement under the jeep. The pain was excruciating, and his trigger finger would not respond. Thoughts of Kip Mather flashed through his mind as he admitted to himself the odds had finally caught up to him. He would probably lose the arm. He found himself wishing the stupid Gideon had never been given to him. He would rather be dead.

Sergeant Richards was up on one knee now. Dazed, but breathing. His entire left side was still smoldering, but the fire was out. He drew the backup pistol from his ankle holster and began peppering the tenement walls down the street, not really sure what or who he was shooting at. Only aware *somebody* was going to pay for the intense pain he was experiencing. After the revolver discharged its last round, the Decoy Squad sergeant continued pulling the trigger against the silence of the oppressive night rushing back in on them. The hammer clicked sickeningly against the empty cylinder chambers, over and over. Down the street, there were no answering muzzle flashes. Only a cat, screeching, running a terrified, zigzag pattern through the parked cars.

"Move it, *Anthony*!" Broox was trying to sound authoritative, but the words left his lips in a strained wheeze. "Cuff that motherfucker!"

Thomas turned on his heels, but "the Torch" was gone. Running for its life. He barely caught sight of the green rain poncho disappearing down a narrow corridor between two tenements. Several balcony tenants were yelling now too, pointing in the direction the suspect had fled. As he rushed past the spot where "the Torch" had crumpled onto the ground, as he saw there was no puddle of blood where the suspect had briefly lain, he wished the Vietnamese screaming excitedly above him would shut the fuck up and mind their own business. And he ran. Faster than he had ever run before in his life, he fell into pursuit behind "the Torch."

Julian Ramirez had not moved an inch—had not blinked an eye since the handful of pocket flares had been set off by the Molotov cocktail. Now that all the activity was settling down, he let out the breath he didn't even know he had been holding in. "Whoooooooee!" he laughed. "Been a hot night in ol' Saigontown . . . and I almost slept through it!"

He walked back over to the twelve-year-old girl lying on the floor beside the bed and gently kicked her in the side as the two MPs below his third-floor window sat in the street, unmoving, catching their breath and their wits. "You still among the living?" he laughed down at the girl. She stirred slightly and turned onto her stomach, mumbling something before falling back into unconsciousness. "Fuckin' teeny-boppers," he muttered, glancing about the room, his memory failing him just then, but she appeared to be the only one present in the room beside himself.

He looked up at the wall clock, then at the calendar below it. He had almost slept past the date he was scheduled to meet with the Indian, also. To discuss more shipments of kiddie porn for the Frenchman's club on Pasteur Street.

Outside, several dozen MP jeeps were rolling up to the scene now, sirens bouncing back and forth off the tenements walls, lights throwing a brilliant collage of flashing reds and blues through the night mist. Julian Ramirez returned to the window and settled in across the bamboo sill to watch. He had two hours until curfew was lifted, and about twelve hours to kill before his meeting with the turbaned Calcuttan. And he could think of nothing, just then, that would better pass the time than watching pig coppers bleeding in the street.

*   *   *

212

Greg Marsh had been watching the men standing out in the street, waiting for him, for several hours now. Even with the fall of curfew, they had stayed on, and once, when a lone *canh-sat* patrol had rolled past, some of the cabbie's friends had even waved to the officers, like they were old acquaintances.

Around two in the morning, one of them had come up and tried to force the door, but it would not budge, and he had returned to wait patiently in the street outside, with the others.

Greg was beginning to suspect they wanted him for more than the simple three-dollar fare he had refused to pay the hack driver for driving him around in circles. Perhaps GIs had been making trouble for months—or years—and he had just been the straw that broke the camel's back. He did not know. But he felt the men beyond the window would not stop at rifling his pockets. He felt suddenly naked without the firearm on his hip, yet he had been an MP barely a week. The room, his fortress, was without a phone.

He did not feel like he was flirting with death, but the situation did appear hopeless. Earlier, the air had been alive with sirens, and several MP jeeps had raced by, lights flashing and sirens screaming. But after they had passed, the cabbie and his friends had emerged slowly from the shadows, reappearing where he had last seen them. He should have used the excitement for a diversion, but it had all happened so fast. One minute the street outside the window was quiet. The next, dust was flying as the American patrols roared by. But now, for the last hour or so, calm had returned to the neighborhood.

Marsh could not believe any hack driver would waste so much time over a lousy 1500 p fare. The cabbie could have made up for it with a couple dozen trips to the airport and back by now. It was obvious now to the newbie that it would take several months for him to understand the Vietnamese.

His eyes caught the dim glow of yellow headlights down

the street, several blocks distant. He knew American MP units were often equipped with the yellow lights, both to help with fog and to cut down on illuminating a combat zone's dark streets too much after sunset. He found himself praying the patrol would not turn down any of the three intersections between where it was at now and his block.

One of the men had spotted his St. Christopher's medal at that first guardmount inspection, and several of the guys had razzed him about taking God to ride shotgun with him on patrol. "Oughta get you a Buddha's charm," one of the two-tour privates had told him. "Christ done forsaken this land . . . ain't you heard? The 'Nam's the asshole of the earth, newbie. Buy yourself a Buddha necklace down on Le Loi. . . .

But Marsh had kept wearing the medal. His mother had promised to send him one graced by the patron saint of policemen, as soon as she found out who that was, but no medal had ever arrived. Judy had gone and given him a Vietnamese amulet instead.

Encased in a plastic seal, it was a small, inch-long red stone, shaped into a spirit-god, which she claimed all the *canh-sat*s wore for good luck, but he had dropped it into his souvenir bag back in his locker. He knew a lot of policemen lost their faith in religion after years on the street. After lifetimes of scooping up the corpses and pieces left of corpses. After too many lights-and-siren runs to the scene of crimes so ghastly there could surely be no God above . . . only evil. Evil in the hearts of men. Men who tore out the hearts of other men to satisfy that evil.

Greg knew there were those cops who got through their tour of duty on the street only through their unwavering belief in God, too. Men who went to church regularly. Lawmen who felt that, without policemen, their world—and their children's world—would decay into a rampant, hostile hell far worse than it already was. He was already feeling his convictions change with each new night patroling Saigon,

214

but he prayed he would retain his belief and trust in the Almighty.

And he watched, holding his breath with anticipation now, the yellow headlights approaching from only two blocks down the street. He could see there was only one man in the unit. And he watched it turn down the intersection one block away. Had the lone MP seen the group of rowdies up the street? Had he purposely avoided the group? Marsh knew there were those soldiers whose motto was "Don't volunteer for nothing." There were also those policemen who responded only to those calls Dispatch assigned them. They were not paid enough to get involved in more than that. Spilled blood was precious.

Greg Marsh let out a disheartened sigh. The group's patience had peaked. This time *all* of them were starting up to his door.

Moments later, two sledgehammers were tearing into the bolted door. The only weapon Marsh could find in the room was a pair of chopsticks. Not even a kitchen knife. He broke them into sharp splinters.

Two dim shafts of yellow light appeared down the opposite end of the block at the precise moment the door came crashing in on Marsh. And then the MP jeep's headlights were drenching the apartment as it rolled to a stop on the crabgrass along the front of the tenement.

The unit had circled back! "In here!" Marsh was yelling now. He wanted to charge the nearest Asian, like they did in the Chinese Kung Fu movies Judy had taken him to, but the room was not filled with high kicks or martial-arts screams. Only bewildered faces, splashed with lights the color of flares. "I'm an American! In here! I need some help in here!"

The tense air was shattered by the sound of a shotgun round being injected into the chamber. "I hear ya, Marshmallow . . . don't get so excited. . . ."

Greg's eyes lit up as the towering form of Sergeant Stryker appeared in the splintered doorway behind the taxi driver and his friends. "Mark!" the private forgot GI discipline as the relief poured over him in the form of sweat above his eyebrows.

Stryker made as if to pop a round into the ceiling, but held off at the last second. *"Di di mau!"* he snapped instead.

But only a few of the men bolted out into the night at the sight of the Ithica. These Orientals had been around firepower all their lives, and they weren't all that impressed by the monster of a man squeezing through the doorway either. "I said *Di di mau!*" the MP sergeant repeated, flashing his teeth at them, but only one Vietnamese slinked out of the room.

The cabbie launched into a torrent of obscenities mixed with half truths about Marsh's failure to pay his fare. Gathering what the driver was saying from his expression, the private countered with, ". . . But he was running me around in circles for forty minutes just to go a few blocks. . . ."

Stryker glanced down at the woman lying on the bed. He did not like what he smelled in the air just then. Whether it was the sweat from all their bodies mingling, or the smog from outside, he didn't know. And he didn't care. He fired a blast into the ceiling, chambered another round of rifle slugs into the shotgun, and sent a second discharge thundering skyward.

He did not stop until the Vietnamese had all scattered out into the night and stars shone down on the dead woman's ashen face.

"What happened to her?" Stryker motioned toward the girl.

"Overdose," Marsh muttered, rubbing his ears as he started toward the jeep.

"You knew her?" Stryker hesitated leaving the scene where a body was collecting gunsmoke. He wanted to hear Greg was no doper.

"My brother did." The three words seemed to answer his

question. "Why did you just happen to be in this neighborhood, anyway?"

Stryker placed the Ithica's firing mechanism on SAFE and flipped the live round out of the chamber. "Decoy Squad got ambushed down the street couple miles," he said dryly. "Thomas is still chasing the suspect. . . ."

"Jesus . . ."

"Yah . . . I've got units crisscrossing this whole sector. I don't like the thought one of my men foot-chasin' some punk out there on his own, without backup. I couldn't resist your little gathering here. . . ." He scanned the shadows beyond the parked cars, hoping not to see any of the cabbie's friends lingering behind. Waiting for a retaliatory strike.

"You think you could maybe run me up to around Cach Mang," Marsh asked. "Judy's probably really worried about me," he added, but his thoughts were of Sharon's swollen, upturned nipples.

"You paid the rent this month?" Stryker grinned slightly, and Marsh answered with an affirming nod. "Then the woman can wait."

"But—" but Stryker shot him an irritated glare, and his attitude, like the signal lights above the intersection of Tu Do and Le Loi, changed from green to red with no yellow in between. "Okay . . . you're right. I'll ride patrol with you until we find Anthony."

"First I gotta get a VNP jeep over here," the sergeant said. "We can't just leave that cunt in there to rot."

"Why not?" Marsh asked sarcastically, ignoring pangs of conscience that told him she might have spent years sleeping with his brother.

Stryker just frowned at the off-color remark. "In fact, why don't *you* call it in to Dispatch. That oughta wake up Schell! Drives him crazy when voices not on his roster come over the Waco net." And Stryker chuckled to himself.

As they approached the jeep outside, both men stopped short when they spotted an out-of-breath Anthony Thomas sitting on the gutter curb alongside the street. He turned back to face them upon sensing their approach. "I lost him," his voice was drenched with disappointment, "the fucking 'Torch' got away from me, sarge."

"Obviously." Stryker rested his hands on his hips as he surveyed the street down both ends. Had "the Torch" sprinted past while they were inside with the dead woman? The neighborhood had returned to its usual pre-dawn silence. "Bet you woulda kept chasing shadows till sunrise if you hadn't come across my unit out here, right buddy?" He tried to sound comforting, but the grim NCO in him shone through.

"Something like that." Thomas still had his pistol out, and he finally reholstered it. "Gary's gonna kill me over this one."

"Gary ain't gonna do shit—"

"You shoulda seen him," Thomas interrupted. "I mean, it wasn't like I was chasin' no track star in tennis shoes, ya know? My big bad suspect was hobblin' along like the hunchback of Notre Dame . . . but . . ."

"But?" Marsh was leaning closer now, intrigued.

"But every time I was ready to pounce, he disappeared . . . only to reappear several blocks up ahead. Almost like he was toying with me . . . laughing at me. I half expected him to turn around and flip me off, ya know? I was half expecting a toothy grin each time just before he disappeared. . . ."

"Just like them goofy Honda Honeys," muttered Greg.

"Huh?" Thomas sounded irritated at the intrusion into their conversation by a newbie.

"Probably some Honda Honeys giving your 'Torch' rides up each block . . . just to fuck with your mind."

"Don't go talkin' crazy shit to me right now, okay, pal?"

"Can you ID the asshole?" Stryker asked. "Did you get a look at his face?"

"Naw . . ." Thomas began massaging his right calf. He had twisted something jumping over the last set of fences. "Just like every time before—keeps that damned poncho hooded over his head like a harem whore's veil. . . ."

"Can you run me by my pad now?" Marsh decided to interrupt again. What could he lose?

"Yah . . . hop in," Stryker jumped behind the steering wheel. "After I call in to Waco and cancel the Code One and the search for supercop here . . ." He twisted the starter toggle and the souped-up engine rumbled to life.

"Suppose I gotta walk back to the ambush site, right?" Anthony wasn't in the mood to be ignored.

"No, you stay here with that woman inside," Stryker pointed into the apartment he had just left. Visions of a rape victim or damsel in distress filtered through Thomas's mind. He could not see the bed through the open doorway. Gunsmoke was still drifting in and out of the moonbeams lancing down through the gaping hole in the roof.

"Until the *canh-sat*s get here," Greg added, "To look after her."

Thomas began straightening out his clothes and tightening his belt. The nineteen-year-old Black Belt ran calloused fingers through his short blond hair, as if to comb it back. "Is she a real looker, sarge?"

"Definitely a real 'looker,'" remarked Greg Marsh.

"Doesn't talk much," Stryker added.

"A real body in there, though, wouldn't you agree sarge?"

"Haven't seen even a *cherry girl* that ripe in years. . . ."

"But definitely not the kind you'd take home to mother," hoped Thomas, licking his lips now.

"No, not the kind you'd wanna take home to mother," both men agreed.

"Just leave her to me." Thomas, all his energy back now, turned and started toward the doorway as the MP jeep rolled off down the street.

11. HAIRBALLS BURN BEST

Sgt. Gary Richards would survive his brush with death. He would spend many days in the burn ward, being treated for first- and second-degree wounds, but the scars would be minimal. And confined to his left side, below the throat. He had been lucky. His elbow had shielded his face, and the mixture in the Molotov cocktail had been more soap flakes than gasoline. The desired result, a destructive fireball, had hardly been achieved. It had been more like a muffled blast from a malfunctioning tear gas canister. The suspect had escaped, but the provost marshal's office had assigned five more CID investigators to the case, and the Decoy Squad had been beefed up with three fresh troopers, ready for action, striving for an arrest.

"Christ," Marsh shook his head and slammed the newspaper down on the table. "They're telling the damn news media everything. 'More men assigned to the case . . . the controversial Decoy Squad to be staking out this neighborhood tonight. . . .' How the hell are we supposed to nab this lowlife when he can read about our strategy in the *Vietnam Guardian* every morning? This PR with the press is getting ridiculous!"

"Perhaps your MP friends lay trap for him, using newspaper people." Judy had floated up to his side from the kitchen, where she had been cleaning the shrimp. "Maybe they *hope* he read paper so they lead him toward jail . . . same-same I catch bird on grass outside with box on top stick. . . ." She leaned over his shoulder and kissed Greg on the earlobe. It made him think of the scar on Sergeant Stryker's ear, and he brushed her away irritably as he turned the pages to the comics.

"I think our 'Torch' is a little more intelligent than that," he disagreed, wondering how he could try to sound like an intellectual when his favorite part of the newspapers was the "Nguyen-Charlie" strip.

Without protest, Judy went back to preparing dinner, humming softly to the Vietnamese music that drifted, dreamlike, from the stereo speakers in the corners of the little room. She didn't seem in the least disturbed by his cranky mood.

Greg was only halfway through the comic strip when his eyes were drawn to her shapely hips, a few feet away, swaying to the tune. Judy wore only a string-wide bikini bottom when they were home. The kind that let her haunches blossom out in the rear and barely covered the crack in between. Sometimes, like this evening, she stood balanced atop high heels, and he thought maybe this was how the girls dancing atop bar counters on Bangkok's Patpong Road looked—they were the only thing some of the men who had just returned from an R&R in Thailand talked about at the guardmount briefings. Not that Greg had attended that many guardmounts. Here he had only worked a few nights on the street, and already he was on his three-day break. A nine-and-three, they called it. Nine twelve-hour shifts, a day for training, and confinement to the compound for Alert duty, then two glorious days to himself. He watched Judy glide to the left to mix the shrimp in with the boiling rice. She was always topless when they were home alone together. Tonight was no exception. He watched her full breasts, the nipples flat and wide, unaroused, sway from

221

side to side slightly with the movement; then she was busy over the sink again, her back to him, thigh muscles flaring, calves sleek as she easily balanced herself atop the high heels. He wanted to rush up and devour her.

Instead, he tried to concentrate on the newspaper, but his eyes kept returning to her curves, and he wondered how many men before him had been treated to that same sight. And how many of them had been MPs.

Just then he wanted to look at her lips more than anything, though. *Her lips.* He by no means considered himself an expert on women, but he had never been kissed before the way this tiny little Asian tigress named Ngoc-Nga kissed him. Her lips were a short story unto themselves . . . a front-page investigative critique on passion, sound, touch, pressure, and flesh against flesh.

In the past, he had always been quick to get through the kissing stages with his dates at the drive-in. Keep 'em happy, blow in their ear, lock tongues for an hour, then it was flop over into the back seat for an hour of sucking on nipples still supported by baby fat, then, if he was lucky, a couple hours of pelvis grinding with their clothes still on.

But this woman standing before him . . . with her, there was no rush to the sack. He'd be content just holding her on some grassy hill above the Song Saigon, listening to the waves slapping at the bank, the birds chasing each other about in the trees, the sound of her lips gliding across his, wet as the waters below. . . .

No, Greg Marsh had never before been so mesmerized by a woman. By her ability to whisk him off to never-never land just with the pressure of her lips across his. Kissing this Asian woman was like dining at a French restaurant, where the appetizers alone became a complex meal, so involved, so succulent, you were left yearning for little else. The main course could wait. You wanted to spend your entire time against her warm, wet, all-engulfing lips. Greg felt like she could massage his soul with them. And no other woman had ever left him with that feeling.

That first night they had finally made love she almost got him angry. Toying with his body . . . pulling away every few minutes, enflaming his passions with a drawn-out kiss again or a dance with her magic fingers, when he wanted to plunge into her and finish it. So they could start all over again.

Could she sense he was a cherry boy who had, nevertheless, spent that afternoon romping on the floor with a nympho-stewardess? Did she want to savor the moment, realizing that it was rare—that the chance might never come her way again to be his first . . .

And when he finally got past her little maze of games and hesitations, the nights unfolded for him. And they had not stopped until the sun had risen, and the rays were filtering in through the bamboo blinds, and it was so hot and they were so slick with sweat that not even the twirling ceiling fan overhead helped.

There came a knock on the door, and Greg put down the newspaper and casually walked over toward where his revolver was lying on the counter. He did not flip the cylinder open to check on the bullets like they always did on TV and in the movies, because a good cop already knew whether his service weapon was loaded or not. And although this was not his on-duty .45, but rather a maverick Colt .38 he had bought on the black market, like all the MPs who had come to Saigon before him had done, he still was aware there were six steel-jacketed hot loads in the cylinder, for this was real life, and it *weren't no adventure novel neither*.

Judy turned slightly to face him, eyeball language telling him not to let anyone in because she was half naked *for goodness sakes*.

Greg responded with a give-me-some-credit-okay? expression and slipped on his thongs, then started over toward the door. He was hoping it wasn't an MP patrol, stopping by to tell him they were going on Alert status and he had to report to the International. He hadn't logged his off-duty

223

address with the company clerk yet, but Stryker knew where he lived, and Stryker would tell. He could hear him now. . . . *"After all, you didn't wanna miss out on your first honest-to-God rocket attack, did ya?"*

A young girl in pigtails was waiting on the other side of the door. Greg, revolver jammed down in between his belt and the small of his back, stuck his head out and checked both directions down the hallway, but she was alone. He ran his eyes down below her chin. Already blossoming like a healthy little wildflower, he decided, comparing her dixie-cup chest with the woman in the kitchen. Maybe fourteen or fifteen. She had chicken bones for legs, though. . . .

"Yes?" He refrained from resting his hands on his hips. The Vietnamese didn't like that. Tough-guy images were frowned upon.

The girl let loose with a high-pitched, low-volumed speech that was obviously a previously rehearsed sale pitch of some sort, and though it was completely in the singsong dialect common to Sin City, Greg listened to her politely.

"Tell the girl we don't want to buy any flowers," Judy responded from the kitchen, overhearing everything. For the first time, Greg glanced down below the harsh ridge pushed out by the bra under her orange T-shirt. He said, "Oh . . ." and started to say something else but halted abruptly. "You come and tell her," he changed his mind. "I don't think she speaks my lingo—" he started to say, but the girl made a little curtsey and smiled up at him, narrow almond eyes radiating total innocence.

"Never mind, kind sir," she all but chirped like a frightened bird. "Sorry for bother you . . . pleasant evening for you, sir," and she vanished.

Marsh gently closed the door and started back toward the table and his newspaper, when Judy said, "That was Val. She lives down the hall. Always trying to sell me something. Last week it was a newspaper subscription to some Chinese rag. I don't even read Chinese. . . ."

Greg's ears perked up at her sudden lapse from pidgin English into near total fluency, but then his eyes fell across her figure as she balanced against the sink in front of him. She had her long hair piled up atop her head, and the bare, smooth shoulders were driving him crazy. He could feel himself growing hard against the thin fabric of the silk pajama bottoms.

"Oh really?" *Keep her busy*, he thought. *Women love to talk*. . . . He silently took the small revolver from the imitation leather belt around his waist and then removed the strap itself, letting the pajamas fall to the floor. He slipped off the thongs and started toward her.

"Yes," Judy was still talking, eyes on the shrimp in front of her, ignoring him for the most part. Greg's eyes ran down along the lightly tanned back, to where the bikini string rested across the slight swell of hips. Then they fell farther. To where the powerful thighs tapered down to long, tight calves. It all finally ended at the high heels. Black, glistening high heels. Feet so small and immaculate he could kiss them. And he had never felt *that* way about a woman back in The World!

And then he was upon her.

Grabbing her gently around the waist, lifting her out of the high heels. She carefully dropped the paring knife into the sink, atop the shrimp, as if on cue. A little scream, a protesting giggle. He carried her that way, back against his stomach, feet a few inches off the floor, the back of her head against his throat, over onto a sleeping mat, where he plopped down, naked, on top of her.

"Gregory!" she squealed loud enough for the other girls on their floor to hear as the noise swept along the veranda outside the kitchen windows.

"Yes, my dear?" he was breathing hot into her ear now as he untied the bikini and slipped it off. She liked *that*. He was coming to know, quickly, what she liked in her man.

"Let me over . . . onto my back." She was whispering now

too, fighting to twist out from under him, yet giggling the entire time. "I don't like it this way. . . ."

"You been teasing me all afternoon in that kitchen over there." He bit her ear a little. "Shaking your tight little ass at me, daring me. Now you're going to get what you've secretly wanted all week," he laughed, spreading her thighs apart with one knee. She fought to keep her legs closed, but not very hard. Greg wondered if her thighs might not be even stronger than his. Squatting all their lives, instead of sitting, the MPs back at the International had often told him, left Asian women with a powerful set of legs envied by others the world over.

"*Gregory!* I'm warning you," she hissed playfully, but the thighs slowly came apart.

He leaned hard into her then, his lips against her left ear, his right arm wrapped under her, the hand cupping her breast. The fingers of their left hands were tangled together, the arms outstretched above their heads, and as he slid into her, Judy's sudden gasp could be heard throughout most of the housing project. A brightly colored parrot often perched in the branches of the tamarinds outside their kitchen window, and, after flapping its wings at the savage sound, it quietly tiptoed in onto the windowsill and began stealing curled-up morsels of shrimp from the bowl in the sink.

The French rock music was blasting so loudly from the wall speakers that Mohammad-from-Calcutta had to lean uncomfortably close to Julian Ramirez to hear what he was saying.

"I said, what do you think of the cunt in the middle?" the deserter repeated, and both men ran critical eyes up and down the dancer with the black and silver bikini bottom.

"Professionally," the Indian grinned tentatively, "or for my own personal, perverted purposes?"

She was European, with wide, jutting breasts and high

cheekbones. Streaked brown hair fanned out about her shoulders as she kicked her legs high with the beat of the music and smiled down at the two men beside the front table.

"Doesn't matter," Ramirez sighed. "Give me an offer . . . and I'll have her for you . . . tomorrow. . . ."

But the Indian's attitude changed abruptly, and his smile faded. "Burnt-out whores are of no interest to me," he said. "You are beginning to sound like you do not have the funds to complete our deal." The man had a large briefcase under one arm and was shielding it protectively.

"Nonsense," the snickering deserter waved a hand. The girls to either side of her had dropped back a few feet as the music wound into a dull crescendo, and the woman center-stage was kicking off the bikini bottom now, to the whoops and cheers of several Asian businessmen at the front row of tables. Ramirez pulled a thick envelope from his front pocket and slid it in front of the man with the blue-silver turban. "Payment in full, honorable arrogant-one."

Mohammad slit the envelope open along its top with a long, sharp fingernail and spent a few seconds glancing at its contents. Then he pushed the briefcase over in front of the Mexican. Ramirez didn't bother to open it. He knew where to find the Indian, and Mohammad was no fool: He had seen what the deserter did for fun, just to pass his free time.

"There is a new market in flesh opening up to us," Mohammad said slyly as he motioned toward the woman up on the stage. "What you need to invest in are not these old, wrinkled crones with silicone jugs, but white meat, my friend. White meat."

Ramirez tried not to act overly interested when he said, "What?" but Mohammad caught the gleam of intrigue in his eyes.

"There is a club in Cholon . . . the Villa . . . which has succeeded in spiriting several young would-be starlets to Saigon . . . signing them here in a go-go capacity, dancer-only contract . . . but when the hicks finally arrive . . ." The

Indian smiled broadly and glanced up at the ceiling, waving his hands about slightly as if he had no control over their fate after the Americans stepped foot in Vietnam.

". . . They dope them up and turn 'em into expensive tricks," Ramirez finished the sentence for him. "But you would need contacts stateside for an operation like that," he frowned, thinking about the people back in the U.S. who had refused to help when he first fled the army. Now, he could own them all. But he could still not trust any of them.

"That is no problem," the Indian replied. "Cash flow is what my obstacle happens to be just now . . . and you, my devious friend—"

"Let me think about it," Ramirez cut him off. His eyes were glued to the three women on stage. They were all naked, had oiled each other down, and were now mounting one another in the most vulgar positions imaginable. The crowd roared its approval.

A few moments later, calculations still running figures through his mind as he surveyed the lust-greedy mob all around and estimated what these Orientals would pay for white meat, Julian Ramirez slipped from the bar on Bac Hai street without bidding the Indian farewell.

Outside, shielding his eyes from the glare of headlights running south along Le Van Duyet, the deserter cursed the convoy of bumper-to-bumper traffic racing toward the heart of Saigon from the airport's west gate. There was no way he'd make his eight o'clock appointment with the Pham Dinh Phung banker—a man the turncoat was setting up for a long-run con game, just to pass the time, of course, and a crafty genius himself—the access to whose vaults had become a personal challenge to the Mexican.

No sweat, Ramirez decided. Maybe if he hoofed it down Bar Lei to Tran Quoc Toan he could short-cut it across to Cholon and phone the greedy bastard requesting a change in their rendezvous point.

But Julian Ramirez had not walked ten paces from the

private establishment on Bac Hai street when he turned and found himself face to face with a short, hunched-over figure concealed in a rain poncho. Barely protruding from the flaps along the "Torch"'s right side, a small rag, stuffed down into a green wine bottle, was burning with hungry, flickering flames.

"You got the wrooooooong motha . . ." Julian's first reaction was to saunter right past, then beat feet out of there—he had read all about this arson maniac in the papers. He couldn't imagine why the man would be interested in a lowly army deserter just trying to eke out a living in Sin City. Their paths' crossing had surely been a monumental coincidence. *So if you'll just excuuuuuse me . . .*

But the caped figure was not stepping out of the way. It was suddenly doubling almost over, winding its arm back. *Like a mechanical toy*, the thought flashed through Julian's mind. It was Ramirez's last brain function.

Except to scream. Ramirez let out a sharp cry as the Molotov was hurled at him. And the cry exploded into a long, drawn-out wail as the wine bottle splattered across his forehead and he was blinded by the sizzling soap melting into his eyelids, burning the skin away, rushing in to devour his eyeballs. His hair was afire and the liquid flames rolling down over wildly twitching shoulders and arms were igniting his clothes as the deserter turned and ran. Smack into the corner of the nightclub he had just left.

A human fireball now, he bounced off and rolled across the ground, contact with the earth tearing loose huge chunks of flesh from his face where long strips of skin were already charred and curling up away from the bone. Ramirez wanted to beat out the flames . . . fight the pain with his fists, the way he had survived all his life already, but the heat was so intense and the fire so all-consuming, the tendons in his wrists and ankles were shrinking taut, drawing his fingers and toes back unnaturally until all he could do was slap his gnarled limbs helplessly against the dust.

A few blocks away, Sgt. Mark Stryker and Corporal Malboys were parked on the shoulder of the roadway, two blocks up from the establishment on Bac Hai, observing traffic. Watching the faces of commuters, hoping to run across a face here or there that was also on their deserter bulletins.

"Yah, me and the old bitch got back together again," Malboys was saying. "Now she claims she never put no temple curse on me, but I have a feeling, after I ran her down in Mui Dinh and hog-tied her young ass . . . dragged her back to Saigontown, she's had a change of heart and paid a visit to the Xa Loi pagoda to buy a remedy for my voodoo malady. . . ." Malboys slipped off his wire-rim glasses and dusted them with an o.d. green handkerchief, chuckling about something he didn't care to share with his temporary partner just then.

". . . Important thing is . . . you're not suffering from a run of bad luck anymore, right?" Stryker laughed himself now, and waved out at the occupants of a black jeep cruising past. The new Decoy Squad, Reilly, Uhernik, Sergeant Schultz, and the old-timer, Thomas, was also cruising the outskirts of Tan Son Nhut airport.

Thomas returned a bored, look-who-they-stuck-me-with wave, Reilly responded with his notorious Bugs Bunny impression, Nasty Nick was busy comparing license plates of oncoming vehicles with stolen tags on his hot sheet, and Raunchy Raul was busy driving, elbows so high with pride they were almost horizontal with his shoulders as he glanced about from left to right, chin up, scanning all but seeing nothing for the glare of his shiny web gear.

Malboys spent a few seconds contemplating Stryker's remark, then said, "Well, they *did* stick me out on the street with *you*, didn't they?" He made it sound like punishment.

Stryker's smile dissolved as he set about mentally planning his response, when, "Car Nine, this is Waco, over . . ."

Both men reached to pick up the mike, and Malboys

230

snatched it up first. "This is Car Niner," the corporal said in a gruff tone, totally businesslike. "We're at Bac Hai, just southwest of Le Van Duyet, over. . . ."

"Car Niner, request you start in the direction of Tran Quoc Toan and Nguyen Van Thoi . . . getting a report of a serious Tango Alpha that one-four . . . possible foxtrot involved . . . several civilian vehicles and an army bus . . . I'm trying to break a unit free to handle at this time . . . request you check on injuries and advise . . . your call is Code Three. . . ."

Malboys ran the military jargon through his decoding banks: Tango Alpha meant traffic accident, possible foxtrot meant a fatality at the scene. . . . He flipped on the lights and siren, waiting for the wail to reach full pitch before he depressed the microphone lever. "Roger . . . en route," he said dryly, in his best unemotional tone.

Before Waco could clear the net with the time, Private Uhernik's voice broke squelch and beat back the static. "Car Niner, this is Twenty-two Echo . . . uh, correction: this is Delta-Sierra Three . . . we're close . . . we'll cover you. . . ."

Stryker was busy steering the jeep in and out of the heavy traffic now, and Malboys didn't bother to acknowledge the Decoy Squad's transmission. There'd be other units too, thought by Dispatch to still be busy with paperwork at a call somewhere, rushing to the scene to help, witness the gore, gloat when the unlucky sector jeep finally arrived to fill out the lengthy Form 68 and take pictures. Such were the games in the MP Corps, as well as other police departments across the globe.

"Christ! Will ya look at that!" Stryker was bringing the jeep into an abrupt skid as they raced past the crowded nightclub in the middle of the block.

What appeared to be a human corpse, charred black, arms and legs outstretched, still glowing with crackling flames as they twitched up and down in after-death spasms, was lying in the middle of the parking lot, a group of curious spectators gathering around it. Some of them, even though they were drunk, were dashing to the edges of the parking lot, between parked cars, and vomiting at what they had just seen.

Stryker, his jeep's dual sirens still winding down, swerved into the lot and coasted past the nauseating stench, through the wisps of human smoke, swallowing as he let his jungle instincts take hold and they screeched at him, warning him spirits floated in the flesh-turned-vapor. And he spotted, despite the death lurking in that parking lot and the superstitions instilled in him by his old tribeswoman, Lai, what he was searching for. "Over there!" The ex-Green Beret pointed with one hand as he guided the vehicle through the mob of bar patrons with the other.

A slender figure cloaked in a green rain poncho was rushing away, out of the ring of street lights, sprinting toward the edge of darkness and the dingy tenements beyond. Stryker didn't call it in. He didn't yell "Halt!" or identify himself. He just flipped off the jeep's engine and leaped to the ground, giving chase.

And they ran.

The three of them. Stryker, Malboys, and "the Torch."

In and out of tenements. Over fences. Through the broken windows of countless deserted warehouses.

Until the MPs were almost out of breath, and "the Torch" was fleeing down a narrow corridor between two tall buildings. A half block away, freedom. It was beginning to look like the suspect was in better shape than the cops after all, despite previous reports that described "the Torch" as a frail, bent-over Arvin veteran who had a thing about setting Americans on fire but couldn't run very fast afterwards. CID had hired a shrink to do a psychological profile on the suspect, and the results told of a psychotic and probably disabled, perhaps even horribly mangled, Vietnamese soldier who had once been the victim of an accidental American napalm bombing run, and now returned each night on a twisted vengeance kick, haunted by his memories, what had happened to him, and the ghosts of his fellow soldiers who had not survived the regrettable incident.

But Stryker didn't give a frog's fart about all that.

He pushed his .45 out to arm's length and flipped off the safety, too winded to cry out a warning.

But before he could even pull in the trigger, a black jeep had skidded up at the far end of the alleyway, cutting off "the Torch" before he could reach the maze of compound walls that would mean freedom to him and future opportunities to light up GIs in the night.

Reilly and Uhernik, ignoring the .45 barrel staring at them fifty feet away, both leaped onto the caped figure at the same time, and after the three of them tumbled roughly to the ground, the private who had already lived his whole life in Saigon and wasn't shocked by many things, yelled excitedly to the others, "He's got tits!" as the two MPs wrestled with the wildly thrashing suspect on the pavement.

Stryker forced in a lungful of the warm, sticky night air and holstered his weapon, then willed his legs to carry him down to the scene of the arrest.

Seconds later, he was jerking the rain poncho off.

"Jesus Christ," muttered Thomas softly. He was still slowly climbing out of the jeep, allowing the rooks their moment of glory, content to let the gung-ho types wrestle with the felons. Now he remembered all the times the woman had been right behind him, often draping her slender wrists across his and Bryant's shoulders as they casually cruised downtown Saigon.

The pretty policewoman, Miss Nguyen, stared up at the Americans. She was breathing hard, and both fear and embarrassment were etched across her features. Stryker was sure her eyes would have appeared wide with terror were it not for the fact that they were still slightly swollen purple from the punches Kim had inflicted on her.

There was a tense silence for several seconds as the six MPs stared down at the Vietnamese policewoman, now handcuffed behind her back. In the distance, three patrol jeeps were racing each other down Le Van Duyet, in and out of traffic, headed for the traffic accident on Tran Quoc Toan. *They could have it*, Stryker decided.

"What are we going to do?" Stryker glanced up at Thomas, ignoring the other MPs in the circle.

"What do you mean by that?" Malboys was all over him. "We take the cunt in. Book her: Murder One."

Stryker didn't immediately respond to the corporal's comment. Instead, he looked down at Miss Nguyen. "Who was that human inferno back there?" he asked, ignoring this unauthorized questioning procedure. "Tell me you didn't torch that poor son-of-a-bitch in the parking lot."

"I'm afraid I *did*, Mark," she said almost defiantly. Both Malboys's and Schultz's eyebrows went up a good half inch at her use of his first name. "That poor *son-of-a-bitch* back there was Julain Ramirez. He was responsible for—"

"For murdering several of your fellow *canh-sat*s," Schultz finished the sentence for her, his features mellowing somewhat now at the realization they were dealing with a fellow cop. Of sorts.

"You could have *arrested* him, for Christsake." Stryker tried to reason it all out. "Why did you have to *kill* him like that?"

"He shot my sister," she broke into tears. "He *murdered* my sister at that raid on the child slave auction! She was a police matron, but *she wasn't even armed*, Mark!"

"But still—"

"He was an American deserter!" she continued her side of the street defense. Beneath the poncho liner she wore only shorts and a thin blouse to fight the heat of the thick fabric. There was no bra underneath, Thomas was quick to observe, and the way the handcuffs forced her arms back tightly, her chest swelled forward, taut against the blouse, revealing how well nature had equipped such a tiny female. "Your government would have spirited him back to America . . . to spend a life sentence in some plush stockade somewhere," she said bitterly. "All he did was smoke a lousy gook, right? He would be back out on the street in ten years, if not sooner.

234

Well, *I* smoked *his* fucking ass, Sergeant Stryker! Do with me what you must. . . ."

Stryker thought back to all the loyal years she had given the Vietnamese National Police Force. "Take off the cuffs," he directed.

"Bullshit!" Malboys stepped between Reilly and the prisoner. "We're going to do this by the book, Stryker. I can sympathize with your conflict of interest here, but—"

"We're taking her to the station," the big MP sergeant said, to set his fears at ease. "But there's no reason to humiliate her in front of the desk cops by bringing her in handcuffed," and he turned to look back at Miss Nguyen. She was pulled to her feet by Uhernik, and he was inserting his key into the cuffs. "You're not really 'the Torch,' are you?" It was a statement more than a question. He didn't know how he could manage to smile at a time like this, but he'd be damned if she wasn't smiling right back!

"No," she admitted softly.

"It was a copy-cat murder?" Schultz muttered every man's thoughts aloud. Their Molotov maniac was still on the loose.

"I decided that imitating 'the Torch' would throw investigators off my trail," and she broke into tears. "My God! You men fail to catch him at all these past encounters, but look what happens to me!" And she dropped her face in her hands.

"I say let her go," mumbled Uhernik.

"We can't do that," Stryker said irritably. "And you know it."

"Why?" said Thomas. "All she did was snuff some scuzzball deserter."

Miss Nguyen looked up at them, a gleam of hope in her eyes fighting off the desperation.

"Because there's too many of us here," Stryker grinned back. "I love this little crate of dynamite," and he draped a massive arm around her shoulders as he made to walk back to his jeep. "But too many careers could be wrecked . . . too many lives ruined if we didn't play it straight this one time."

"This whole thing sucks to high heaven," muttered Reilly.

"It's the only *right* thing to do," Malboys agreed with Stryker's assessment of the situation, and he reached out to grab Miss Nguyen's arm to help "escort" her back to his unit.

Schultz, still standing with his .45 out—*Never trust a woman* was his motto—started to move aside to let them pass, and Stryker said, "You can put your heater away now, Schultzy . . . the excitement's over."

"If a rotten apple's gotta put in twenty behind bars to keep the rest of the profession's image untarnished, then so be it," Malboys added, but Miss Nguyen jerked her arm away from him and moved closer to Stryker.

"Don't touch me!" she hissed softly, and, like a reflex to his own hand's snapping back, she hesitated then suddenly bolted ahead, slamming herself into Sergeant Schultz's pistol.

In the blink of an eye, she had her arms around him, squeezing with all her might, throwing him off balance, and as they tumbled into the shadows the .45 barked twice, knocking her loose, away. Both rounds exploded forth from her back in a bloody spray, chasing her soul toward the stars.

And when she came to rest on her stomach at Stryker's feet, face on its side, eyes staring up at the men, unblinking, lifeless, the big MP sergeant folded his arms across his chest and let forth a disheartened sigh. It still amazed him how such fragile, beautiful creatures, full of life and love and emotions one second, could be made so still and inhuman the next. Never choosing to return. The warmth gone from their bodies, their souls sucked from their eyes by the demons of death.

All on account of a ten-cent slug of lead.

A flock of birds fluttered overhead just then, low beneath the clouds, shadows against the moon. And he wondered if, should he shoot one down, could he talk the life back into the woman at his feet?

12. ON RAPE AND REVENGE

Stryker stared out at the somber collection of MPs draped across chairs, leaning against roof supports, sleeping standing up in dark corners of the immense briefing room. The entire battalion was exhausted. The 716th not only had to contend with extended hours on patrol because of more Torch murders and an increase in downtown units,but a battle raging north of Gia Dinh was pulling more infantry companies out of Saigon, and MACV had requested additional Alert teams be confined to post, ever-ready if needed.

"I'll make it brief," Stryker announced the start of the guardmount. He wondered how many, if any, of the men were really listening. "Sergeant Richards should be back on the street in a few days, per his request, and Broox has refused medevac stateside, so we'll be seeing him soon, too. The only reason the Docs at Seventeenth Field didn't shove an Article Fifteen up his ass is 'cause we're so shorthanded here. They figure, 'If he wants to stay in the 'Nam that bad, more power to him. . . .'"

A scattering of mild applause, but Stryker knew both men *were* missed.

"Until they're back, Schultzy, Thomas, Reilly, and The Uke will be working Decoy. Hue Chean, Tim's wife, was

237

taken off ICU last night, so Bryant will be back too, and these four chumps," he pointed down to Raunchy Raul and his crew, "can be returned to their regular assignments so the rest of you can return to twelve-hour shifts."

The applause increased this time, but, even though his gut feeling told him to stand up and take a bow, Schultz remained seated, aware they might just be clapping about that Chean woman's recovery.

"Got a letter from Mather here," a cheer rose up from the back of the room, "and some nice photographs from his wedding. In case some of you don't know . . . he and Hoa tied the knot a couple months ago . . . there's a long story behind those two . . . Farthing back there can fill you in on it, if you're interested. These pictures will be on the bulletin board for two complete nine-and-threes, then they go in *my* fucking scrapbook.".

He got no arguments, other than a feigned snore somewhere from the back of the room.

"Everyone's hero, Calloway, has been reassigned to Ninety-five Charlie," he announced then, and half the room suddenly came alive, with several men giving a standing ovation to word the new lieutenant was on his way to supervise tower rats at the LBJ stockade. "I thought you'd like to hear that,"he smiled. "Now I won't say I told you so, but didn't I mention I'd handle the problem?"

More cheers and hearty applause, sincere whistles that almost made him blush with mock modesty.

"Okay . . . okay. You all know your patrol sectors, so hit the streets," and the room was suddenly a din of a hundred clomping boots as the MPs filed out to their jeeps.

"Looks like another no-good sun dog fucking up my day," Stryker muttered a few minutes later, after he stepped out onto the Orderly Room veranda and surveyed the bright ring encircling the sun.

Buck sergeant Farthing paused beside him, on his way down the steps to his unit. He shielded his eyes against the late afternoon sun. "That ain't no damn sun dog, Stryk. . . ." he argued.

"Sure it is. I know a fucking sun dog when I—"

"So do I . . . and I'm telling you there ain't no lousy sun dogs over Saigon. What you're seeing are smoke particles from that battle outside Gia Dinh . . . they're collecting up there and the sun's hitting them just right to form that eerie ring. Unusual, but ain't no sun dog."

Stryker frowned at this new revelation. Why was he arguing? He had considered sun dogs bad omens, despite legends saying they were forest spirits sent to watch over hunters.

"Now what's going on down *there*?" His attention shifted to a congregation of MPs circling the old *mama-san* who had been hired to bake the pizzas at the bowling alley. "Christ, that old geezer is moonlighting on us, Farthing . . . Selling her damn sugar cane cubes when they only gave her a pass to remain in the bowling alley. See what you can do about—"

"Can you spare a dime, brother?" Farthing nudged Stryker with an elbow. "So I can buy a baggie of that stuff? I've loved steamed sugarcane cubes ever since I ended up here in the 'Nam. . . ."

Stryker lapsed into another frown and dug deep into a pocket. Both NCOs started down the steps toward the old lady and cut in at the head of the line. The men around them didn't seem to mind. They appreciated the sergeants not breaking the cluster up and ordering them out to the street.

"How's your daughters?" Farthing was asking the old woman in pidgin Vietnamese, humoring her.

"They working hard downtown," she answered, also in Vietnamese. "Busy civil servants, my daughters . . . make me proud, you see? Work, work, work . . . all day long so someday I don't worry about my future. . . ."

That was it!

That was where Stryker had seen the Honda Honeys

before. They were this old crone's whoring daughters! Only they weren't civil servants, working for the government downtown . . . *they were prostitutes tricking on Tu Do!*

"Hey, hey, hey!" he was pulling Farthing aside now, excitement dancing in his eyes. "Now I remember where I saw them Honda Honeys before! They were this old bag's cunt kids! Do you remember what hotel they were working?"

"But she says her daughters are civil servants for the government." A third NCO had listened in and joined the conversation without invitation.

"We know that," Farthing responded with a scowl. "She tells all the men that. What did you expect? She's got *some* pride." And he turned to Stryker. "Hell, I can't remember where those two used to hang out, Mark . . . but I do know who you're talking about now."

"The one who lost her face after that chase with me and Marsh was the short one," he said. "The tall one's been joined by another cunt."

"*Mama-san* here *did* claim to have three daughters, total," Farthing replied. "Christ, I just can't remember where I last saw them whores flashing their thighs. . . ."

Stryker was waving one of the gate militiawomen over.

"Ask her where she lives," he told her. "And write it down carefully for me. I want her address. . . ."

The woman, dressed in a blue and white *ao dai* and armed with a sawed-off version of an M16 slung over her shoulder and resting against her hip horizontally, pulled out a notebook and ran a jabber of rapid Vietnamese past the old *mama-san*. But the sugar cane vendor kept her eyes on the ground the whole time, remaining silent for several seconds, before saying, ashamed, "I live *here*. . . ."

"Yes, yes . . . I know she *works* here," Stryker said in English, "but where does she *live*? Where does she sleep at night?"

"The old woman was given quarters in the shack behind the bowling alley," the militiawoman snapped back at him. "Her daughters have abandoned her long ago . . . can't you see that? Can't you see how you hurt her with this questioning? Must you embarrass her so?" But the girl answered her own question. "Leave her alone!"

Christ! Stryker threw his hands up into the air. *Women! What did I do to deserve all this crap?* He sidestepped from the semicircle around the *mama-san*, walked over to his jeep, and hopped in. At least he knew who they were now. . . .

Now all he had to do was find them, somewhere in this sprawling city of over three million.

Greg Marsh leaned against the balcony railing of their second-floor apartment overlooking the Minh Chieu rail-yards. He could never recall being so happy in all his life. Judy had made him forget what he was seeing nightly on the street—the darker side to her people. She was even making him forget about his own brother, Nathan. *That* was almost unforgivable, but it was true.

All his leads . . . all the clues at the bottom of his duffel bag had led to dead ends. The closest he had gotten to anything was the woman who had overdosed in his presence. And what had he gotten for his trouble? Practically beaten out of his boots by a mob of sledgehammer-wielding cabbies.

Greg was slowly changing his attitude about his mission in Vietnam. He was gradually becoming content with his life here, regardless of how his search for his brother had failed. Judy was treating him like a king. He was falling in love with her. He could even envision marrying her . . . taking her back to The World. . . .

Back to Chicago? The windy city? Maybe he would just remain here in good ole Saigon, sucking on coconuts *and his warm, beautiful Judy. . . .*

Icy Chicago? Visions of his woman floating around the apartment, gliding from chore to chore, topless, the heat of the tropics filtering in through the kitchen window, parrots squawking in the trees outside, filled his head. *Yes, welcome home, Greg*, his thoughts seemed to answer him. *Man is born abroad . . . and he is constantly searching for his home. . . .* Greg smiled: The words in the Walter Sheldon novel he had read on the plane over were finally having some meaning.

There came a tugging at his elbow, and he looked down to see the girl from a few doors away smiling up at him brightly. "Well hello, Val." He hoped he had remembered her name correctly.

"Hello, Etan . . ." She displayed a straight set of white teeth, just like Judy's. In her hand, she was holding out a platter of pink papaya. "You like?"

"Eaton?" he pulled his chin in. "My name is Greg, honey," he said the word "honey" the way you would address a child, not a bar girl. He reached down and took a sliver of the fruit. "Thank you."

"You welcome, *Etan*. . . ." she giggled.

"*Greg*," he insisted.

"Very well," her smile dropped slightly, then she decided to play along. ". . . If you insist. . . . But you will always be *Etan* to me. . . ."

Goofy kid, Greg decided. He turned his attention to the brightly colored parrots lining a branch only a dozen feet away. All four white-feathered birds were eyeing his papaya enviously, tilting their heads to the side or upside down while they kept beady little eyes locked on the pink sliver and Greg's fingers. He broke off a little piece and tossed it at them gently. Two of the birds flew off, startled, but the one in the middle caught the morsel with its beak, almost casually.

"I'll bet you were the rascal who snuck in and made off with half our shrimp last week, too," he laughed, impressed with the bird's bravery. Probably someone's pet, sent out to shit on passersby below.

"You like another slice maybe?" The girl was tugging his elbow again, "*Etan*?" Her smile was ear to ear, and contagious, but Greg became annoyed with her.

"Who the hell is this Eaton?" he demanded, snatching

242

away her platter of fruit. "And you don't get it back unless you tell me."

"You know," she kept smiling, sliding her shoulders from side to side now, shy at talking to such a tall foreigner so much, all at once.

"No I don't!"

"*Etan!*" she raised herself up on her toes, closer to him, as if body movement would make him remember their little games in the past.

"What's his whole name?"

"Etan . . . Etan H. Sram," she said the name slowly. Proud she could remember it in its entirety.

"And where does this Mr. Sram live, if I may be so bold as to ask?"

"You may be so bold," she giggled.

"Damnit, girl!"

Her smile vanished, and Val leaned over the railing and pointed down to a cluster of tenements a half block away. "You know!" she insisted, "Numba two, two, and two!" and as he was staring down at the cluster of white stucco two- and three-story apartment houses, she snatched up the platter of papaya and ran off down the hallway, laughing.

Brother! he thought, shaking his head. "Vietnamese kids are weirrrrrrrrrrd. . . ." he muttered out loud as he made his way back down to his own apartment. "Definitely fucking weird. . . ."

"What's your problem?" Judy asked as he sauntered in toward the kitchen, still grumbling about something.

"That kid Val is hanging around again, acting strange, as usual."

Judy was by the sink again, rinsing a bowl of bean sprouts, but today she was wearing a pair of shorts, tight though they were, and a bulging halter-top. She had put the high heels into storage for a while—until her cherry boy wore himself out or she could walk normally again, unlike a duck. Whichever came first. "Oh, you know how little kids are," she said. "Especially Val. She gets a kick out of you goofy round-eyes . . . although I don't, for the life of me, know why . . . Americans are so fucking weirrrrrrd!" and she tossed a limp bean sprout back at him.

"Why you . . ." Greg, suddenly invigorated by the sight of her, chest damp with perspiration as she slaved over the hot plate, charged.

They tumbled out of the kitchen, onto the floormat, and, as they rolled around, soon naked, Judy managed to turn the stereo up.

And, like clockwork, the parrot waiting patiently outside their window quietly hobbled in onto the windowsill and began snatching up morsels of seafood soaking in a large bowl.

Later, that evening, after the stars had come out and they had feasted on what the birds had left them, Judy lay in his arms, staring up at his eyes while Greg watched the black and white TV tube flickering silver light out into the dark room. It was the first time a soldier had ever bought her a television, and the expensive gift had made her ultraromantic tonight.

"I hate it when you have to work nights," she said. Greg swallowed hard, thinking back to the warnings Stryker had given him. *He said there'd be days like this.* . . .

"It's how I bring home the paycheck," he said softly, bending his head low to lick her nipples erect again. But she cupped her hand around his chin and lifted his eyes back up to hers.

"May-Lynn, down the hall, has a boyfriend who works daytime. He is a soldier too," she cooed. "But he sleeps with May-Lynn, *at night*."

"May-Lynn's old man is a clerk-typist," he countered. "I work the streets, Judy. I wouldn't be happy doing anything else. . . ."

"But—"

He checked his wristwatch and made a movement as if to get up. "Someday, perhaps, I'll have the rank and seniority to land a dayshift job at PMO, but . . . speaking of the night

244

shift . . ." and he glanced at his wristwatch again dramatically, ". . . duty calls. . . ."

"But I get so worried when you are out at night. There are so many VC out there . . . waiting . . . just waiting for you. . . ." She was on her feet now too, obediently preparing his uniform, still nude.

"Don't exaggerate." Greg slipped on his fatigue pants. It was a little after 10 P.M. He had about fifty minutes before guardmount.

"Will you be riding *papa-san*'s scooter to work tonight?" she asked, referring to the old man downstairs who, for a modest fee, gave the night soldiers a lift to their destinations. He was even available on a weekly contract basis, so long as the fares were spread out reasonably well, timewise.

"No," he was slipping his gunbelt into place now, running his eyes along the mound of pubic hair that beckoned back at him. He glanced at his watch a third time. *Enough time for a quickie, maybe?* "Sergeant Stryker's working the six-to-six relief shift. He wanted to pick me up tonight, if things stay quiet, so he could meet you. . . ."

"Meet me?" Judy's hands flew protectively across her breasts. "He's already seen me. . . ."

"Introductions while lying prone atop blacktop in the middle of Checkpoint-Six-Alpha with a sniper blasting away down at you is hardly what I would call *proper*," he smiled. "Why don't you put on some chrysanthemum tea?"

There seemed to be an unusual amount of noisy activity in the street outside, below their window—had been for the last few hours, but the two lovers had been so involved with each other and the stereo had been cranked up so loud that they hadn't really noticed. Now curious, Greg slipped his .45 from the bureau drawer into its holster, and, thinking it might be Stryker and the boys, started over toward the window to look out for the first time—

When the front door to the apartment came crashing in.

Marsh whirled around, hand on his gun, but he froze at the sight of all the glowing QC helmets, *canh-sat* hats, and

245

weapons pointed at him.

"I'm . . . an . . . MP. . . ." he mumbled slowly, bewildered, but they were upon him like tigers, knocking him flat, disarming him, cuffing him behind the back, slugging him a few more times for good measure. All the time, Judy stood back in the shadows, hands to her lips, eyes wide . . . wanting desperately to scream, but unable to. Frozen to the spot. Petrified . . . confused.

One of the Vietnamese policemen spotted her quickly enough, and they were dragging her into the center of the room, barking commands, throwing her down beside Greg, ignoring her nakedness, kicking her in the side once or twice. Three times.

"What is this all about!?" Marsh demanded. "I'm a cop! *Canh sat!*"

The policeman appearing to be in charge went down on one knee and unleashed a torrent of accusations at Judy, then slapped her and motioned for her to translate.

"He says they are arresting you for rape . . ." she swallowed hard, tears streaking her makeup, ". . . and murder. . . ."

"Murder!?" He fought against his bonds, but he was no match for them. "When? Where?"

"They say woman down the hall, May-Lynn . . . they say you rob her house . . . they say you rape her and Val . . . they say Val dead now . . . little Val dead, Greg!"

"But when?" His neck was twisted around so that he could see her eyes.

"They say two hour ago!" She lapsed back into pidgin English.

"But I was *here* two hours ago! I was with *you* two hours ago! I been here all fucking evening!" The apartment was heavy with the scent of lovemaking. A policewoman in the doorway was staring down at them, sniffing at the room now and then, pretending she was disgusted. "They got the wrong man! I'm a cop, for Christsake!"

"I know!" Judy was crying nonstop now, a *canh-sat*'s boot

246

in the small of her back. "But they say—"

"*Fuck* what they say!" he yelled, twisting his face inward as the boot, aimed at his teeth, impacted aginst the side of his head.

The policemen were dragging him to his feet now.

"They say they take you police station," Judy said. "They say you in a lot of trouble, Greg. . . ." The floor was wet with her tears.

As they dragged Marsh across the teakwood planks, the first two Vietnamese out the door were propelled right back in, and the lot of them tumbled to the floor on top of the American.

"What the flying fuck's going on here?" Stryker, huge as a gorilla, sturdy as granite, squeezed his arms against the bamboo rods, impressively filling the narrow doorway. "Where's my MP, Marsh?"

Outside, two other units, lights flashing, were pulling up behind Stryker's vehicle. Both were gun jeeps with Hog-60s in the back.

"He's going downtown for questioning!" The *canh-sat* in charge spoke fluent English for a change.

"By whose fucking authority?" Stryker demanded. "He's wearing an MP armband, isn't he?" Stryker's hand was gripping his gun butt. The .45 remained in its holster, but the flap was open. The MP sergeant had the highest respect for the Vietnamese National Police, but one of his men was *not* going downtown with them in handcuffs!

"They say I killed some broad down the hall!" Marsh was wide-eyed. "They say I killed some broad and her kid, for Christsake! *Me*!"

"He is accused of robbing Apartment twenty-six," the *canh-sat* corrected him, calm now, "and raping the mother and her fourteen-year-old child there. The girl has died. The mother is badly beaten . . . we don't know if she'll make it yet. Her throat was cut, *sergeant*. . . ."

Four American MPs crowded into the hallway behind Stryker, one cuddling the M60 in his arms. Stryker had radioed for backup upon finding all the activity at Marsh's apartment complex.

"What's your alibi?" Stryker was not making accusations.

"I was with Judy all night!"

"Alone?"

"Of course," Marsh snapped, then, seeing Stryker's train of thought, he added, "unfortunately. . . ."

The ex-Green Beret-turned-cop frowned. "And *unfortunately*," he said, "wives and live-in girlfriends don't make the best alibi witnesses in court. . . ."

Saigon policeman Jon Toi appeared in the doorway just then, and he squeezed through the MPs. "What's up, Mark? Anything I can help with?" Stryker breathed a rare sigh of relief.

"You can accompany my man here down to the stationhouse," the American with the stripes requested. "Make sure they don't break any bones during the trip, too. Ride with Greg here . . . he'll fill you in on the details. . . ."

The *canh-sat*s acknowledged Toi's presence with slight nods, but they were already hustling Marsh out the door.

"One other thing, sarge," the rookie blocked the doorway painfully with his shoulder, causing the entourage to halt abruptly half in and half out of the hallway. "I don't know if it'll help you clear my ass or not, but the little girl, Val, kept insisting my name was Eaton. She seemed to be mistaking me for some motherfucker down the road . . . maybe that's why the *canh-sat*s are on my case like this. The white stucco buildings . . . number two-two-two. . . ."

"Got ya covered," Stryker was staring down at Judy now. "I don't suppose you clowns are taking her in for interrogation, too?" he asked the *canh-sat* in charge.

The man ran his eyes down across the nude woman's back and shook his head, fighting off his desires. "The woman is free to remain here," he said. "But she must remain *here*, in this apartment. Investigators will be by to question her at a later time."

"That's fine," said Stryker, reaching for a towel in the

248

bathroom. He draped it across Judy's backside. She was still lying on the floor, sobbing quietly but uncontrollably.

And then all the police vehicles were gone, and slowly the neighborhood returned to normal. Except for the woman, all alone on the third floor, crying herself to sleep because, once again, she had lost her man to the street.

In an unusual break from the traditional bog-down of red tape and pretrial delays, the Saigon government rushed this extraordinary case of the Vietnamese People vs. Greg Marsh through the court system, and, amid widespread attention and even commercial exploitation, the military police private was found guilty of murder in the first degree. The little girl's mother, May-Lynn, was unable to testify because she was still in a coma, but the tenants in the building Greg shared with Judy stuck together in their testimony that the American had been a frequent visitor of the dead girl's mother. There had been numerous heated arguments between them, and violent disturbances, where the *canh-sat*s had been called. All this damaging evidence was admitted into the trial, and further testimony from the apartment complex's security guard seemed to portray Marsh as a maniac whose idea of entertainment was keeping two mistresses in the same building.

All this came to light, soap-opera style, exciting chapter after chapter to the approval of the bloodthirsty public, even though Sergeant Stryker's personal investigation had shown that Pvt. Greg Marsh was attending the Military Police Academy, thousands of miles away, when he was, according to the government's witnesses, beating May-Lynn silly on Friday nights. But Stryker was also uncovering damaging evidence as well, and he didn't have much time to sort it all out.

Marsh was sentenced to die by firing squad, in a public execution, in two weeks' time.

13. MONSTER IN THE MIRROR

Mark Stryker sat in his jeep, parked alongside the towering statue in Lam Son square, staring at the framed picture in his lap. A notepad was balanced across one knee, and now and then he would scribble something on it, then cross it out.

"Sure looks like Greg Marsh to me." Carl Nilmes was back on patrol, his helmet liner concealing the bandage wrapped around his forehead.

"Yah . . ." the sergeant muttered under his breath. "Sure does." The comatose victim, May-Lynn, was posing arm in arm with the man in the photograph. Stryker and his boys had gone through the apartment at 222 Vang Chay and had found the picture on a wall shelf, among other assorted items of memorabilia that seemed to place the young private in Saigon long before he had actually arrived. Could it be that his in-processing papers were forged and he had been in the city for quite some time? Perhaps a deserter from another unit?

Stryker felt like bashing his head against a brick wall. *That* was as far as this investigation was taking him. The apartment on Vang Chay, just down the hill from Judy's flat, contained few other clues. Some dresses that were too small to fit the victim, May-Lynn, so *that* seemed to say that Greg, or whoever this was in the picture—*of course it was Greg!*—

was keeping still a *third* woman in his stable.

Stryker had paid the recruit, if that's what he was, several jailhouse visits during the last ten days, but, even after numerous in-depth talks, neither of them could come up with anything that could explain the youth's dilemma. Although the experienced sergeant, trained in all aspects of field interrogations, often got the feeling the kid was holding something back. If only he could try some of the "techniques" they had used so successfully up in Pleiku . . .

But this *was* Saigon. *And Greg* was *one of the good guys!*

The private had taken the photo Stryker had shown him and compared it with his likeness in the mirror in his cell. Stryker had asked him to try and explain the picture—*anything!*—but Marsh could only stare at his face in the mirror, glancing down at the black and white photo every few seconds, lips trembling, but unable to speak . . . until tears had finally welled up in his eyes, and Stryker had called it a day.

"The little girl, Val," he told Stryker, "kept calling me 'Eaton.' She said my name was 'Mr. *Sram*,' Mark. 'Eaton H. Sram.'" He seemed to be chasing the truth. Grasping at straws, yet slipping the MP sergeant clues only Greg knew the answer to. Stryker was beginning to feel like a store detective, watching a kleptomaniac rushing through the shop recklessly, begging to get caught.

It sent a shiver up his spine.

Stryker wrote a few more words down on his pad in different combinations, then just as quickly scratched them out, while Nilmes watched the girls of Saigon float past in their tissue-thin *ao dais*. "Can we pay a visit to the zoo now?" he'd ask Mark every few minutes.

"Your girlfriend in the gorilla cage is doing just fine." Stryker grinned for the first time in days. "She can wait . . . I got important detective work to do here. . . ."

A Vietnamese fire truck screamed past, heading away from the river, along Tu Do Street.

"Tango-six, this is Delta Sierra Two," a transmission broke squelch on the static-laced radio net behind them.

"Car Niner," Stryker answered, ignoring the "Training" designation.

"Activity at the target location . . . how copy? A light just went on in the west end of the apartment; over,"

"I'm on my way!" Stryker said, slamming the mike into its dashboard clip and turning the engine over with the same movement. Nilmes watched him circle a name on the clipboard instead of scratching through it, and reached over and flipped on the red lights switch, sensing the urgency in the air.

The MP sergeant slid the clipboard under his seat and made the rear tires spin, pointing the jeep down the road toward Vang Chay Street.

For the last ten days, he had persuaded Richards, who was out of the hospital, to alternate his Decoy Squads on an intermittent series of stakeouts of the apartment in which he had found the photo of Marsh and May-Lynn.

And now somebody had returned there. The first time he knew of, since the double-rape and murder. Stryker was banking on finding a certain female in the building, scooping up possessions, trying to make a clean sweep of the apartment, her property. And her past.

"Whatta ya think we'll find at two-twenty-two Vang Chay?" Nilmes leaned over toward Stryker as they came across a traffic jam and countless water hoses crisscrossing the street at the scene of a travel office fire. "Marsh is scheduled to stop a dozen rifle slugs in the morning. . . ."

Stryker patiently watched as the fire fighters fought a losing battle. Floor-to-ceiling posters in the front window, depicting nightclub scenes on Le Loi boulevard below the caption SAIGON: THRILL CAPITAL OF THE WORLD, were curling up from the heat and flames. He felt that's how his investigation was going.

But there just might be a breakthrough awaiting him on

Vang Chay Street.

"I don't know," he finally said. "I'm just not sure. . . ."

Curfew was falling across the thrill capital of the world by the time Stryker and Nilmes pulled up alongside the Decoy Squad. He noticed Thomas and Bryant were both riding in the back seat. Richards and Reilly, in front, waved at Car Niner upon its arrival.

"We been watching the windows with binoculars," Richards briefed them. "Some movement, but no positive ID at this time."

"But I'd wager a female's in there," Reilly had the sergeant's folding binoculars back up to his eyes, "and I'd say she's alone."

"Possibly waiting for somebody," Richards added.

Stryker checked his watch. "Almost midnight. It won't hurt to wait a while . . . see what goes down . . . who, if anybody, makes a dramatic rendezvous." He picked up his mike and switched to Channel 2. "I'll advise Waco we'll be unavailable until further notice. . . ."

"And that we'll need two more units down on the other side of the hill," Richards suggested.

"Just in case," Reilly added, his attention diverted to a group of flares floating along the outskirts of the airport now, over Fort Hustler.

Stryker and Richards exchanged humored grins and both rolled their eyeballs toward the stars good-naturedly.

"Patience," Bryant, trying to keep the ice broken, elbowed Thomas. Anthony was rubbing gun oil into his AK stock so vigorously it appeared the rifle might burst into flames, but the PFC just wasn't feeling at ease around an old friend whose wife's belly he had put a bullet into.

And patient they were.

The ten MPs who eventually surrounded the ground-floor apartment at 222 Vang Chay waited until the crack of dawn, but they spotted no one else arriving at the dwelling.

"We better make our move," decided Stryker, stretching his arms and back muscles. "Before people down there start waking up—"

". . . And venturing out into the crossfire," Reilly cut in, anticipation in his trigger finger. It had been a good two weeks since he had been in a fire fight, and that sniper, like most rooftop Cong, had melted into the night before reinforcements could clear the tenement, floor to floor.

Reilly had been slightly wrong in his calculations, though.

When they kicked in the door, the MPs found not one, but four people in the apartment.

Three of them—two women and a man—were in one bed, sharing body heat under the sheets.

A half-dozen rifle muzzles were pointed at the two Honda Honeys when they popped their exhausted almond eyes up from under the pillows. And sleeping right between the whores was a man whose face brought a relieved smile to Stryker.

"Greg Marsh!" Richards's jaw all but dropped across the bamboo floor out of shock.

14. THUNDER IN THE SUN

"Not quite," muttered Stryker.

"But—"

"Greg's in Chi Hoa jail."

"But—" The resemblance was uncanny.

"I want all three of you to show us your hands . . . real slow. . . ." Stryker ordered the man and two women. Without taking his eyes off them, he then told Richards, "Have two of your men clear the rest of the apartment, Gary."

Just then a shaft of the orange dawn broke through the clouds along the eastern horizon, and, like a beacon, the sunray splashed through the filmy bed sheets.

"Tim!" PFC Thomas called out as he spotted the outline of the pistol beneath the sheets. He pushed Bryant to the side, an instant before the automatic discharged, creating a smoking black hole where the sheet lay across the Honda Honey's lap.

The slug struck Thomas in the belly, against his flak jacket, but before the impact knocked him off his feet, his own weapon was barking in reply.

The wild burst of AK rounds practically split the woman in two, from the chest up to her forehead.

"On the ground!" Stryker and Reilly were jerking the man

out over the surviving woman, slamming him roughly to the floor. "Spread-eagle!" But he was unarmed.

Nilmes was up across the bed on one knee, jabbing his rifle between the survivor's sweat-slick breasts, but the woman made no move to resist—only glared at him defiantly, snarling like an animal. Uncaring . . . fearless.

"Anthony! Anthony!" Bryant was back on his feet, rushing over to his fallen partner. "You okay, buddy? You all right?"

Thomas rolled over, onto his back, groaning slightly. One eye was turning scarlet, rapidly swelling shut from the fall against the sharp dresser. And there would be a nasty bruise over his stomach, but he'd be fine. "Yah . . . yah, you'll be fine," Bryant was helping him to his feet. "You'll be okay, brother. . . ." Neither MP looked over at the woman who had been stitched up the middle—smoked with hot tracers—and who now looked like pared shrimp, split open in front. Once full breasts now hung to the sides, lifeless, drooping, separated by two feet of mangled muscle and punctured ribs.

Reilly was cuffing the man on the floor. "If this cocksucker ain't Greg, who the hell is he?" the Spec4 demanded an end to the mystery.

"Hey, Stryk!" a voice—Richards—was calling from the back of the apartment. "Come on back here . . . you gotta take a look at this. . . ."

"I just don't know how all these people got in here without us seeing 'em," Nilmes was complaining out loud to himself.

Stryker glanced over at the dead woman, still lying in the bed beside his rook partner. Nilmes's knee was creating a depression in the mattress, and the blood oozing from the horrible wound was collecting around it, filling the valley like a pond at the end of a slowly trickling creek. A crimson-colored creek. Even though her face was also torn in two by the pounding slugs of lead, the MP sergeant was confident she was the same woman who had led him on the chases downtown. If he had to, how could he explain it to the other men? He probably couldn't . . . he could only *feel* it. He wished Bryant had his pocket camera. Carmosino would be proud.

In the back, in a cramped storage room illuminated by a single dim ceiling bulb, oblivious of all the death and gunfire down the hallway, Stryker found the old *mama-san* sitting amid piles of laundry, smiling up at the Americans with her black, betel-caked teeth as she calmly moved the iron about.

"So your civil-servant daughters had abandoned you, eh *mama-san*?" Stryker asked in English. The question was laced with mild sarcasm, and pity, but the woman just smiled back at him stupidly, nodding her head up and down. Proud, *like the pizza lady*. . . .

"So what do we do with this one?" asked Richards.

"Just leave her," Stryker replied, checking his watch. "For the time being. The *canh-sat*s oughta be here any moment—they can have her if they want. *We* got what we came for. Now we gotta rush the son-of-a-bitch in the bedroom back to Lam Son Square before the firing squad takes a bead on Greg. . . ." He was already darting back into the hallway.

"Hustle his ass into the jeep!" he was directing Reilly seconds later. "We gotta rush this 'evidence' downtown . . . before it's too late!"

"Who is he, anyway?" Reilly asked again, feigning patience when he wanted to grab Stryker and *attempt* to shake the story out of him. But too late: Everyone was hustling outside to the jeeps.

"Etan H. Sram?" Nilmes had pulled Stryker's clipboard out from under the seat and was reading the name the sergeant had circled just before receiving the radio call from Richards.

"Deserters resort to little games in order to stay one step ahead of the law and insanity," Stryker attempted to explain as their prisoner was strapped into the back seat. "And sometimes, when little children are involved, like Val," the big MP glared back at his prisoner, "the 'games' become ridiculously simple. . . ."

"I don't get it. . . ." One of the gun-jeep MPs was crowding close to Stryker's unit.

"'Etan' is 'Nate' spelled backwards," Nilmes had figured it out . . . was still piecing the puzzle together as he fired up the jeep. "And 'H. Sram' is 'Marsh' spelled backwards. . . ."

"Greg thought all along the girl, Val, was calling him 'Eaton.' He had no way of telling how she spelled it, just by the sound. Or maybe he did. . . ."

"So who the fuck is Nate Marsh?" the gun-jeep private had his head cocked to one side out of curiosity.

"Greg's twin brother," Stryker revealed.

"His twin!?" several MPs strained to get a better look at the man. Up close.

"You decide!" the sergeant grabbed the deserter's chin and turned him sideways to face the men. "Added a little hair over the ears and this shitty excuse for a mustache . . . picked up the scar there somewhere, but take all that away—"

". . . And you've got Greg Marsh," said Reilly.

"So screw all you dudes," the prisoner muttered, forcing his head back.

"What a way to treat your own flesh and blood," the gun-jeep MP said, climbing back up behind his Hog-60 as Stryker's vehicle began to pull away.

"Greg never mentioned he had a twin," said Reilly, who was now seated beside the prisoner in the back seat. "And in the 'Nam."

"He never even mentioned he had a *brother*," Stryker growled, feeling somewhat betrayed. "Nathan here has been roaming the bush the last few months with his renegade buddies . . . two of them were the jerks me and Tim and Anthony ran into down at Tim's place. Nathan here, at first disenchanted with Uncle Sammy and the Green Machine's way of conducting business, decided to desert and take the war to Charlie in the jungles . . . man to man, without all the

258

heavy hardware and the hierarchy that went with it.

"But a few months in the rain forests north of Gia Dinh would sour even the most idealistic freedom fighter, right Nate, ol' buddy?" he continued sarcastically. "It's hard to combat evil in the form of the Red Menace, with a small ragtag band of AWOLs, when, all around you, the Vietnamese themselves are getting wealthy off the fortunes of war.

"So you decided to go for a piece of the action yourself. Ambush the drug runners coming down from the Golden Triangle instead of the Cong . . . until you found that the drug trade in these parts was 'protected' by several powerful Arvin commanders. . . ."

"That's what all the fighting north of Gia Dinh is all about," Reilly decided.

"When Nate's group here found out they were outclassed and outgunned, they simply turned the tables on some people—easy to do beneath a rain forest canopy, right Nate?—and sent opposing dope kingpins in after each other."

"So all that arty out on the horizon all night ain't even part of the war," concluded Nilmes.

"Just a bunch of South Vietnamese unit commanders fighting over territory," said Stryker. "Nate here, enraged by the way things went down, tried to lay low at one of his old haunts in Saigon . . . on Vang Chay street. Where he took his anger out on his old tealock and her kid . . . and we all know what that led to."

Stryker glanced at his watch again. "You better get on the tubes and tell Waco to notify the VNP to halt the execution . . . that we're coming in with—"

"Otherwise we'll never get there in time," Reilly cut in.

"I already tried," Nilmes said. "You know how the Saigon government is. Dispatch said they couldn't promise any-thing. . . ." Already they were swerving in and out of early morning traffic, some cars headed for Lam Son square and the much publicized event.

"Jesus . . ." muttered Stryker. Nilmes punched the accelerator, and the jeep, snarled in traffic briefly, jerked back into motion.

"How about a little code, boss-man?" the private driving asked the sergeant beside him as he reached for the siren toggle.

"You can bank on it, Carl," came the predictable response, "'cause if you snooze—"

"You lose."

The three Vietnamese policemen struggled to restrain Judy, and they finally had to drag her from the fenceline, kicking and screaming. After she was deposited roughly behind the barbed wire, the squad of twelve soldiers resumed its march toward the hastily erected clay wall, stepping smartly to the somber beat of the lone snare drum. Beyond the fence, hundreds, perhaps thousands of Vietnamese stood, fingers clinging carefully to the sharp strands of concertina, struggling to get a better view of the proceedings. Behind the crowd, two vans were parked. And atop them stood TV cameras and an assortment of international newsmen.

In front of the twelve-foot clay wall stood ex-Private Greg Marsh, stripped of his rank and his U.S. citizenship, manacled to a stout pole, staring out at them all, prepared to meet his fate, physically, but a shambles mentally.

"I love you, Gregory!" Judy was shouting through the wire, above the clamor of the crowds, and suddenly an odd assortment of television and radio personalities were rushing up to interrogate her, but she was ignoring them, hiding her face, slapping them away—the whole time jumping up above the heads of the men crowding in front of her, trying to see Greg again . . . trying to let him see her. See that she was still here. Still loyal. After all they had gone through. After all the jailhouse visits. *The nights she lay awake, alone*. After all they had *not* gone through.

There was no podium near Greg. No speeches in English. Not even a politician around. Only a bent-over *canh-sat* jabbering instructions to the firing squad over a bullhorn, and then they were lining up twenty-five meters away from him, taking their stances. . . .

Greg shook his head from side to side when a tall Oriental appeared out of nowhere, offering him the mask—a deceptive blindfold to hide the muzzle flashes, which would do little to protect him from the sheet of sudden hungry lead. Some of the Arvins would probably shoot past him, or into the ground. Some would even miss accidentally, but out of a dozen soldiers, some of them had to despise what he stood for. One or two or three would take special care not to miss. And one or two of them, the way things were going *these* days, might even be a damn Cong.

Greg stared out at the crowd, past his executioners, trying to find his woman . . . trying to make some sense of all this . . . visions of his brother Nathan filling his head . . . flashbacks of that afternoon with Sharon . . . memories of his mother cabling him—how could she be by his side? There was no money . . . no cooperation from the State Department toward the mother of a convicted murderer, now dishonorably discharged from the Armed Forces. He would die without seeing any of them again.

And the pain came because he knew he was not to blame for any of it.

The last ten days had been a swirl of dizzying confusion, and he still wasn't convinced he might not wake up from this nightmare yet.

A siren in the distance. Several sirens.

Like angels, pangs of conscience, trying to wake him.

Then they were roaring into Lam Son Square, a dozen American MP jeeps, rooflights flashing, sirens screaming, and big bad Sergeant Stryker leading them!

Greg Marsh felt his whole body release a thin coating of perspiration as the shiver ran through him, and his eyes were locked on Judy's now.

He had found her, breaking through the line of *canh-sats* running up to him . . . newsmen surrounding the hand-cuffed man in the MP jeep . . . Judy's eyes wide with relief, her arms outstretched for him . . . the policeman with the loudspeaker demanding order, being totally ignored by everyone—the crowd, the press, the MPs, the firing squad itself . . . Judy's breasts bouncing wildly as she ran, calling to him . . . the mob all around the square tearing down anti-American banners—bewildered, angry, jubilant . . . Stryker's ear-to-ear grin a frame in the corner of Greg's eye . . . Judy half across the grassy field now, running faster but her steps registering slow-motionlike in his mind . . . faster and faster . . . her straight white teeth . . .

The mortar, whistling down onto her from the quiet sky.

Splashing her body across Lam Son Square, like a sledgehammer slamming down on a cluster of fruit . . . grapes . . . *red red wine.* . . .

"Judy!" he screamed, but she was gone. Nearly dis-integrated. A memory.

The Viet Cong were walking their mortars from one side of the park to the other, crisscrossing through the crowds of South Vietnamese with hot, smoking shrapnel.

MPs all around Greg now, cutting his bonds, releasing him, some diving away from him as the attack increased in intensity, grew nearer, ignoring him now before the straps around his ankles were off, trying to protect themselves. *Every man for himself!*

Better him than me. . . .

Grief, pain, sorrow at the loss of such a buddy, such a fine MP . . . *but better him than me.* . . .

But Greg was free now. Was racing toward Judy . . . what was left of her.

But she was gone. Vanished, except for the pool of blood

262

and slabs of meat. Pieces he could not bring himself to look at.

This was not Judy! This was not the woman whose lips carried him off to never-never land every night. . . . *This was not his woman!*

Greg was on his knees, thigh-deep in the slick of crimson death, fingers coated with it, hands raised to the rising sun in disbelief. Thunder in the sky answering him . . . mortars exploding all around.

No storm to cause the thunder. No clouds. Just a tempest of silver smoke and swirling, screaming shrapnel.

He was running now. Toward his brother.

His long, lost brother, Nathan.

Somehow the prisoner, in all the confusion, had escaped. Was running to freedom, wrists still handcuffed but in front of him now, bashing terrified Vietnamese out of the way, Greg hot on his heels.

Stryker, sitting in a pool of his own blood, dazed, a sliver of mortarshell in his back, lowered the pistol's sights from Nathan Marsh's back when he saw the deserter's twin brother flying through the air, tackling him.

He tried to concentrate on getting the .45 back into its holster without an accidental discharge, tried to get his thumb to work . . . flip the safety into place, but he was falling backwards now, into the pit of pain, shaft of darkness . . . listening to all the people screaming on all sides, their voices hopeless cries ringing in his ears. Shock . . . trauma. The last thing he saw before blacking out was the two Marsh brothers fighting, hand to hand, fingers around each other's throat, locked in combat . . . battling to the death: good versus evil.

Fighting over a goddamned woman . . . his thoughts laughed at it all, making his lips curl up in a smile, despite the waves of pain, before he lost consciousness.

Sgt. Mark Stryker did not see the dual mortars that crashed down upon the Marsh brothers, like bolts of justice

263

on Judgment Day, killing both Americans instantly.

Gary Richards sat at Stryker's desk ten hours later, dwarfed by the piles of paperwork balanced precariously all around him. And more reports were still coming in.

Two MPs had been killed in the surprise mortar attack on Lam Son Square.

After the Alert teams were deployed, and after the wily VC disappeared across their rooftops . . . after the final count was in, 35 military policemen had been wounded. Thirty-five Purple Hearts would have to be requisitioned . . . even though it was a private little joke among the men of the 716th that "They" never gave Purple Hearts to MPs.

Stryker was in 3rd Field Hospital. He would recover.

And crime in Saigon did not skid to a stop merely because all hell had broken loose on the battleline with communism. Richards glanced up at the color-coded map on the wall. He had just briefed the 11 P.M.-to-11 A.M. shift—they were now returning to the street after putting in the ten hours in the V100 assault tanks.

He had even talked to that crazy ex-Green Beret over the phone—Stryker was insisting their "Torch" suspect would more than likely strike again tonight, taking advantage of all the confusion in the streets. He had the scenes of each Molotov murder plotted on his little map, and it would now be Gary's responsibility to see the pattern developing week to week, and deploy the Decoy Squad appropriately: in the most likely neighborhood to intercept the suspect.

Richards could still hear the man yelling over the phone . . . complaining the damn nurses had him strapped into his bed because they considered him an uncooperative problem patient.

Never mind about the Marsh brothers, Gary told himself, rubbing his temples, amazed his thought processes were still working after all he had just gone through . . . experienced

. . . survived. Never mind that people he had grown close to were now vapors on the breeze. . . . He forced himself to concentrate on the map, and, sure enough, after a few minutes, he saw the circular pattern in the red pins with the yellow flames.

He picked up the desk phone and called Dispatch. Schultz was in charge of the Decoy Squad again, in his absence. "Have Raunchy Raul set up his stakeout in the vicinity of Hong Thap Tu and Xguyen Vinh Khien," he said.

And then he started in on the report nearest him, resolved to take it easy the next few hours, trying to imitate a supervisor for a change. Behind him, the MP radio net monitor was audible but turned down low.

An hour later, as curfew settled across the City of Sorrows, Richards glanced at the set of reports he had just checked over, then at the stacks piling up all around him, and decided the latter had nearly doubled in size. He thought about Saigon's clerk-typists, who were all home with their women now, snuggled up against warm flesh . . . bumps in the night. *Size 36 bumps* . . .

"Waco to any units . . . vicinity Minh Chieu and Cach Mang," the dispatcher's droning voice broke through the shuffling sound of papers and boots rushing in and out of the room, adding to the piles that were now above his head. "Report of man down, that location . . . on fire . . . nothing on suspect . . . a Vietnamese fifty-two en route. . . ."

The transmission continued without Dispatch's allowing air time for any street units to reply, ". . . Attention all units . . . vicinity Vo Thanh and Truong Tan Buu . . . second report of possible 'Torch' victim . . . in the alley . . . exercise Code Zero. . . ."

A brief break in the transmission, then, "Waco to any car to handle ambulance call at Cach Mang and Nguyen Vai . . . man on fire . . . one *canh-sat* unit en route . . . VNP pretty much tied up right now. . . ."

"Christ!" Richards was on his feet now, running out to the

265

nearest MP jeep parked in the long line of units beside the Orderly Room. The assaults were all going down miles from where he had deployed the Decoy Squad! "Delta Sierra Three to Car Ten-Alpha," he could already hear Schultz calling him over the air.

On the run, he pulled his pak-set off his belt and muttered, "Send it!"

"Did you copy Waco, Gary?" Their jeep's engine could be heard in the background, its strained roar mixed with the sound of squealing tires.

Richards could not believe none of them had thought about her before. "Respond to two-twenty-two Vang Chay!" he said, snatching up his jeep's mike.

"Roger," came Schultz's unemotional reply. "That's right where we were headed for; over."

Richards all but blew his jeep's engine speeding to the apartment complex where they had arrested Nathan Marsh.

He pulled up to it five minutes later, only moments after the first Decoy unit arrived. The last man out of the Black Beast was still jumping from the rear seat. Nilmes.

"Witnesses said we just missed our man!" He was out of breath. They had been doing some running. Down the street, another corpse was smoldering, pieces of its unburned clothing still glowing. Another drunk GI had lost the odds gamble. Richards glanced at the white stucco building they had staked out only twenty-four hours ago.

Was it that long ago?

Schultz was deploying his men around all sides and next to the windows. More jeeps were rolling up now, blacked out, silent as shadows moving in the night.

"Let's do it!" he muttered after running up to the NCO with the perpetual smile. Schultz gave him a 'be-my-guest' wave of the hand, then both sergeants put their shoulders into the door. It collapsed with the first hit, but before either man could rush inside, a stocky figure had dashed between them, gun hand outstretched, portable radio crackling on his web belt.

"Stryker!" Both men all but gasped the name, astonished. What they found inside was even more disturbing.

The old *mama-san*, who was always so proud to claim her whoring daughters were civil servants downtown, was squatting in the cramped storage cubicle in the rear of the apartment, a rain poncho crumpled in front of her tire-tread sandals, grinning her usual black betel-nut smile, drenched in gasoline, a kitchen match in her hand.

Stryker had both hands out now, motioning for calm, his eyes pleading with the woman. "Whoa, *mama-san*," he was saying. "Settle down now . . . no need to . . ."

Richards was frantically waving the other MPs out of the structure. Fumes were thick and heavy throughout the apartment.

"Just calm down," Stryker was grinning, his eyes taking in the old woman's collection of brass jewelry around her neck—the same thick plates that had saved her, like bulletproof armor, from MP slugs twice in the past. "Everything's gonna be all right. . . ."

And she nodded back at him happily, smiling the whole time as she struck the match against the cement floor, visions of burning monks dancing in her eyes as she herself burst into flames and a fireball chased the Americans out the open windows in the rear of the building.

The old woman squatted there, unwavering, as the fire consumed her withered, ancient form, and the structure burned down around her. The smile remained on her face, like a wallet photo of an old girlfriend thrown into a crackling fireplace, until she toppled over, rigid and black as charcoal, the sound of Buddhist temple gongs ringing in her ears instead of the popping flames and collapsing lumber . . . like the snapshot in the fireplace, slowly turning black until it curled up into nothing but a hint of ash.

"The Torch" was finally out.

Saigon policeman Jon Toi plopped his boots up on

Richards's desk, ignoring the piles of reports scattered all over the floor. He glanced up at the stuffed tiger head on the wall behind the MP sergeant. "Been a damn hot tour of duty in ole Saigontown tonight!" he sighed, cupping his hands behind his head.

"Yah, I don't know how much more 'excitement' I can take." Gary reached over and turned off the radio scanner. "Sun oughta be up any minute now. . . . How many nonstop hours on the street does this make for *you*?"

Richards didn't want to try and count them. "So tell me about that crazy *mama-san*," he said instead.

"Crazy is the right word," the *canh-sat* sighed again. "Did you know her oldest son was one of the Buddhist monks who torched himself four years ago . . . back in sixty-three?"

"You're shittin' me. . . ."

"The old crone lost her marbles after that. Sat in on all the bonze barbecues—the radical Buddhist movement saw to it she was notified in advance, as a courtesy to her privileged status as mother of one of their religious martyrs."

"I guess she just got . . . burned out on all the suicides, so to speak." Toi suppressed one of his grim chuckles. "Got to the point where she couldn't separate her love for the foreigners from her son's obsession to rid the country of them. She began torching easy targets: drunk GIs . . . out of her own twisted compassion . . . feeling, somehow, she was doing them a favor . . . sending them straight to Buddha."

"She tried to equate murder with her son's noble sacrifice for the cause," Richards muttered sarcastically.

"Something like that. Her three daughters were just along for the ride—for kicks. Fuck the GIs, and all that."

"For kicks," Richards almost groaned.

The door to the office swung open again, and Bryant and Thomas stuck their faces in. "How's the Stryk doing?" Tim asked.

"Oh, I relieved him of duty and had Raunchy Raul drag his ass back over to the hospital before he bled to death."

Richards forced a refreshing grin, though inside he felt like crying. Two MPs had died over all this, not including Greg Marsh—he'd have to work on changing the dead private's miltiary status. *Good men had died over this farce.* This "Torch" incident, the Marsh affair, the Ramirez racket. *Lives wasted!* And that didn't include all the *canh-sat*s who had been killed. Defending their lady, Saigon.

Richards couldn't bear to think about what he'd do if Stryker was ever dusted out on the street. Despite all their well-known in-fighting.

"Well, we're gonna call it a night," said Anthony.

"Call it a *couple* nights," Richards corrected him, but they were already gone.

Jon Toi rose to his feet also, deciding to leave without a long drawn-out farewell. "And stay away from the tamarinds at the embassy," he called after the two enlisted men.

"Haven't you heard?" Richards listened to their distant reply in the hallway. "That's why that kiss-ass Calloway got his butt shipped off to guard duty in Long Binh. Sergeant Stryker caught *him* under the ambassador's tamarind trees . . . red-handed, with a whole harem of housegirls. . . ."

Laughter filled the building, then quickly faded as doors slammed.

Richards allowed himself a small snicker of disrespect, then returned his attention to the matter at hand: paperwork. The Decoy Squad sergeant-turned-watch commander picked up another set of reports, wondered briefly where the hell all the damn lieutenants were at times like these. (they couldn't all be hiding out at LBJ. . . .), then attempted to focus his eyes on Jeff Reilly's handwriting.

When a mind-jarring bell began clanging next to his right leg!

Inside the top drawer.

Richards jerked back in his seat, but quickly caught himself, keeping his composure, and smiled, ignoring the racket, content to let the alarm clock locked in the desk drawer run its spring down.

"So you think you're gonna rattle ole Gary's nerves, eh Stryker?" He laughed out loud, folding his arms across his chest, proud of his calm demeanor.

After the alarm clock bells wound down, he resumed, trying to collect his thoughts and decipher Reilly's enemy-action report.

Five minutes later, there came a sudden roar from the gaping jaws of the huge Bengal head mounted on the wall behind him, and Richards, taken off guard this time, flew out of his chair, knocking another pile of reports off the desk and onto the floor.

But the Decoy Squad sergeant quickly skidded to a halt and drew his pistol, burned out on the 'Nam himself now, as he turned to face the growling tiger head. Without any second thoughts, the veteran Saigon Commando aimed at the provost marshal's stuffed trophy, captured somewhere near Pleiku, and slowly fired off eight deafening rounds, then calmly saw back down and resumed checking reports as if nothing out of the ordinary had happened.

As the hidden recorder, undamaged and jammed down behind the gleaming fangs deep in the beast's mouth finally bellowed its last roar, Richards tried to ignore the gunsmoke settling over his desk, and the satisfied laugh of Sgt. Mark Stryker on the final two feet of tape.

"Payback is a bitch, Gary-baby," the metallic voice taunted him. "Don't get mad . . . *get even. . . .*"

NEW ADVENTURES FROM ZEBRA